"My goal is to agency like the *New York Times*. Who knows, you may be sitting here with the next Woodward or Bernstein."

"A reporter?" He stared at me for a moment and then looked down, dusted off his hands, and rose to his feet.

I stiffened. "Is something wrong?"

He didn't answer. Instead, his gaze searched the house's dark interior. "I have to go. Will you be okay waiting by yourself?"

"Well, uh…yes sir, of course." I scrambled to my feet and handed him the wet dish towel. "I appreciate you tending to my injury. Mama will want to thank you personally. We'll stop by sometime and—"

He had taken a step toward the door but spun and thrust out his palm like a stop sign. "That isn't necessary. Good luck with the healing." He vanished into the house, closing the screen door, and the oak door behind it, and bolted the lock.

Seriously? Dazed by his icy send-off, I slumped to the steps and mentally repeated my words, wondering if I'd said something offensive.

Praise for Sheila Hansberger

Her debut novel: *The Gardener's Secret* was awarded first place honors in the women's fiction category for the 2023 Florida West Coast Writers contest [formerly the TARA].

The Gardener's Secret

by

S. Hansberger

The Gardener's Secret

Cover Art by *The Wild Rose Press, Inc.*

The Wild Rose Press, Inc.
PO Box 708
Adams Basin, NY 14410-0708
Visit us at www.thewildrosepress.com

Publishing History
First Edition, 2024
Trade Paperback ISBN 978-1-5092-5301-2
Digital ISBN 978-1-5092-5302-9

Published in the United States of America

Acknowledgments

Writing a novel is a team effort, and lucky me, I have a wonderful team!

The first team captain, Marilyn Cram Donahue, mentored a group of fledgling authors at SCBWI. I was the newbie and will always be grateful for her guidance.

Thanks go to the beta readers from The Joy Book Club for reading my first draft and offering words of encouragement.

To Linda and Shenoa at Lustre Editing, kudos for your honest suggestions, even when I just wanted to hear praise.

Cousin Lauri Quick, I humbly appreciate your advice about all things southern.

To the Florida West Coast Writers, thanks for sponsoring an annual writing competition. Without you, my manuscript might not have caught the eye of a publisher.

And to Editor Kaycee John at The Wild Rose Press, you have my undying gratitude for your patience and helping me get my debut novel published.

Last, but not least, heartfelt hugs to my family who has always supported my creative endeavors. Where would I be without all y'all?

Chapter One

Mama, a genteel southern lady, rarely voices her opinion. Her motto is "If you can't say somethin' nice, don't say nothin' at all." And yet, double negatives aside, she'd probably be embarrassed if she knew I saw her nod in agreement with a neighbor's derogatory comment. Over the fence, gossipy Miz Brown complained that the young people of today view the world through rose-colored glasses. Well, there may be some truth in that statement, because I'd been guilty of doing exactly that. At least in the beginning.

Once upon a time, when my world was rosy and bright, I was out west at UCLA, enjoying my junior year as a journalism major, working toward the day when my byline would crown the front page of a prominent newspaper. Hunched over a text book and overwhelmed by a flurry of finals, I got a phone call that made my heart stop—an ambulance had just taken my father to the hospital.

Mama could barely speak between sobbing and blowing her nose. Daddy's emphysema had worsened, and his oxygen tank wasn't keeping up with his fight to breathe. He had only slim odds of returning to the home he shared with the woman he'd married thirty-nine years earlier.

"Don't cry, Mama. I'll be home on the next flight." I hoped she would draw strength from my take-charge manner, because that's what she needed. But after the call ended, all my imagined maturity vanished, and I folded into a ball, wishing someone would hold me while I cried like a baby.

Later, while fastening the plane's seatbelt, I wondered if other passengers could hear my heart pounding. Worry consumed me, not only for my father, but for my mother who'd never spent a night alone since the eve of her wedding. Pressing my forehead against the cabin window, I scowled at the ground crew's slow-motion efforts while they loaded a tram full of suitcases into the baggage compartment. Didn't they know I had an emergency?

Then it hit me...I had absolutely no control over anything. Tipping my face heavenward, I leaned back against the seat, closed my eyes, and prayed in silence until sleep visited. In a restless dream, I saw myself as a young child, fretting about grades while my father smoothed a strand of hair from my face. He told me not to worry, everything would be fine. Little did I know, as the plane idled on the tarmac, God decided Daddy couldn't wait for me.

Even with three years of college under my belt, my real education began when I returned to my southern roots. I viewed moving back to Willoughby, Georgia, as temporary, and as much as I regretted giving up a partial scholarship, it was the proper thing to do. Dedication to my grieving mother had to come first, and my lifelong dream of a college degree—the first in our family— would have to wait.

I shoved anxiety into a cubbyhole in the back of my mind and focused on a new goal—keeping my journalistic skills intact. I wrote freelance articles for any publication that would accept my quirky style of writing. The pay wasn't great, but I stayed busy, and my résumé grew.

Losing my father was my heartbreaking reason for coming home. Over the coming weeks a new worry emerged—I might never leave. The longer I stayed, the more comfortable I became. Mama's southern cooking and all that familiar, homey stuff started nibbling away at my resolve. Would my dream of an education vanish like a wounded butterfly?

Chapter Two

The cursor on my laptop screen blinked, daring me to continue. I sat cross-legged on the sofa, camped out with notepads and resource materials scattered about, trying to decide how to finish my latest freelance article. I'd been back in Georgia for three months, grinding out assignments for various magazines, and had finally developed a decent rapport with several editors. I could usually turn vague ideas into smart words, but that day, I couldn't concentrate, because of *him*. I'd given him ample attention earlier, but he wanted more. This time, I refused to acknowledge his sulking, even though his dark eyes tried to penetrate my psyche.

"Callie Lou James," my mother drawled from the kitchen doorway. "He's been waitin' patiently for an hour. Please take that poor dog for a walk."

I was about to mumble a complaint when my southern upbringing kicked in. "Yes, ma'am. One more minute." Then I made the mistake of glancing at Rascal. He sat up and shifted his weight from one paw to the other. When his hopeful whine finished me off, a huff of a sigh escaped my lips. "Okay, Rascal, you win. Get your leash."

Besides his fondness for eating and sleeping, there's one thing we could always count on. Whenever we uttered the magic phrase, "Get your leash," he'd take flight and rush around the house in a panicked search for the leather harness that meant fresh air and a chance to bully the neighborhood cats.

Golden retrievers are known to be intelligent and easily trainable, but I'm not sure Rascal got the memo. However, his brain wasn't what tempted me to choose him from the animal shelter seven years before. Soulful eyes hinted that he was an affectionate sweetie pie with a gentle disposition. I'd hate to imagine a burglar breaking in, but if one did, Rascal would probably greet him with a wagging tail and help carry loot to the getaway car.

He found his leash on the console in the entryway, the same place he usually found it. Stretching up, he gathered it in his teeth and slid his paws to the floor.

Not sure when that sturdy piece of oak furniture received his first toenail mark, but I do know, long after he leaves this earth, I will envision his silly antics with a little melancholy whenever my dusting rag polishes those familiar scratches.

"Come here, you funny boy." I patted both knees, and he jumped up, the leash dangling from his mouth. I nuzzled a cheek against his soft fur, then cradled his head in my hands and rubbed thumbs under his ears while admiring that sweet, innocent face. "What a bootiful doggie you are. Yes, you are. Callie wuvs you."

Minutes later, the old wooden screen door, with impatient doggy imprints, banged shut behind us. We stepped out onto the covered porch and down the faded blue, weathered steps. Or at least *I* did.

Rascal zoomed by and bounded to the front yard, clearing the entire staircase with one impressive leap. Bursting with pent-up energy, he ran around and around in circles and rolled in the grass before landing at my feet. *Crazy dog*. He seemed happy just to be outside.

Before clipping the lead to his collar, I threaded my arms through a cozy sweatshirt to ward off an early morning chill. I shivered and rubbed cold hands together, puffing a frosty breath between them, trying to warm numb fingers as a light breeze filtered through my hair.

Depending on the whims of Mother Nature, the final days of September can be hot, and the next one cool. The trees are often confused by this, and not all agree to let go of their greenery at the same time. Some had already started to shed; some would wait. But by the end of October, all would be fully committed to the changing season, and I'd be out in the yard raking up bushels of multicolored leaves.

An earthy smell from the previous night's rain persuaded me to breathe deep. My thankful lungs drank in the fresh Georgia air, reviving my foggy brain from the grip of writer's block. Lucky me, I was blessed to be back in the safe, rural atmosphere where I'd grown up.

Rascal strained on the leash, drawing me back to the present. He cocked his head with an eager look that begged me to get going.

"Okay, you feisty mutt, where to?"

With eyes set on the horizon, he put his legs into first gear, as if knowing he had permission to forge ahead and investigate outlying neighborhoods.

Not twenty minutes later, the breeze died, and the sun on my back caused my sweatshirt to live up to its name. I made Rascal cease his full-throttle pace. Tongue lolling from one side of his mouth, he circled, wrapping the leash around my legs twice before plopping down atop my feet. He seemed relaxed, almost content to take a timeout.

With shoes buried under Rascal's golden fur, I crisscrossed my arms, grabbed the hem of my sweatshirt, and tugged the fabric skyward…just before I heard the rustle of dry leaves.

Rascal's leash tightened like a noose around my ankles. A millisecond later, he bolted.

With arms still in the air, I watched a cat zip by. Then my body twisted in a spin, and darkness claimed the light.

Chapter Three

"Ow, it hurts," I whined, waking to pain. My head rested on a striped porch-swing pillow. I couldn't bend my left arm. Someone had created a splint by using two wooden spoons and strips of cotton rags, efficiently wrapping them around my elbow. My blood-stained sweatshirt lay nearby. The frayed knee of one pant leg revealed a nasty scrape, but most of the throbbing stemmed from my arm. With blurred vision, I tried to focus on the figure in faded overalls who hovered above me. "What happened?"

"You fell," said the gray-haired man. "Your arm doesn't appear broken, but I immobilized it, just to be safe."

He handed me my damaged eyeglasses—not shattered but tweaked. Embarrassed that a stranger had witnessed my clumsiness, I shoved the glasses into my jeans pocket and nonchalantly tried to rise. When the sudden movement revealed a new ache, I collapsed back onto the porch swing and cradled my head with the only hand I could lift.

"Stay still," he warned. "Okay if I take a look?"

I parted my bangs and mumbled something that must have sounded like a yes.

He bent over and squinted. "Skin's not broken, but you have a sizable contusion. Swelling needs to be reduced. Wait here."

"You sound like a doctor," I joked. My smile faded when my words fell unnoticed as he disappeared into the house. Feeling guilty I'd already taken too much of his time, I called after him. "Please, don't trouble yourself any further."

The only response was the crackle of cubes being dispensed from an ice maker.

Within seconds, he returned, twisting a dish towel around a clump of ice. He leaned forward and pressed the makeshift cold pack against my forehead.

I tried to appear calm, but my brain thought it was being turned into a frozen kids' treat. I winced, squeezing my eyes shut.

He adjusted the compress. "Hold that in place."

When my aching head grew numb, I opened my eyes and sat up. "How did I get here?"

"I carried you."

No doubt about it, he looked like he could have, even at his age. He was probably in his late fifties or early sixties, almost six feet tall, rawboned, with broad shoulders and sturdy arms.

I, on the other hand, was five foot five, twelve pounds overweight, and not diminutive in any way, so it would take someone of his size to carry me very far.

As my mind pieced together a scenario, I remembered my dog had a hand—or rather a paw—in my accident. "You didn't happen to see a Golden Retriever, did you?"

The stranger pointed to the side yard. "Looped his leash over the faucet." He waved away my concern. "He's fine. There's shade."

I started to rise. "I should get him some water."

"No need. Spigot drips continually."

Southerners don't usually speak in clipped sentences, so I figured this man wasn't a local. Since I'd been taught to be hospitable, even to strangers, I smiled and nodded a thank-you-for-the-information. Then I craned my neck to check on Rascal. Without standing, all I could see was his backside, twitching as a dragonfly lit on his blond fur. Keeping my head down, too embarrassed to look at my rescuer, I ran fingers across my makeshift bandage and mumbled, "Sorry about my dog chasing your cat." I looked up to judge his reaction. "Is she okay?"

"Not my cat, but she's fine."

Before I could ask if he knew the cat's owner, the stranger's gaze settled on my arm.

"You need to address those injuries. Do you have someone who can take you for medical attention?"

Setting aside the ice pack, I reached for my sweatshirt to search a pocket. The shattered glass on my phone's readout made it obvious it had bitten the dust at the same time I did. "Darn. May I use your phone to call my mother?"

He studied me for several seconds before answering. "Of course." He led the way into the parlor and stood nearby, arms folded, watching me put the receiver to my ear.

Was he afraid I'd steal something?

After the call, he strode across the room and held open the screen door.

I assumed that was my cue to leave, or at least go outside. "Is it okay if I wait on your steps?"

"Sure."

Curt answers didn't suggest someone who'd been raised in the south. At my house, southern hospitality would have taken the lead with Mama seating the stranger in our most comfortable, overstuffed chair and then putting a frosty glass of sweet tea into his hand. I walked to the edge of the porch, took a seat on the top step, and propped a shoulder against a wood post.

He did the same on the opposite post.

A gentleman after all? Or maybe he just wanted to keep an eye on me and my dog.

I stared at my bandaged arm, then turned to face him. "Thanks so much for your help."

He nodded.

"You don't have to wait if I'm keeping you from something."

He drew up one leg to a higher step. "That's okay."

His nervous gaze flitted from one end of the street and back every minute or so. He appeared to be watching for a car. Was he *that* anxious to get me out of his hair? We only lived a few dozen streets away, but Mama had just stepped out of the shower, so it would be a while before she arrived.

My rescuer didn't seem comfortable with small talk, but I couldn't imagine just sitting there twiddling my thumbs in silence. Since my focus was always on that future reporter job I hoped to land, this seemed a perfect time to hone my interview skills. "Silly me, I forgot to introduce myself. I'm Callie Lou James." My grin widened as I waited.

He nodded. "William."

"Glad to meet you, William. And your last name?"

He blinked. "Smith."

William Smith. Really? Thousands of people must have had that same name. Oh well, not everyone could claim a fancy one. Although I went by Callie Lou, I'd been named for my grandmother, Callista Louise.

I wasn't sure how far to take this practice interview, but eventually he leaked sufficient information that allowed me to form a mental sketch of him and his family. Not ample enough for a news article, but solid enough to appease my curiosity.

Mr. Smith and his daughter Mary, and her eighteen-month-old son, Johnny, had just moved into the rental. Mary waitressed at the Lakeview Dinner House three nights a week and at the Kopper Kettle during breakfast and lunch shifts.

"I'm retired, so I'm the babysitter." He drew his legs together and folded his hands into a tight knot.

I sensed he meant to end his comments there, but I wanted to know more. "You're retired? From what?"

His nostrils expanded as he breathed in. "Gardening."

An image of Daddy pulling carrots from our red Georgia soil wandered through my thoughts. "My father loved growing plants, but not professionally. What made you quit?"

His jaw tightened, then he reached to rub a knee. "An injury made me rethink my options."

Not sure why he seemed to struggle with letting go of that less-than-vital info. In the end, he had described an ordinary man, living an ordinary existence. Yet, something didn't add up. His polished mannerisms, and even his choice of words, suggested a more refined individual. I assumed he was highly educated, maybe even at an Ivy League school. "I don't detect an accent. Where are you from?"

He swallowed. "Well, uh...all over. No special place is home."

I felt sorry for him. How could a person not take pride in a particular town or city and call it their own? Maybe he just didn't want to play favorites, or maybe he thought I'd be offended if he didn't choose Willoughby.

He shifted his gaze, as though gathering his thoughts, then turned his focus on me.

"You don't have an accent either."

I cocked my chin. "Really? You don't hear a hint of a southern drawl?"

"Barely."

"Probably has something to do with me being away at school."

He propped an elbow on a bent knee. "Whereabouts?"

"California." I grinned. "Hard to be out west and not be influenced by the speech of surfers and Valley girls."

He rested his head against the post. "Hmm, California. I remem—" He cleared his throat. "Sounds like fun."

"Yes, sir. It was."

"Was? Will you finish school in Willoughby?"

His comment didn't surprise me. Most people assumed I was still a teen because of my round, babyish face. "No, sir. Willoughby doesn't have a college. But it does have a high school, and I graduated there three years ago."

His cheeks flushed. "My mistake. I thought you'd been away at boarding school."

I didn't want to further his embarrassment, so instead of meeting his gaze, I lowered mine and brushed imaginary dirt from a pant leg. "No, sir. Entirely my fault. I should have made it clear I attended the University of California in Los Angeles. I'd almost finished my junior year when Daddy died." The memory brought a lump to my throat. "Not returning to California was an easy decision. My mother needed me more than I needed an education."

"Sorry for your loss. No one else to stay with her while you finished?"

"No, sir. Not really." With a twinge of sadness, I realized I could have been sitting in a classroom at UCLA at that very moment, just beginning the fall quarter of my final year. But Mama was still in the throes of grieving, and I refused to abandon her.

"No siblings?"

"Just one." A smirk threatened to make my feelings known. "Might as well not have any. My brother is fourteen years older than me. After Zack was born, Mama was told she'd never have another child." I forced an exaggerated smile. "Then, surprise…I happened."

Mr. Smith's eyebrows rose. His reaction shouldn't have caught me off guard, but it did. After all, I'd blurted out something personal without thinking. My gaze dropped to my sneakers as I tightened a shoelace. I knew my humor had fallen flat when my audience didn't react with even a tiny grin. Instead of covering my humiliation with yet another joke, I picked up a fallen leaf from the porch and twirled the stem between my fingers, hoping a silent second or two would allow my embarrassment to fade. "Anyway, Zack left home for parts unknown when he turned twenty-one"—I dropped the leaf and crooked my fingers to represent quote marks—"to find himself." I sighed. "He'd always wanted to explore the world, and he's still out there. Months go by without a single letter or phone call."

Mr. Smith shook his head. "If you'd known how to

contact him, would he have come home?"

Would Zack have come home? I squirmed. Even though I'd gotten used to covering for my brother's aimless wandering, my jaw usually tightened whenever I made excuses for him. So, this time, I decided not to. "I doubt it. If he had, he wouldn't have been a trustworthy caretaker. And he would've bolted at the first opportunity. Besides, Mama and I are very close. I've chosen to be here as long as she needs me. I'll finish my education when the timing is right."

"Sometimes life gets in the way. You're sure you'll return?"

Determination inspired me to sit up straighter. "Yes, sir. Definitely. I promised my father years ago that I'd get a degree and make him proud." A knot formed in my chest when I realized Daddy wouldn't be sitting in the audience at graduation.

I stared at the abandoned cold compress laying on the porch beside me. The ice had melted, leaving the dish towel soggy. I couldn't bring myself to ask for fresh cubes—my pseudo doctor had already been more gracious than necessary. And even though my head still ached, it did so less and less with each passing minute.

"UCLA has an excellent pre-med program...or so I've heard. Are you planning on a medical career?"

"No, sir. Journalism. My goal is to work as a reporter for a big news agency like the *New York Times*. Who knows, you may be sitting here with the next Woodward or Bernstein."

"A reporter?" He stared at me for a moment and then looked down, dusted off his hands, and rose to his feet.

I stiffened. "Is something wrong?"

He didn't answer. Instead, his gaze searched the

house's dark interior. "I have to go. Will you be okay waiting by yourself?"

"Well, uh…yes sir, of course." I scrambled to my feet and handed him the wet dish towel. "I appreciate you tending to my injury. Mama will want to thank you personally. We'll stop by sometime and—"

He had taken a step toward the door but spun and thrust out his palm like a stop sign. "That isn't necessary. Good luck with the healing." He vanished into the house, closing the screen door, and the oak door behind it, and bolted the lock.

Seriously? Dazed by his icy send-off, I slumped to the steps and mentally repeated my words, wondering if I'd said something offensive.

Recognizing the hum of my mother's vehicle before I did, Rascal sprang up on all fours and whined with excitement.

Mama left the car running, opened her door, and put one foot onto the ground. I motioned for her to stay put before rounding the house to untie Rascal's leash. With him in tow, I strode to the curb.

My dog wasn't happy about getting inside— probably noticed a lingering scent from the neighbor's kittens, who were born on the backseat a week before. Grunting, I lifted his overweight frame with my one good arm. When he finally hoisted himself up onto the carpeted floorboards, I wedged my feet in next to him and pulled the door closed.

Mama twisted to look over her shoulder. Concern wrinkled her brow. "You sounded calm on the phone. Why didn't you tell me your arm was in a cast?"

"It's not a cast, Mama. It's a splint. The doctor wanted to prevent further damage."

"Doctor?"

"Did I say doctor?" I chuckled. "He did treat me like one. But, no, he's not a doctor, he's a gardener. Just an ordinary gardener."

Or so he said.

Chapter Four

Late that afternoon, following a trip to urgent care, I sat on the living room sofa and extended my arm to examine a fresh cluster of bandages. I had always taken a lot for granted, never thanking God for healthy limbs, but I was sure thanking Him now. Nothing was broken, it just appeared that way. Mounds of sterile gauze wrapped my arm, from a damaged elbow all the way down to a scraped palm, replacing the makeshift dressing created by Mr. Smith. I cringed, realizing his wooden spoons were probably in the trash at the medical clinic. I'd have to buy new ones and deliver them with a forgive-me note.

I continued to stare at my arm, knowing bulky bandages would make typing difficult. Yet, I had to give it a try, because a scheduled deadline loomed in the near future. My shoulders tensed as I thought about the consequences of delivering the piece late. The assigned editor had the reputation of being an impatient ogre. This would be our first time working together. Although he might forgive me if I explained my situation, begging for mercy wasn't my style. Instead, I would do whatever it took to impress him. Otherwise, he might return my work without payment. And my tenure at that magazine would come to an end.

Opening my laptop, I accepted the inevitable, that the current article would be written in the hunt-and-peck method, by a one-handed author. Just locating each individual key required sharp focus. But every teeny, tiny sound around me pelted my concentration with one interruption after another: the grandfather clock monotonously ticked, Rascal's snoring mimicked distant thunder, and Mama's favorite Christian radio station blared old-fashioned hymns. Who was I kidding? There would be no writing that day. I needed a change of scenery. "C'mon, Rascal, let's go outside."

He awoke with a start but willingly followed. I tossed his chew toy into the yard and watched him scramble down the steps and plop his furry body onto the grass, obviously content to maul the familiar armless teddy bear for the millionth time.

My fingers skimmed bare wooden slats as I sat on the top step. I couldn't remember when the house's weathered boards had last seen fresh color. The white trim didn't look too bad, but the powder blue siding had faded. I made a mental note: *Stop by the hardware store and buy a gallon of paint.* When my deadlines were met, I wouldn't have the nerve to tackle the entire house, but at least I could give the porch a quick touch-up.

Cotton ball clouds, tinged with orange and pink hovered over the horizon. The quiet setting should have calmed even the most restless heart. Yet, my agitated mind fought against the tranquility. I sighed, frustrated that so little was known about the stranger I'd met earlier that day. Maybe then I would understand why he suddenly wanted to be rid of me. Did he really have somewhere to go? Or was his chilly reaction caused by something I'd said? Whatever the reason, I had to find out. The investigative reporter within me wouldn't let the subject die.

Chapter Five

My nature didn't lend itself to leaving things unfinished. Daddy used to say I had the stubbornness of a mule and the curiosity of a cat. I guess you could say those qualities helped my writing. Not too many years before, as the editor of the Willoughby High School newspaper, I uncovered a scandal related to the school district's food services. A little snooping led to the discovery of two employees receiving kickbacks whenever they bought from certain overpriced vendors. My tell-all article earned a special award from the school board and recognition from the governor's office. I went on to write other pieces and entered national competitions. My efforts garnered prizes, but the prizes were secondary. For me, writing was like a drug—and I was addicted.

The screen door creaked, jarring me into the present.

Mama stood on the threshold, a hand on her hip. "Callie, didn't you hear me? Supper's ready."

"Yes, ma'am, I'm coming," I grumbled. "I was in the middle of problem solving." Feeling guilty for snapping at her, I kept my head down and stood.

My dog pushed his blonde, furry body ahead of us and ran to claim a space on the floor next to the kitchen chair I always occupied. He sat at attention, licking his lips.

After Mama asked the blessing, I opened my eyes

and found Rascal edging closer. "Rascal, stop that!" His disappointed face pricked my conscience. My delivery of harsh words had even surprised me. I should have apologized, but instead I avoided his gaze by focusing on my napkin and unfolding it across my lap. "Begging is rude. Go sit somewhere else."

"Honey, what's wrong?" My mother paused, holding a serving spoon mid-air before helping herself to a scoop of fried okra. "You seem a little irritated."

"I'm fine," I protested, dodging her question and the sight of her pinched brow as I tore apart a biscuit and slathered it with butter.

Being a typical mother, she wouldn't let it go and continued to prod her grumpy child.

"You havin' pain from your accident?"

"No, ma'am, my physical pain is only minor." With a pouting lip, I stared at my dinner plate while aimlessly pushing food around, letting the day's events take priority over my appetite. "My mental pain is the problem."

"Well, I'd be happy to lend a sympathetic ear."

Grateful to have someone else's opinion, I inhaled. "Why is it, when you think you're using your best manners, some people don't have the courtesy to return the favor?"

She tilted her chin. "I don't understand."

Setting aside my fork, I rested both hands in my lap. "I'm just saying, I thought I was being polite today, but I must have done something wrong."

She flattened a hand to her chest. "Did *I* make you feel like you did somethin' wrong?"

I shook my head. "No, Mama. Not you. I'm talking about what happened after my fall. The gardener and I were carrying on a friendly conversation. Then, all of a sudden, he turned distant, almost rude, and got up to leave."

"Callie, not everyone's as extroverted as you. Think about what you said that might have changed his mood. Maybe he felt uncomfortable. Were you flirtin' with him?"

"Mama!" Eyes wide, I stiffened. "Why would you say that? I am *not* a flirt. Besides, if you'd seen him, you would know Mr. Smith is ancient."

"Ancient? How old is ancient?"

"I don't know exactly. Just old."

"Older than me?"

"Maybe younger."

"Younger?" She blinked. "And *he's* ancient? Gee, thanks."

After we both had a good laugh, I relaxed, ready to clear the matter from my mind.

Mama twirled her fork in a mound of mashed potatoes. "Did you have a chance to read the newspaper today?"

I knew better than to talk with food in my mouth, so I just nodded.

"Did you see the nice article about our local auto dealer?"

I raised an eyebrow; I knew where this was going. She was segueing into a topic that had been an on-going battle between us for weeks—her concern about my aging vehicle breaking down in the middle of nowhere, versus my objection to having a car payment.

She poked at the okra on her plate. "The article says the dealer just got the biggest fall shipment he's ever had. They quoted him as sayin' this is the year to buy a car, and this is the month to look for the best deals." She glanced up. "Callie, maybe it's time you looked for somethin' dependable."

I heaved a sigh. "Mama, as I said before, Daddy's old truck suits me just fine." I knew she had to be distracted, or we would end up bickering, so I launched into another subject, one that was dear to her heart. Baking. "Speaking of today's newspaper, did you notice the grocery ads? Shameful. Halloween is still five weeks away, but they're already advertising ingredients for Christmas goodies."

"My favorite cookin' program on TV is doin' that, too." A slow smile crinkled the corners of her eyes. "By the way, they're showin' a new episode tonight. You wanna watch it with me?"

"Thanks, but no. Got a deadline." I sheepishly held up my wounded arm. "Can't let anything but this come between me and the article I need to finish."

Her fingers wrapped a frosty glass of sweet tea. "What's the article about? Or is that privileged information?"

"Pfft. Hardly important enough to be called that. It's about building materials—how they've improved over the past fifty years." I patted my lips in a sarcastic yawn. "Ho hum. Can't imagine the Pulitzer Prize committee holding their breath for it."

"Maybe you shouldn't hold your breath either. Can't you write somethin' that makes you feel good?" She dabbed her mouth with a napkin. "If a magazine asked for an article on your favorite subject, what would it be?"

"Hmm." I rested an elbow on the table and stared off into space. "Probably a human-interest story. Like, 'Adopted Siblings Reunite' or 'Soldier Surprises Family with an Impromptu Visit' or—"

"So why wait? Why not write the story you love and send it to one of your editor friends?"

I opened my mouth to object, but she was faster and held up a wait-a-minute finger.

"I know. You're about to tell me why you can't do that. But just consider this. I'll bet your talent would shine even brighter if you let your passion lead the way. And a story with real heart in it will surely get *someone's* attention."

My mother often surprised me with her advice. I'd be a fool not to follow it as soon as the inspiration hit.

****

Since we had only one upstairs bathroom, bedtime tended to remind me how inconvenient it was to live in a one-hundred-year-old house. With legs crossed tight, I waited my turn, sitting on the edge of the bed, thumbing through Mama's recent issue of *Good Housekeeping*. When the bathroom door opened, I leaned sideways, peered across the hall, and watched Mama shuffle toward her bedroom. I skipped across the bare floor and yelled a quick good night to her retreating backside.

Minutes later, with my head perched over the sink and my face lathered up for a good scrubbing, I heard a knock from the hallway.

"Callie?"

Soap bubbles stung the rims of my eyes. I squeezed them tighter. "What is it, Mama? I have soap on my face."

"That's okay, hon." She hollered through the closed door. "Stay at the sink. I don't want you drippin' on the bath mat. I just remembered somethin'. Sorry I didn't think of it earlier, but with all the excitement over your injuries, and the trip to urgent care, I plum forgot." She huffed a sigh. "Some days there's just too much goin' on. You're keepin' your bandages dry, aren't you?"

"Yes ma'am." I waited. "And…?"

"And what?"

I had to smile. She got sidetracked so easily. "Mama, what did you remember?"

"Huh?" She paused. "Oh, yes. You got a phone call today. Mr. Barton from the *Willoughby Tribune* was tryin' to reach you."

Almost forgetting to breathe, I splashed water on my face and stood upright, letting suds slide from my chin. I stared at my reflection in the mirror and blinked. "Did he say why?"

"The newspaper has a part-time position available."

Part-time? Not quite what I'd prayed for, but at least another step toward my dream career. Maybe even a chance to show what a great investigative journalist I was.

Chapter Six

I confess, I'm impatient. Always have been, probably always will be. So, waiting for a timepiece to slowly move its hands is a particularly painful occasion in my world.

Believe it or not, the clock on our stove still functioned after multiple decades of kitchen grease. Or did it? Were the hands stuck? I kept watching as I downed a serving of grits with milk and honey, washed my dishes, and fed the dog. Now I was on my second glass of juice, waiting anxiously for eight o'clock to arrive. I only hoped someone would be at the *Tribune* by then. But what if they didn't open until nine? I'd have a heart attack.

I called at exactly eight o'clock. "Hello. My name is Callie James. May I speak to Mr. Barton, please?" I angled the receiver away from my mouth while clearing my throat. "This is regarding a message he left yesterday." My stomach churned as I speculated about his opinion of me. Would he think me ill-mannered because I had delayed returning his call? Or, worse yet, would my delay result in someone else getting the job?

"Good morning, Mr. Barton...Yes, sir, I did. I'm sorry I didn't call yesterday. I was in an accident and didn't get your message until last night...No, sir, just a bandaged arm...An interview? Yes, sir, I'm available all day...This afternoon? Absolutely!"

****

Ahh. I sucked in the intoxicating scent of printing ink floating through the lobby at the *Willoughby Tribune*—the smell had permeated those walls for over ninety years. In today's newspaper publishing business, a parent company often owns several small-town newspapers and combines their printings at one off-site location, making the operation much more cost-effective. However, occasionally you'll find an independent out there doing it the old-fashioned way, with dedicated reporters gathering timely news, and one lone technician down in the basement operating an off-set press. That's how it's done in my hometown.

The lady at the reception desk, sporting retro clothing straight out of the 1940s and wearing more makeup than I'd ever owned in my entire life, seemed perturbed I had chosen this day, of all days, to show up and ask to speak to the editor. Before shoving a pencil behind her ear, she used it to gesture to the chaotic activity in the newsroom. "Yer gonna have to be patient. We're puttin' the weekly edition to bed today. Mr. Barton is up to his eyeballs in last-minute problems, and he don't have a minute to spare."

"But I'm only here because he called—"

She heaved a sigh and waved me toward the lobby bench.

My mother always taught me to greet rudeness with politeness, so I shrugged an apology, put on my best forgive-me countenance, and sat down to wait. Even though a little put off by her attitude, I knew she was just doing her job.

I sat there, marveling when she went into action. First, she reached for the ringing telephone, nodded to whatever the caller said while jotting something on a piece of paper, hung up the phone, folded the note, addressed an envelope, stamped it, tossed it into a basket, took a bite of a breakfast sandwich, and used her free hand to dust crumbs from her desk before smearing another layer of bright red lipstick on her pinched mouth. And, still chewing, she gathered a stack of last week's edition and trotted it to the recycling bin. All this in less than sixty seconds. Whew, I was exhausted.

I'd met people like her before. They functioned at a different level than the rest of us. They didn't need caffeine—they were fueled by an internal blend of high energy. Their goal was to get things done…without wasting a nanosecond. Woe unto the person who got in *their* way.

I picked at the bandage on my arm and tried not to stare at any of the employees. To pass the time, I let my mind explore the surroundings—the dusty light fixture, the cracked ceiling, and the smudges of fingerprints on the wood framed glass doors. I counted all the windows and each plank of worn oak flooring.

Fidgeting, I turned my attention to my appearance. I patted my hair. Did it look okay? Was my skirt too short? *Let me think, when was the last time I even wore a skirt? The sixth grade dance?* The memory of that one particular night would haunt me forever.

I was painfully shy during those early years and rarely attended dances, and only then with a group of other girls. If we didn't get asked to dance, at least we could huddle and gossip about those who did.

Because the school janitor insisted no one scuff *his* highly polished floor with street shoes, we left our footwear at the front door. We sat in metal folding chairs on one side of the gymnasium, the boys on the other. We tried stifling our giggles whenever a young man requested one of us accompany him out onto the dance floor. But truthfully, those giggles only masked our adolescent nerves. This was serious business. After all, someone might be expected to hold a boy's hand.

And then, J.B. Taylor, one of the best-looking boys in my class, invited me to join him for a slow number. I was thunder-struck. With stockinged feet, and shaking hands, I followed him to the center of the varnished basketball court and nonchalantly wiped sweaty palms on my hips, hoping he hadn't noticed. When the music started, we took the formal dance position. On his shoulder, I rested my wrist and secretly puffed into cupped fingers to make sure I didn't have bad breath.

Ah yes, a night to remember...or maybe a night better forgotten.

The audible click of the lobby clock's hands interrupted my youthful memories. Another ten minutes passed while I waited at the *Tribune*. Every time one of the staffers walked by, I quickly rose, hoping they'd been sent by Mr. Barton to fetch me. Instead, each was either headed out the front door or into the restrooms adjacent to the lobby. That was okay. I figured I'd gotten a much-needed workout. Up and down, up and down. My thigh muscles felt tighter, making me sure I'd burned at least a thousand calories in the space of those ten minutes. My subconscious even tried to convince me I could have dessert with lunch.

The sound of someone clearing her throat brought me back to reality. Miss Multi-tasker announced the editor would see me, and she gestured toward his office.

When I walked into the room, Mr. Barton, the editor,

stood. "Miss James, thank you for comin' in today." His gaze flicked to my bandaged arm. "You mentioned an accident. I hope you're not in pain. Was anyone else hurt?"

I lowered my gaze. "No, sir. Just me. And my pride."

He grinned.

I studied the room while he shuffled alternately crisscrossed stacks of papers off a chair.

The *Willoughby Tribune* was housed in one of the oldest brownstones in town, and the editor's office fit in perfectly with the stately theme. High ceilings, tinged with cigarette smoke from long ago, featured decorative crown molding, carved by hand. The desk and bookshelves could have been featured in an ad for office furniture…from 1900. The room was either messy or tidy, depending on how you wanted to describe it. Papers and books and files littered every flat surface, but Mr. Barton could undoubtedly find whatever he needed at a moment's notice because of color-coded sticky notes peeking out from strategic places.

He gestured for me to take a seat. "We have a tricky situation here. The *Tribune* needs an instant employee." He rounded the desk and dropped into a swivel chair, folding hands on a manila file in front of him. "A member of our staff has been talkin' about retirement, and this is the week she chose to do it. Her husband won a trip to New York, and he wants to go while the weather's still mild. So yesterday, Etta came in and told me it was her last day."

He opened the manila folder and pulled out the form I'd submitted weeks before. "Out of all the applications we have on file, yours impressed me the most."

Really? Or is it because I'm the only unemployed fool still available after all this time?

He lifted the various papers littering his desk and mumbled something about misplaced eyeglasses. Finally, he leveled the application a few inches from his face and squinted. "It says here you've won honors for your writin'." Lowering the page, he grinned. "I guess we have somethin' in common. I did the same thing when I was your age."

His gaze fell to a lump under the empty folder, and upon raising a corner, he grinned. "Ah, there you are, you little devil." Extracting a worn black leather case, he pulled out wire-rimmed glasses and rested them on his long, narrow nose. Once again, he scrutinized my application. "You didn't finish college?"

With crossed fingers, I hid both hands in my lap, hoping that piece of information wasn't pertinent to me being hired. "No sir, I left college after three years. I moved back to Willoughby to help my widowed mother."

"Well, not a problem. Most of our employees don't have a degree either." He laid the page on the desk and tilted his chair back on its swivel, clasping hands behind his neck. "I'm more interested in your experience as an intern. Can you tell me about it?"

My mind did a happy dance. "Yes, sir. I'd be happy to." I took a breath and searched my memory for something that would impress the heck out of him. "Last year I worked for a small Southern California newspaper, at least ten hours a week, in between classes. They gave me responsibilities in almost every department. I answered phones, input computer data, and sat in on various staff meetings. I accompanied reporters on interviews and even had my byline used on a few articles."

"I see." He tipped his nose until his eyes peered above his glasses. "And what type of articles were those?"

I swallowed hard, not wanting to spill the whole truth. "Several were in Community News, and a few were in the Sports section."

"Sports? Really?" His chair creaked as he leaned forward. "Did you cover any prominent teams?"

Phooey. He had me. I looked down into my lap, locking nervous fingers together, and blushed. "Well, I guess you could say they were prominent…for a suburb of L.A. My articles had to do with local Little League teams."

He slapped the arms of his chair, threw his head back, and laughed. "Miss James, I was afraid you were over-qualified to work for our modest little publication. We let the big dailies cover the national stories and the major sportin' events. Hometown news is the *Trib*'s specialty."

I exhaled the breath I'd been holding and let an anxious smile light my face. If he hired me, I could use this experience as a stepping stone to become a *real* reporter for some famous news agency. "Are you saying I've got the job?"

"Maybe." He sat back in his chair, but his gaze never strayed from mine. "What do you know about gardenin'?"

So *that* was the purpose of this interrogation. They needed someone to write the gardening column. Not exactly the juicy reporter job I'd hoped for, but at least a chance to rub elbows with newspaper people. Sadly, though, I knew absolutely nothing about gardening—*nada*, zip, zilch—nothing.

"Well, I know a lot more than most people." I managed to produce a small grin, hoping to inspire confidence—not only in Mr. Barton, but in myself as well. "I haven't gardened for quite a while, but gardening is one of my favorite hobbies."

I'd started down a path paved with lies. No turning back, but I needed a better map to provide directions. I searched my mind and remembered the weed patches my parents had assigned me as a child, and how I would procrastinate as long as possible. "In the past, my green thumb has coaxed lots of plants into thriving."

"Really?"

"Yes, sir." Heart racing, I forged ahead. "In fact, as soon as my latest freelance article is finished, I plan to put in a big garden."

His brow lifted. "At this time of year?"

"Of course." I babbled without hesitation, like I knew what I was talking about. "You'd be surprised at all the wonderful things that can be grown right now."

Did I just say that? Didn't sound like something I'd say because I didn't know if my statement held any truth. Yet, it sure seemed like those words had tumbled from my mouth. Some part of me wanted to make a good impression, and I assumed this was the best way. However, I could feel embarrassment creeping up my neck. If Rascal had been with me, he would have been happy to dig a nice, deep hole, and I would have willingly crawled into it.

Mr. Barton donned a wide smile, stood, then reached across his desk to shake hands. "Congratulations, Miss James. You've got the job."

He escorted me to the newsroom and introduced me as the reporter who would take over Etta's column. He boasted that I was an experienced gardener and asked the staff to welcome me as the newest member of the *Tribune* family.

Over polite applause, one of my new *siblings* narrowed her eyes. "My, my. You're so young. How is it you know about gardenin'?"

Although I didn't actually lie, I proceeded to dig my grave a little deeper. Plastering on a firm smile, I continued to tweak the truth. "My family always worked outdoors. They convinced me to join them at an early age. You could almost say it's in my genes."

Each conversation had me closer to burying my pitiful corpse. If I didn't get out of there soon, some skeptic might decide to grab a shovel and finish the job.

****

"Mama, where are you?" I hollered, bursting through the back door.

The sewing machine hummed in the guest bedroom. "Up here, honey."

I took the stairs two at a time and ran into Mama as she approached the landing. I'd always done my best to make her proud, but I was about to admit I'd procured a job by lying. Standing there, looking into her sweet face, I felt my eyes cloud.

She took my clammy hands into hers and held them tight. "Callie, what's wrong?"

I swallowed a nervous breath and whined, "They hired me."

She squeezed my fingers. "That's good news. Right?"

"It should be." I withdrew my hands and stood back,

hoping to separate myself from her disappointment when she heard my confession. "But my assignment is writing the gardening column, and I'm afraid Mr. Barton will discover I lied about my experience with plants."

Her mouth dropped open.

I lowered my gaze in embarrassment. "I know. Not exactly the way to get a job, huh?" I looked up to see her shaking her head slowly and folding stiff arms across her chest.

Leaning against the wall, I slid to the floor and hugged my knees, regretting the bold lies I'd invented earlier. Reporting was supposed to be about reviewing the facts and telling the truth. Wasn't it? If word got out that I told *half-truths*, my credibility as a journalist would be on shaky ground, and my reputation would end up in the toilet.

Chapter Seven

The next day, I was again summoned to the *Willoughby Tribune*. I'd made peace with myself for lying and was on a mission to prove I was the best gardening columnist the newspaper had ever hired.

Ten minutes after arriving, I had filled out all the various employee forms, thanks to the organized receptionist who had gathered the materials in advance. She even led me through my very own copy of the *Tribune*'s overly-thick policies and procedures manual, paper-clipping the important sections, allowing me to bypass all the blah-blah-blah legalese. Guilt nipped at my conscience. Here she was, going to all this trouble for me, yet I viewed this job as temporary, almost beneath someone who only wanted to become a serious reporter.

Last of all, we tackled setting up my "office." She propped a wad of newspaper under one leg of a rickety corner desk in the main room, proclaiming the space all mine, complete with a computer monitor resembling a bulky TV from a previous decade. I offered to use my own laptop but was told, "Thanks, but no thanks." Even though ancient, the office computers were networked into a system the staff and the pressman understood. Also, the *Trib*'s computers only had slots for floppy discs, so I couldn't even transfer data via a flash drive. At least an equipment upgrade was scheduled for the near future. For now, I would have to work with outdated technology. My southern upbringing told me not to complain. After all, I was the new kid on the playground.

The receptionist became my new best friend that day. When we first met, I'd secretly made fun of her. Shame on me. I'd called her Miss Multitasker, which seemed an appropriate robot name for someone so efficient who appeared to be molded from steel. Her real name was Mazie Lewis, and although a little abrupt at dealing with strangers, she had a heart the size of Atlanta hidden under a no-nonsense exterior. Her boney frame carried not an extra ounce of fat, probably because of the lightning speed that drove her life. However, she did take a leisurely timeout that day and treated me to lunch and brought me up to date on all the office gossip.

I'd been made to feel welcome, which inspired confidence. Unscathed, I had sailed through orientation, set up my work area, and even had another meeting with my new boss.

He'd scheduled a phone chat with Etta, my predecessor, who was on vacation in New York. After placing the call, he pushed the speaker button. "Good mornin', Etta," he bellowed.

Was he afraid she wouldn't be able to hear him in that faraway city?

"I'm sittin' here with Callie James, our new hire. Hope you don't mind offerin' a few pointers to get her started."

We both went through the pleasantries of introducing ourselves. Each offered a brief background—her first, then me. An awkward pause lingered when I finished. I held my breath, afraid she'd want to delve into my experience with living plants, and I'd be exposed as a charlatan. Luckily, she didn't. I mostly listened; she was a talker. She outlined a few simple rules on writing for a newspaper, which I already knew, but generally she wanted to tell me what a glorious time she was having in the Big Apple. Less than fifteen minutes later, I was out of there, still unidentified as an impostor.

Relieved to be sitting in my truck, I leaned back my head and stared at the roof of the cab. No use regretting what I'd gotten myself into, so, for what seemed like an eternity, I gave myself a pep talk. Finally, I sat up straight. *No more excuses. You can do this.*

But how? My first column, "Gardening with Callie," was due in five days. I shuddered, knowing my creativity needed a jumpstart. Even though my next move wasn't clear, I refused to be defeated. *What about growing something?*

Living in a small town, twenty miles from the closest plant nursery, I knew my choice of stock was rather limited. Other than a few potted herbs in the supermarket produce section, or the seasonal pony packs at the drug store, the only live plants sold in Willoughby were at the feed store.

I cruised the parking lot at Martin's Feed, checking out the plant collection displayed on racks next to bales of hay by the front entrance. I'd gone to that location, because that's where Daddy always purchased packets of seeds. But I didn't have time to wait for seeds to sprout—I was on the hunt for mature vines that would produce fruit soon.

My fingers lifted the leaves of a thirsty plant. Describing the feed store's greenery as "live" was a joke. The wilting victims probably hadn't seen water since the day they'd arrived. Even *I* knew you had to give them an occasional drink.

The gangly teenager who waited on me had no clue why the store didn't have tomato plants in stock. He suggested I check back to see if the next day's shipment had any. I later learned the end of September is not the time of year to sow tomatoes. That is, unless you're a farmer in Australia.

I left there with two identical four-inch containers—one of them with a worn plastic tab stuck in its soil identifying it as a bell pepper. That tab was a mini-encyclopedia of information and advised me to locate the plants in full sun. I did, of course, but just imagine my surprise when the plants bloomed a few weeks later, and yellow chrysanthemums sprouted between the leaves. That probably says something about how inexperienced I was at the gardening business.

Escaping the work in Daddy's garden was something I excelled in as a child. I shook my head in remorse. Who knew all those green things could have taught me something useful? Where could I get my hands on a little education? I decided to contact my friend…the Internet.

Perched on the sofa in my usual cross-legged manner, I Googled the word "agriculture." Found 72,000,000 results. No kidding. Narrowing my hunt, I typed "home gardening" into the search engine. The number increased to 180,000,000. No way! If I chose to search all those sites, I would be on the computer 'til Armageddon.

Three hours of eye strain later, I had sifted through hundreds of specialty sites. Some dealt with raising perennials, some described every vegetable known to man, and some gave detailed step-by-step instructions for pruning fruit trees. There were even "green" sites, encouraging the use of organic remedies instead of pesticides to control insects. Where to begin? I yelled toward the kitchen, "Mama, what was the best vegetable you ever planted?"

"What?" She walked into the parlor, wiping hands on her apron. "Sorry. Couldn't hear you over the mixer."

"I wondered about the most successful thing you ever planted."

She skewed her mouth sideways and shrugged. "That would be nothin'. Your father always did the plantin'. My job was to water everythin' when he couldn't get to it." She leaned against the door frame and folded her arms. "Why the question?"

"I want advice for next week's column."

"Well, don't ask me. I only cooked the vegetables." She tilted her head. "Want advice on cooking?"

"Maybe. Maybe for a future article. Gotta tackle this one first. I want to emerge as a super star by showing how brilliant I am at growing things."

She didn't have to say a thing—her grin said it all. She, too, must have remembered the weeds I'd spurned.

My mother had a habit of reviewing her day just before bedtime. That's when she would recall something she meant to say earlier. That night, as I surfed the web for more ideas, she kissed me on the forehead and told me not to stay up too late. She started up the stairs, stopped mid-step, and called over the railing. "Callie, why don't you go visit that gardener who helped after your fall? Maybe he has some suggestions."

Great idea. Or was it? Our parting had been so cold, so sudden. Would he agree to see me again? I needed a plan, as they say, to get my foot in the door.

Chapter Eight

My stomach rumbled. The mouth-watering aroma of homemade chocolate chip cookies invaded the entire house. Pulling them from the oven, I knew they had to be packaged immediately. If not, I'd soon find myself reaching into the fridge for a milk carton to accompany my uncontrollable lust as I gobbled down the whole batch.

A dozen cookies on a sturdy paper plate, covered with plastic wrap, was my thank-you to the gardener who'd taken pity on me after my fall. On the way to his house, my truck found every bump in the road. With the plate perched on the passenger seat, I prayed I wouldn't have to helplessly watch my precious cargo tumble to the floor. Not that I wouldn't be happy to scarf down broken crumbs, but then I'd have to start all over. That would mean exposing my figure to even more calories than I'd already consumed that morning.

Mr. Smith's quiet street had all the telltale signs of an established neighborhood. Although most of the houses couldn't hide their age, their owners had applied layer upon layer of paint to keep the traditional beauties in fresh makeup. Mature sycamores, with determined roots, cracked an occasional sidewalk. The ambitious trees spread healthy limbs outward in an attractive shade canopy that reached across the road to connect with others growing on the opposite side.

The gardener was home. He, and a little boy I assumed to be his grandson, walked their yard with clippers and a large trash bag. When my truck silently glided to a stop at the curb, Mr. Smith whipped his neck around and instantly pulled his grandson into his arms, as if to protect him. When I emerged from the cab, I could see the man's shoulders relax, allowing the boy to wriggle free. Undoubtedly, the bandaged arm I waved helped him recognize me.

Balancing the cookie plate with my good hand, and slamming the door with my hip, was an easy enough task, but as I crossed the sidewalk, my foot caught on a tree root, and down I went.

"I'm not usually this clumsy." I chuckled as he pulled me to my feet. Thank God, nothing was broken, scraped, or damaged…except my dignity. And more importantly, the self-clinging plastic wrap had kept my peace offering intact.

Mr. Smith, still somewhat reserved, sat with me on his porch steps, enjoying a chocolate chipper.

Johnny scampered around the yard, catching air in the empty plastic trash bag.

"Remember I told you I wanted a job at the local newspaper?"

Mr. Smith's mouth was open, ready to take a bite of the cookie he held midair. He stiffened and twisted his head to look my way, saying nothing, staring with a fixed gaze.

In spite of the coldness his glare suggested, I hooked my thumbs under imaginary suspenders. "Well, you're looking at the *Tribune's* new gardening columnist."

His tense face muscles relaxed. "Oh. Congratulations. When do you start?"

"My first article is due in two days. It'll appear in next week's paper." My lips quivered to form a timid smile.

"You seem nervous about it."

"Yes, sir. Scared to death."

"Probably just stage fright. You'll do fine."

"Hope so." I stared at my feet while slipping clasped hands between my knees. "Because at this point, I know nothing about gardening."

"Nothing?"

I looked up to see his raised eyebrows, and then shook my head. "No sir. Absolutely nothing."

"I'd be happy to offer advice if that would help."

"Would you?" My hand flew to my chest as I exhaled an enormous sigh. "That would be great."

We sat there for a while, mulling over ideas for my debut column. Although slightly younger, he reminded me of my father, patiently listening to my excitement and only making suggestions when necessary. In the end, we both agreed autumn was the perfect time to write about pumpkins. He offered to show me some growing in his backyard.

Motioning for me to follow, he gathered his grandson and strode to the faucet at the side of the house. Mr. Smith washed every chocolate remnant from the toddler's hands and face, despite Johnny squirming to break free.

I noticed a gooey mess running down the front of his Winnie-the-Pooh romper and thought it odd his grandfather ignored it. I knelt and thrust out my hands. "Here, let me help you get him out of that."

When he abruptly wrenched Johnny from my reach, the panic on his face made me drop backward. Stumbling through his explanation, he told me all of Johnny's clothes were in the washer. But the sting of embarrassment refused to leave. After an awkward, silent moment, Mr. Smith gestured wordlessly to the backyard gate.

"Wow!" was all I could think of to say. His garden looked as big as a football field. Well, not actually, but healthy plants covered most of the ground inside the fence. My enthusiasm must have broken the ice, because his sullen expression disappeared.

Before directing his attention to me, he lowered Johnny into a sandy play area bordered by old railroad ties. The sandbox made a perfect digging pit, complete with plastic trowel, shovel, and a bright blue bucket.

With his grandson distracted, Mr. Smith led the garden tour just a few feet away. We walked sunlit rows, occasionally squatting to inspect something closer. He told me the official name for each plant and described how it would develop before reaching its peak at harvest. He said most of the plantings hadn't been in the ground very long. This was considered a winter garden where only cool-season vegetables grew.

I hadn't thought to bring anything for taking notes, but the voice recorder app on my new smart phone gathered a ton of information before the battery quit. Did I have enough details to strengthen my article? I wondered about the readers' response to my new-found knowledge. Then I realized, I didn't have to wait for next week's publication—I lived with one of the readers.

****

"Mama, where are you?" I shouted, heart beating wildly as I charged into the house.

"In here, Callie."

I followed the voice and found her in the parlor, bending over an upholstered chair, dealing with a pile of fresh laundry. While my face radiated enthusiasm, my hands cradled an orange tennis ball-sized orb.

"What's that?" She glanced my way and then turned her attention to folding a pillowcase.

"A pumpkin," I squealed with delight. "A teeny, tiny, baby pumpkin."

She snapped a clean dish towel in the air before creasing it into fourths. "Okay. So, what makes that so excitin'?"

"Now I know what to write about."

She furrowed her brow before reaching into the laundry basket for another item.

Her blank look told me she either didn't understand, or she wasn't really listening. Wound up in selfish excitement, I took her hand, led her to the sofa in front of the bay window, and gestured for her to sit. "This is the subject of my first column. It's from the gardener. Remember? You suggested I go see him." I blathered on and on, speaking as fast as my brain could form the words, and letting my hands wildly sweep the air while I described Mr. Smith's delightful garden and how a riot of ideas now filled my head.

Holding up her hands to form a T, she raised an eyebrow. "Time out. Just how much caffeine have you had today?" Her eyes crinkled at the corners, suggesting she was tickled by my behavior.

I giggled. "Probably too much, but I'd be on a high even without a drop. Don't you see? Now that I'm armed with some understanding about this gardening thing, I'm on my way to a Pulitzer Prize."

Chapter Nine

The last of the season's cicadas welcomed me to the shed where my father kept his coveted garden tools. The corrugated tin building hadn't been entered for months, or more precisely, since the day Daddy died. He'd just put away pruning shears when he reeled backward against the siding and struggled to catch his breath. Mama was watching from the laundry room window and saw him grab his oxygen lead. His gaze locked on hers just before he collapsed on the ground.

Paramedics took over a short while later and rushed him to the hospital.

But it was my mother who padlocked the door the day after the funeral.

I stood in front of the structure, ready to face the job head on. Determined spiders had fashioned webs near the opening. They'd snared a variety of insects on which to leisurely munch. With my trusty broom, I showed them I meant business.

A spasm of warm air escaped when I opened the door, bringing forth the scent of aged mown grass combined with a heady mixture of oil and gasoline. Since a local boy had taken over the grass cutting chore, using his own mower, our old red one sat neglected.

I squatted to brush away dried clippings until the brand name shone on the metal housing. Unscrewing the fuel cap, I peered into the tank. Empty. I reached for the gas can, but only the tiniest bit of liquid sloshed inside. Lucky me. If there had been more gasoline, I would have felt obligated to mow the lawn. But the job I faced would already consume most of the day, leaving no time for extra work.

My father always kept his "toy room" in tidy shape, so assessing what I had to work with didn't take long. Every type of tool in the world was crowded into that ten-by-twelve-foot space. Whenever some new gadget showed up at the hardware store, Rawleigh T. James had to have it. A connoisseur of tools, he valued what he collected and took delight in using every single item.

I recognized the shovel, the rake, and the hoe for what they were. Different types of clippers and claws and hose nozzles hung on each pegboard hook, and I could figure out how to use them. But several unfamiliar implements puzzled me.

Why was a ruler engraved into the trowel blade? Was the block of wedge-shaped iron a garden tool? And what was the round cup-like thingy with a handle grip attached? *Hmm.* I placed it and all the other mystery items into a bucket, hoping Mr. Smith would help identify them later.

After closing the shed, I walked out into the yard and leaned on a shovel, envisioning the lush gardens my father had planted on that very same spot. In summer, buckets overflowed with fresh vegetables, but most of our harvest was reserved for Mason jars, to be used year-round. Tomatoes, collard greens, corn, okra, and string beans made for an awesome display on the open shelves lining our basement walls.

As a small child, long before I'd learned the jargon associated with canning, I overheard a neighbor speak of her own efforts. She announced she'd *put up* twenty quarts of beans and *put up* twelve pints of apricot jam. Why would she lie? I'd seen her fruit cellar…she also put jars on the *bottom shelves*. Mama laughed when I mentioned it. A few days later, she put my hands to work and showed me exactly how to *put up* canned goods, and then she let me store them on any shelf I wanted.

My parents were grateful for their annual bounty and willingly shared. Have you ever heard that one zucchini plant can feed the multitudes? I swear to God, that's a true statement. Mama always had extras she could distribute to the ladies at church. Maybe I imagined it, but I think I noticed a few people sneak away in the opposite direction when they saw her approaching with loaded sacks of that one particular vegetable.

I breathed in a lungful of mind-clearing air. As enjoyable as reminiscing was, if I wanted to get today's job done anytime soon, I'd actually have to put my procrastinating body to work.

Rascal, on the other hand, seemed to have his own idea about facing the long day ahead. He yawned while wagging a lazy tail, undoubtedly signaling me to go ahead without him as he flopped to the ground, just far enough away so he wouldn't be disturbed. His message came through loud and clear: he'd nap; I'd work.

In the distance, a breeze ruffled healthy vines of kudzu, known to grow several inches per day. Roaming tendrils crept along the land, searching until they found sturdy trunks of unsuspecting pines. Open fertile fields, separating our land from the kudzu-draped trees, struggled to showcase the last of summer's native wildflowers. Nature would eventually replace the blooms with cool-season grasses.

Our property was bordered by two strings of rusty fence wire, wrapped around splintered cedar posts, planted every six or seven feet, most of them tilting at odd angles. The plot of ground, once home to my father's vegetable garden was rock-hard red Georgia clay, baked into one giant brick by the relentless sun of a whole summer. No, make that two summers. Daddy hadn't felt well enough to do much yard work during his final years, and he could barely summon enough energy to prune Mama's roses.

Mr. Smith recommended adding nutrients to the soil, like manure, vermiculite, and natural mulch, to assure a successful harvest. He added another suggestion. "If the soil hasn't been worked in a while, it might warrant a gas-powered tiller."

"Nah," I boasted, "I'm strong. The exercise will do me good. Besides, I want to be like a real farmer and do it the old-fashioned way."

"Your choice," he mumbled. But that was the short version. What he really meant was you're in for a heap of pain, but it's your funeral.

Well, I'd show him.

I saturated the hardened plot with a sprinkler the day before, which allowed me to easily bust through the top crust with a shovel. Then I broke up the dirt clods, sometimes by smoothing a rake back and forth, sometimes using the rake like a hammer to beat the clods senseless.

Bags of newly-purchased, smelly soil amendments sat nearby, ready to be ripped open. As I emptied the sacks and scattered their contents atop damp earth, I wished I'd also purchased a set of sturdy back muscles.

Flipping shovelfuls of earth over and over was a process I repeated until fatigue begged me to stop. I turned on the hose and let the water run icy cold before allowing my parched throat to enjoy a long drink. Wiping wet lips on the cuff of my garden glove, I scanned the plot. My chore was only halfway done.

Rascal lazed in the shade but occasionally picked up his head to check on me.

"I need your help, big fella," I jokingly called out. Of course, he ignored my plea, groaned, and again closed his eyes. In fact, he ignored me so well, he would have appeared dead to a casual observer. However, when Mama brought out lunch, Rascal sat up and came alive. His tail swept the dirt to show how pleased he was we finally had something to eat. Did I say *we*? Okay, I did give in and slipped him a few potato chips and a tiny piece of bologna. When break time ended, Rascal went back to sleep, and I went back to work.

Shortly thereafter, I formed lines of trenches and was officially ready to begin planting. Without a doubt, my yard had the best-looking soil in all of Georgia that day. I removed dirt-caked garden gloves, slapped them against my thigh, and watched powdered dust float across the empty rows. Squatting down, I brushed a steady hand across the tiny seedlings my gardener friend had donated. Four cardboard boxes, each lined with a plastic grocery bag, were filled with oodles of precious thinnings from his own garden. His generosity astounded me, but he waved away my appreciation, saying he needed to pull out the extras anyway and was happy to see them go to a good home.

Much later, wiping a soiled shirt sleeve across my sweaty forehead, I dropped my tired remains to the ground beside Rascal. As I ran my blistered hand along his furry mane, I couldn't help but feel contentment. I'd worked my tail off, and the garden looked fantastic. Pride wanted me to jump up and down and announce it to the world, but my aching body argued.

I don't know which was worse—how I looked, or how I smelled. I removed my sneakers and grimy cut-offs. In fact, I took off everything, except my undergarments, and left a dirty heap in the laundry room sink. All I could think about was treating my sore muscles to a good soak.

"Don't worry," I announced to my mother as I scurried through the kitchen. "I'll be back down later to clean up the mess I left behind."

As Mama looked up from peeling a potato, a grin lit her face. She giggled.

I stopped short. "What's so funny?"

She didn't say anything, she simply pointed to where my bare legs changed color at the ankles from white to brown. The stark contrast made me look as though I'd been in a tanning bed and forgotten to remove my socks.

Later, however, I realized the application of SPF50 had actually worked. My temporary tan had been just that, and all of it magically disappeared down the drain when I pulled the plug. All of it, that is, except for the bathtub ring which I immediately scoured with cleanser. If I didn't take care of it right then, Mama, aka Mrs. Clean, would have it bright and shiny before I could turn around, and I, of course, would feel like a naughty child.

Chapter Ten

"And what's this?" I stood in the Smiths' driveway and withdrew the fifth item from the galvanized pail sitting on my truck's open tailgate. "My mother thought it looked like a flour sifter."

"No," Mr. Smith said. "That's for broadcasting grass seed."

I grabbed another mystery item—a metal form with four compartments. "How about this thing?"

"I've never used one, but I'm sure it's a soil block maker."

"For…?"

"For making little planting squares…kind of like peat pots."

"Peat pots?"

He raised an eyebrow. "You really *are* new to gardening." Taking the implement from my hand, he pointed to one compartment. "Each of these tiny sections would be packed with soil and then plunged out, making mini-gardens for one or two seeds. You let the seeds germinate in a controlled environment while you wait for ideal weather. Then you plug the whole thing into the ground without disturbing any roots. Make sense?"

A vision from long ago floated through my mind— trays of potting soil squares, lounging on a window sill, while tender sprouts of baby plants enjoyed new life. And me, there I was, standing on a chair, leaning above those trays, tracing my name through the humidity that had trickled down our glassed-in laundry room. With a sigh, I tucked away the precious remembrance. "Makes perfect sense. I think my father did that."

I pulled the final tool from the bucket. "Okay. Last one. What's this pointy thing?"

"That's called a dibber. It's for planting bulbs." He gestured a demonstration in mid-air. "You hold the handle like this and push it into the earth." He glanced toward his garage. "Wait. Stay here. I'll be right back." He returned, carrying a sack of flower bulbs and explained he had them stored in a refrigerator.

We knelt by a maple tree with a circular bed of greenery at its base. He pushed back a clump of leaves and shoved the metal dibber into the ground in a dozen spots. Each fresh hole received one bulb, and then soil got patted over the top.

He crumpled the empty sack and stood. "Pretty simple. You just have to get them into the ground before first frost." He dusted his hands and helped me to my feet. "You might tell your readers it's time to plant bulbs now so they'll have springtime blooms."

"Great idea!" My mind reeled with possibilities. "I'll be glad to give you credit. How does that sound?"

With an expression near panic, he roared, "No! Don't do that. I don't want credit."

Speechless, I stood there, mouth open, eyes blinking in disbelief.

His ears turned red. He lowered his gaze while softening his tone. "I mean…it's too early to give anybody credit. Right now, your readers need to believe all this knowledge comes from *you*. That's how you'll earn their respect."

He'd had similar panicked outbursts before, but within seconds he always backtracked and calmed down. Maybe he was manic-depressive? I didn't know him well enough to suggest medication existed for that sort of behavior. Anyway, his moods were none of my business.

In less than an hour that afternoon, my gardening expertise grew substantially. Mr. Smith even presented me with a bag of miscellaneous bulbs I could plant at home. He told me they were from his grandson.

"From Johnny?"

"In a roundabout way. Last spring, when the blooms finished, I lifted the bulbs and carefully separated each variety." He chuckled. "When I went to retrieve a box of storage bags, Johnny piled all the bulbs into a single mound."

Mr. Smith didn't smile often, but I could tell he had a soft spot for his grandson.

"I couldn't be angry. Johnny didn't realize he was mixing colors." Mr. Smith shrugged. "Anyway, you get to enjoy nature's surprise next spring."

I thanked him, said good-bye, and went to close my truck's tailgate.

Mr. Smith called out for me to wait. He hurried to the garage and came back with one more gift. He'd been cultivating his own hybrid tulips over the years and had developed a unique variety in a color combination not available commercially. Not only did he give me a sample bulb, he included a photograph, showing how the flower looked in full bloom.

****

I had barely walked through the door when the phone rang. The caller was my boss at the *Tribune*. He told me the initial feedback on my prior articles had been extremely positive. He had decided to expand the allotted space from two columns to three. Translation? I'd have a quarter page to work with.

"If you don't have enough copy to fill it, you're welcome to include a photo."

"A photo?"

"Either a head shot of you or anything pertainin' to your theme. A black and white with good contrast will work. But next week, we'll run a full-color edition, and a color photo might dress up your column."

My mind instantly envisioned the photo of Mr. Smith's hybrid tulips. A photo. *Yes. I could do that!* I hung up and flew to my laptop, mind clicking with fresh ideas, and laid down the first few lines of my next newspaper article.

Mama descended the stairs, mumbling to herself, "Where did I put those?"

She often thought out loud, and since she hadn't directed the question to me, I knew I wasn't required to answer, so I continued to focus on typing.

Her voice trailed off as she padded across the room in her terry scuffs. In the kitchen, the sound of her opening and closing drawers echoed off the walls. When the last drawer slid shut, Mama announced, "Ah ha. Right where I left them." Floorboards creaking under her steady footsteps, she walked into the parlor and approached the sofa.

With my fingers dancing on the keyboard, rushing to capture immediate thoughts, I didn't stop to acknowledge her until the weight of a hefty purse dropped down onto a neighboring cushion. I gave her a quick smile as she settled next to me.

She peered into a fat envelope and withdrew a fistful

of supermarket discount coupons. Shuffling them from one hand to the other, she let an occasional sigh escape her lips. "Phooey. Most of these have expired."

I heard her purse being unsnapped and the crinkle of the envelope, but I had returned to my keyboard and didn't look up.

"Honey, I'm fixin' to go to the store. Wanna come along?" She paused but eventually reached over and tapped my shoulder. "Callie—?"

Gaze still riveted to the computer screen, I held up an index finger, indicating I needed a moment before answering. At the end of the paragraph, I removed my glasses and cleaned them on my shirttail. "Sorry, didn't mean to be rude. I was afraid of losing my train of thought."

She reached into her purse and withdrew an ink pen and a rumpled grocery list. "Well, do you want to come along or not?"

"Yes, ma'am." I folded my laptop and shoved it onto the coffee table. "Let me change into something warmer. Finish your list. I'll meet you at the car." I paused at the base of the staircase. "And don't forget to change your slippers." I wasn't being smart-alecky—I just didn't want her to be embarrassed in public...again.

I bounded up the stairs and ditched my cut-offs in favor of blue jeans. Before pulling on a long-sleeved top, I rolled my injured arm forward to examine my elbow. The doctor had removed the dressing after the first week to let the sores breathe and continue to heal. The last of the scab would be gone soon, and it didn't look like I'd have much of a scar. In a frustrated fit of anger, because typing with one hand sucked, I had ripped off the part of the bandage that covered my palm after the first day.

Grabbing a favorite hoodie, I mused that my sweatshirt collection would soon get regular use. The nights had cooled weeks before, the humidity had lessened, and the daytime temps were becoming milder with every passing day.

I gazed out the window at my garden, noting the fading afternoon light and the sunset glow on those tender young shoots. At that moment, I could see more red dirt than green vegetables, but I assumed the look of the plants would change soon enough. Even with less warmth from an autumnal sun, I knew determined little sprouts of life would continue reaching heavenward. I couldn't expect the same bounty as with a summer garden, but the winter garden would produce plenty of fresh veggies that would find their way into our kitchen. And the results would appear in my weekly articles.

Mama eased out of our driveway and glanced at me. "You came home with a paper sack this afternoon. More little plants for your garden?"

"No, ma'am. Today's bag contained flower bulbs."

She grinned. "How nice. I like the idea of seein' more color in the yard than just my roses." A soft smile graced her expression. "I hope you know how proud I am of you. It's fun watchin' my baby girl become an authority on somethin' she seems to enjoy."

I chuckled. "Well, I'm not an authority yet. But considering where I started, I've come a long way."

"Did I mention I've been given permission to add photos? There'll be lots of room in next week's issue for pictures." A mischievous grin found its way to my lips. "I'm not going to tell Mr. Smith I plan to use his tulip photo. Can't wait to see the surprised look on his face."

Chapter Eleven

Mama wheeled the shopping cart up one aisle and down another, leisurely taking her time to compare prices on every item before deciding to buy.

I'd only partnered her on this trip because of my excitement about exploring one particular department. My impatience finally got the best of me. "Mama, when you're finished, come find me in the produce section."

Waist-high bins displayed generous mounds of salad greens, lightly misted and neatly stacked, tempting each passerby. I felt like a kid in a candy store. Why hadn't I noticed these before? There were so many varieties to choose from: escarole, radicchio, curly endive, arugula, and more. The choices blew my mind. I had never given any of these a single thought until I started farming.

We were simple people. I'd grown up thinking a salad meant iceberg lettuce and chopped tomatoes, with mayonnaise as the dressing. If we really wanted to be fancy, we might even add a few snips of carrot. At the college dining commons, I thought I was being so continental when romaine caught my attention.

I yanked a strip of plastic bags off a spindle next to the produce scale and stuck a dozen twist ties between my teeth, determined to take home a sample of every green available. I filled the final bag and grinned, confident I'd gotten one of everything.

"Excuse me. Will you be leaving some for the rest of us?"

I whirled, ready to defend my actions, and nearly bumped into Mr. Smith and his family. Their cart, filled to the brim, hinted they wouldn't have to shop again until winter. Johnny sat strapped into the child seat and kicked his legs enthusiastically upon seeing me. I tickled him under the chin, delighting in his reaction when he ducked his head and giggled.

Mary's smile said she approved. This was the first time we'd met. She was a combination of long legs, a gracious smile, and a thin figure. The light freckles dotting her nose were a perfect match to Johnnie's. Wavy, shoulder-length, dark brown curls with strawberry-blonde roots told me she needed a visit from a bottle of hair color. Not sure why she bothered with coloring; pale tresses would have beautifully complemented her fair skin.

Similarities to her father's mannerisms were present, but Mary was less serious, more animated, probably because she worked among the public at her waitressing jobs. But she spoke haltingly, like her father. I couldn't help wondering if they always monitored their conversations, carefully choosing just how much information to reveal.

"I told your Dad I went to UCLA. He didn't mention where *you'd* gone."

Her gaze flicked to her father and then back to me. "Well...I didn't go to college."

"Did you have one picked out, just in case you changed your mind?"

Her hands tightened on the shopping cart's red handle. "Um...no. I didn't."

"There's still time, and some schools have financial aid for widows."

Mr. Smith reached between us and snapped a plastic bag off the roll. "Pardon me, but we need to finish shopping. Johnny's tired."

At his curt interruption, I stepped back. "Oh, sorry. Didn't mean to delay you. At least let me introduce my mother before you go." I scanned the immediate area.

The wheels on Mama's basket had stopped in front of the apple display. She placed a few, small Red Delicious into a bag and added a twist tie.

I caught her eye and motioned for her to join us.

After a brief nod to my introductions, she glanced at her watch. "Callie, we should get home. I left a roast in the oven. If I don't pull it out soon, you'll be eatin' beef jerky." She turned her cart toward the checkout register and called out over her shoulder, "Nice to have met y'all."

Because Mama's exit had been a little abrupt, I stayed behind to dispel any qualms about her friendliness. "Next time my mother fixes one of her famous cobblers, she'll want to have you over."

I knew Mama would be okay with the invitation— she was the consummate southern hostess, whose primary mission was to feed the world. I waved goodbye and watched the Smiths hurry away in the opposite direction.

****

Mama stepped onto the back stoop with an armload of groceries. She twisted the house key back and forth several times in the rusty knob before shoving a shoulder against the door. "This is gettin' so hard to open. I don't know why we bother lockin' it anyway. Someone could just break the glass if they wanted in."

Onto the kitchen table, I plunked down a total of four reusable grocery bags and started unpacking. "Glad I finally got to meet Mary. Maybe we can be friends." I pulled out a box of grits and wedged it into the pantry. "Isn't that little Johnny a doll?"

Mama didn't react. The groceries held her undivided attention as she searched for items needing refrigeration. I passed her a package of frozen peas. "Mama, what did you think of Mr. Smith's family?"

She still didn't respond. The job of stacking food into the freezer seemed to occupy her thoughts. Without looking up, she reached out to grab the next item.

I gripped it firmly, refusing to let go until she answered. "Well?"

She tugged at the package before meeting my gaze and then exhaled. "They seem like pleasant people." She turned back to the freezer, deposited the final item, and shut the door, letting her hand linger on the handle. "But…"

I blinked. "But what?"

"All I meant was I was surprised to see them at the market, that's all."

"Huh?" I scowled. "People need to eat, you know."

"I know, silly." She tightened the cap on the newly purchased bleach jug and walked it to the laundry room while talking over her shoulder. "It's just…well…I heard they hide from the public."

"Wa…what?" I drew back my chin. "Who'd you hear that from?"

"From the manicurist where I get my hair done." Mama tilted her head. "You know, your friend from high school…Francine Lothner?"

"Francine Lothner, huh." I knew where this was going. Francine was the queen of gossip when we were in high school.

"She lives on the same street as the Smiths. She's seen your truck over there and wondered what was up." Mama lowered her gaze and avoided my stare. "I'm sorry, Callie, I didn't want her assumin' somethin' strange was goin' on, so I told her about the gardenin' thing."

Dread hit me as I realized the significance of one more person knowing I wasn't a gardening expert. "Oh no! You didn't." How much time did I have left at my new job before someone squawked? Eyes shut, I smacked my forehead in frustration.

"Callie Lou, stop that. You needn't worry. I specifically told her not to tell anybody Mr. Smith was givin' you advice for your column."

I rolled my eyes. *Sure, motor-mouth Francine wouldn't blab.* I exhaled a sigh that could have been heard next door. "So, what else did she say?"

"She thought the family was a little weird."

"Weird?" Folding a leg under me, I dropped onto a kitchen chair and braced myself for a story about Francine's latest gossip victims. "How so?"

"Other than Mary goin' to her job, they never seem to get out. And you're the only person who drops by." Mama frowned as she looked off into space. "Hmm. You know, now that I think about it, most of my information really came from Olivia Brown. She was in the shop, too. She said the Smiths keep their blinds drawn. A lot. Sounds kinda creepy, doesn't it?" Mama leaned back against the counter and folded arms across her ample bosom. "I don't feel comfortable about you goin' over there anymore."

I was old enough to make my own decisions about where I went. Indignant, I rose up straight and accidentally bumped an empty grocery bag, sending it to the floor. "Well, Francine's right, they do keep to themselves." I bent over to rescue the sack, and then creased the corners. "They're quiet people. But to believe Francine…let me tell you, she's not my friend. We're only acquainted because we had classes together."

Mama edged closer, pushed wayward hair out of my eyes, and cupped my chin. "Well, *she* thinks y'all are friends."

"Pfft. Yeah, right. She just doesn't remember." My gaze dropped to the bag. I finished folding it and laid it on the table, pressing it flat with my fingertips. "In school, we all kept our distance. She was responsible for most of the rumors at Willoughby High. She'd say almost anything to get attention. Maybe she's still doing that."

"Maybe. But she did appear genuinely concerned."

"Well, I'm not. And as for me going over to the Smiths', I'll be fine. I'm a big girl, so please stop worrying." I turned away and faced the pantry, signaling I was done with the conversation. I gathered the few remaining cereal boxes and placed them onto the shelf, all the while feeling my mother's nervous presence behind me. With my chore done, I folded the remaining bags and jammed them into the crowded space beneath the sink.

The sound of silence made me turn. Her troubled look was still there, so I patted her shoulders and pressed my cheek to hers. "I love you for being concerned, Mama, but remember, you raised a smart daughter. If I sense something's not right, I won't go back." I inhaled a quick breath. "Now then, I'm headed upstairs to wash, and then I'll be down to set the table. Okay?"

But I had lied. Not about setting the table, but about not going back to the Smiths' house. If anything, my curiosity would probably get the best of me, and I wouldn't be able to stay away.

Chapter Twelve

"What the hell were you thinking?" Mr. Smith bellowed.

I blinked at his outburst. Stunned, I returned his roar. "I was thinking you'd be flattered."

"Well, you're wrong! I distinctly remember telling you I didn't want any credit."

My eyes stung, but I willed myself not to cry. "I didn't give you credit. Did you see your name anywhere in the article?"

He whipped the newspaper from my hands and scanned the gardening column.

I brushed away a determined tear while he wasn't looking. "See? I told you." My voice grew softer as I dialed down my furor.

He creased the paper in half and handed it back. Then he headed for the bottom porch step to sit. I followed his lead but waited for him to say something. An eternity ticked away before he spoke. Still not looking up, he grumbled, "I'm sorry, Callie. I jumped to conclusions."

The knot in my stomach slowly unwound. "That's okay. I should have gotten your permission before using the tulip photo. I'm really sorry." I swallowed hard before letting the words spill out. "But can you please explain why my article upsets you so much?"

Again, dead silence as he focused somewhere out in

space. "You never know when danger—" He paused and finally looked at me. "Would you like a soda?"

"Uh…sure," I responded, wondering why he'd changed the subject so abruptly. *Darn it!* I wanted him to finish what he'd started. *You never know when danger—?*

He climbed the steps and disappeared into the house.

His trip to the kitchen, under the guise of getting us beverages, might have been his way of grabbing an opportunity to compose his thoughts. Was he trying to steer me away from a subject he feared would slip out, something he didn't want to reveal?

The refrigerator door closed, and two pop tops released their fizz. The screen door banged shut and Mr. Smith walked down the steps to offer me a frosty soda. We sipped in silence until I could stand it no more. "You were saying?"

He took a long drink before placing the soda can on the step. He folded his hands and leaned elbows on bent knees. "Callie, I'm a very private person. I don't need people fawning over my accomplishments for me to feel worthwhile. My tulips are my very own special thing. Personal. I don't mind sharing them with you, but the whole world doesn't need to be in on it. If anyone asks about the photo, I'd appreciate you saying it's yours. Please don't mention I had anything to do with it." His eyes riveted on mine. "Will you promise me that?"

"Uh…of course." I remembered how alike Daddy had been about his own talents. I could never replace my father, but a similar friendship might suffice for now. On the other hand, could it last? I swallowed hard. If Mr. Smith was this upset now, he would go ballistic come April.

Chapter Thirteen

"Hate" is a dirty word. I refuse to say it aloud because I don't like the sound of it rolling off my tongue. Sadly, it fit the situation, because that's how Mr. Smith was going to feel about me when he found out what else I'd done.

When Mama suggested I write about a subject that truly appealed to me, her words got me thinking. I'd always been drawn to human interest stories, so it made sense to use that as my theme. Who was my subject? A grandfather, whose greatest joy came from tending his garden and taking care of his family.

Every aspect of the article fell together beautifully. It was as if God had directed my hands to type the words. I even had a nice photo to go with it. Days before, unaware of me, Mr. Smith bent down to tie Johnny's shoelace and I snapped a quick picture using the camera on my cell phone. The lighting, the composition—a professional couldn't have captured a better shot, if I do say so myself. Initially, I hadn't meant this photo to be anything more than just a sweet remembrance I would paste into a mental scrapbook. Then I wondered…wouldn't the world also enjoy seeing this slice of life?

Originally, I'd thought of this article as a test piece—one I could chew on until the wording was perfect, one I hadn't meant to submit anywhere until I spoke to Mr. Smith. Then I saw a writing contest's final Call for Entries. The mail-in deadline had passed, but the on-line deadline was just minutes away. The sponsor, *American Portraits Magazine,* with a circulation of over one million subscribers, promised future publication and a monetary reward for the winners.

I debated the consequences of asking or not asking Mr. Smith for his permission to enter the competition. If he said yes, and the article got rejected by the judges, I'd feel like a foolish amateur, and Mr. Smith's disappointment might be even greater than mine. My other choice was to enter, cross my fingers, and hope my article made the final cut. If it did, I would then fess up to what I'd done.

I hit the Send button before I could change my mind. Then, the following month, a certificate arrived in the mail with a confirmation. "Congratulations! Your article will be featured next year in the April issue of *American Portraits Magazine.*"

I'd been published lots of times, so this particular article shouldn't have been a big deal. But it was. This project was my newest baby, and I even considered passing out cigars announcing it. But I didn't. Why? Maybe because I knew I had done wrong by not asking Mr. Smith's permission. Now, I just needed to come up with the right words to explain my hasty decision.

My most difficult challenge was hiding the secret from Mama. I feared if she knew, she might let it slip while visiting the beauty shop and give Francine Lothner something new to post on social media.

I was so paranoid about keeping quiet that the concern even crept into my dreams. In a recurring nightmare, I found myself on a very public street corner, mashed into a mob of scurrying bodies. When the red light changed to green, I got caught up in the surging crowd and stumbled into the crosswalk. Dizziness caused me to stop in the middle of the street. I was about to be sick, so I held out my arms to push pedestrians out of the way.

I yelled, "Nooooo!"

All at once, thousands of words exploded out of the top of my head. Wild-eyed with fear, everyone backed off to stare at me like I was a terrorist. I woke up in a sweat.

But bad dreams were the least of my worries. I wasn't aware of Mr. Smith's privacy issues when I submitted the article. Now that I knew, I shuddered every time I thought ahead to April. That's when I'd have to deal with his anger and maybe lose a friend. However, publication was still five months away. By then, surely, I'd come up with a plan.

Chapter Fourteen

November

My garden looked healthier with each passing day. The radishes now produced crops regularly. The first time I harvested one big enough to eat, I didn't want to. I don't mean I didn't want to *pick* it; I just didn't want to *eat* it. Some things in life must be cherished, treated with respect. You know, kind of like bronzing a pair of baby shoes? Not that I'd go that far—at least I don't think I would—but I did drop the radish into a baggie and keep it with me. However, after two days in my backpack, the shriveled vegetable wasn't fit for human consumption. Even though it was painful, I gave the radish a decent burial in a trash can.

The greens growing in my rich garden soil came from tiny seedlings, beginning their first signs of life in Mr. Smith's plot. The various plants were still relatively small, but they were wonderfully tender. Every now and then, I selected some worthy leaves and made us a salad. Salad was *not* my mother's favorite—she only tolerated my choice, because she didn't like to see good food go to waste. As time went on, she shared bags of the stuff with the ladies at church.

Meanwhile, I used most of the vegetables as subject matter for my column. Whenever I borrowed the *Trib's* professional camera, along with a close-focus lens, I shot respectable photos of what appeared to be mature plants, lush enough to fool my readers. Using a photo to accompany each article had become tradition. A little early to call it tradition? Probably. I'd only been on the job for seven weeks.

I'd written the pumpkin-themed article for my inaugural *Gardening with Callie.* If I'd had a chance for a do-over, I would have included a photo of bulging orange pumpkins, featuring a golden-crusted pie in the foreground. The composition would have made a heck of an impression. So far, my garden had only produced miniature pumpkins. But I was okay with that, because they would make lovely table decor on Thanksgiving.

For all the November issues, my theme was "Autumn Harvest." Each column would include a picture. If desperate, I could buy a stock photo—heaven forbid—easily purchased on the Internet. Not my choice, but Mr. Barton gave me permission to do so if I couldn't find suitable subject matter to shoot on my own. I also wanted to use one of my mother's favorite recipes to enhance each article that led up to turkey day.

Mama ceased thumbing through handwritten index cards in her recipe collection and paused, wedging a finger inside the file box as a place holder. "Persimmon cookies?"

"Not quite what I'm looking for."

"Well, you said fall, and it's filed under fall."

My mother had great recipes, but she was the only one who could navigate her creative filing system. I reached across the table and squeezed her arm. "I know, and everyone raves about your persimmon cookies, Mama. But this week I want *vegetable* recipes, not desserts."

She nodded and pulled a three-by-five card from the box. "Here you go," she announced, using her fingernail to scrape off a lingering spatter from a past holiday. "Cranberry-Orange Sauced Beets. Your father loved them."

I clapped my hands like a little kid. "Perfect. Will you make some for Thanksgiving?"

Mama had already asked the couple from next door, along with our minister, to join us for turkey dinner. I invited one of my new friends at the newspaper, Savannah, who worked in the accounting department.

I also stopped by Mr. Smith's house and extended an invitation to him and his family. "Mama suggested coming early, about one o'clock."

"Thanks for asking, but we have other plans."

The Smith family celebrating with someone else had never occurred to me. Feeling a tiny bit jealous, I lowered my gaze and scuffed a shoe against his driveway. "I'm disappointed. Mama will be, too. She always cooks enough food to feed an army." I looked up and cocked my chin. "I'm glad you have other plans, though. What will y'all be doing?"

"Well, um, we...I mean...my daughter has to work. The restaurant is serving special Thanksgiving meals."

I brightened. "Gee, if that's all it is, what time does Mary get off work? Mama will be happy to postpone dinner 'til later."

He shook his head. "Don't change your plans for us. We'd feel guilty. And truly, after working a heavy shift, Mary will want to come home and put up her feet."

"Oh. Of course." I resigned myself to his refusal, until an alternative idea hit. "Then why don't just you and Johnny join us at one o'clock? We'll package up some leftovers you can serve Mary after she gets home."

"Uh...I don't think that will work either. Johnny takes a nap each afternoon, otherwise he gets pretty cranky. Besides, how long since you and your mother ate with a toddler? His manners aren't the best. Thanks for the invitation anyway."

Obviously, he wasn't going to budge, so I gave up. He probably would have just invented more excuses anyway...as he had in the past. I began to wonder if Francine Lothner was right. Were the Smiths afraid to go out?

Chapter Fifteen

Thanksgiving has always been my favorite holiday. How could anyone not love a day centered around food? I would consume a week's worth of calories within a few hours. And if that wasn't enough, we'd have a refrigerator full of delicious leftovers I could savor all weekend, in spite of the extra pounds that would haunt me later.

Mr. and Mrs. Brown from next door were the first to arrive. Olivia Brown was a round, jovial woman, a chatterer who had to be taken in small doses. Her third husband, Roy Brown, never had a chance to say much, and after almost seven years of marriage, things were not about to change.

Miz Olivia exuded her own version of the daily news and delivered it with calculated speed so her listeners had no chance to escape. Single-handedly, she could pin down an entire army with her incessant talking. That day, we were the army being held captive.

"Did y'all hear the new bank manager already got himself engaged?"

"Really?" Mama mumbled, mildly distracted as she poured servings of sweet tea from a frosty pitcher.

"Uh, huh. To Lilly May Tindal…of all people."

Then, as if the four of us were in a crowded room, she peered over her glass of tea, shielded her mouth with a cupped hand, and confided in a loud whisper.

"I hear they met only three weeks ago." She cleared her throat. "I don't think he knows what he's in for, but I'd be surprised if they're still together a month from now." She turned to me and added, "You young'uns would describe her as high maintenance. A year ago, I seen her buy three pairs of shoes…all on the same day. I think she set her sights on Mr. Orton when he first came to town." Miz Brown giggled. "Yep, Lilly May probably figured a banker could afford to keep her in high fashion."

My mother's Christian upbringing didn't favor gossip, but she'd also been taught not to be rude, so she politely kept her tongue. However, Mama couldn't hide her relief when an interruption rang the doorbell.

We both rushed to answer it, but I got there first.

Opening the front door, I found our minister standing on the welcome mat, wearing a nervous grin. He thrust his arm past me and handed Mama a cellophane-wrapped bouquet. I should have been red from embarrassment, standing there witnessing little sparks between the two of them, but my mother was the one who blushed.

"Oh, Pastor Dan, you shouldn't have," she cooed, dipping her nose into the flowers.

He stepped inside and removed the hat concealing a bald head fringed with white hair.

His head couldn't have shone more brightly if he'd worn a halo. But, then again, maybe he did. He was a genuine, selfless man who ministered to a congregation of just over two hundred, not only on Sunday, but every day of the week. The word "no" was not in his vocabulary where his church was concerned. Whether you were a Southern Baptist, a Methodist, or whatever religion, you had to admit you admired him. He embodied the wholesome goodness that came from clean living and an eye fixed upon the Lord.

When Mama excused herself to hunt down a vase, I escorted our newest guest into the parlor. "Pastor Dan, this is Mr. Roy Brown and his wife Miz Olivia Brown."

"Mr. Brown," he said, nodding a greeting. "Callie, you don't have to introduce me to Olivia Bedford, um, I mean Olivia Brown. We both graduated Willoughby High in—"

"Now, now, Dan," she giggled, fanning her face. "Let's not give away what year. Let's just say we're old friends." She directed her gaze toward me. "We met when he dated my cousin Wanda."

He shyly confirmed it with a nod, rolling the brim of his hat before allowing me to place it on the entry hall console.

"You shoulda stayed with Wanda," Miz Brown scolded, wagging her finger. "She came into a lot of money when her daddy died. Anyways, where'd you run off to?"

"The Lord called me to seminary school."

"Oh," she replied, her neck turning a bright pink. "Well, that couldn't have meant but a couple years. How come you took so long to get back to Willoughby?"

"God had other plans, I guess. I spent six years as a navy chaplain."

"Good for you." She glanced at his hand. "I don't see a wedding ring. Wanda's between husbands right now. Maybe you—"

He raised a palm. "I appreciate the offer. But I'm pretty busy at the church."

Shame on him. He'd lied. In truth, the church had

just hired a new assistant pastor. Translation? More free time for Pastor Dan. Although he wasn't quite ready to retire, he had asked for a break now and then to invest in a personal life. Seven years prior, he'd lost his wife to pneumonia and hadn't remarried. Since then, all his attention had been devoted to his church—his parishioners depended upon him more than any earthly bride ever could.

At sixty-seven, he was just a few years older than my mother. Since he'd already weathered the death of a spouse, he knew firsthand what Mama would experience with her own loss. He had practically carried her through the initial grieving and was still her closest ally. I knew he wanted more. And in time, maybe she would, too. But for now, I sensed she didn't want to betray Daddy by letting herself love someone new. Obviously, she and the minister made a good match. But I wouldn't be the one to push them together, mostly because I didn't know if I was ready for a stepfather.

The next time the doorbell chimed, my new friend Savannah stood at the door…a half hour overdue. Southern hospitality dictated I pretend her tardiness wasn't an imposition. We would have been ill-mannered if we had started eating without her, no matter how long she took to get there.

"Sorry, Callie," she said, out of breath, stepping into the entry and slipping arms from a wooly sweater. "My sweetie called. He forgot his lunch."

A grin revealed my amusement. "Too bad the convenience store doesn't carry anything to eat."

She laughed. "Just because he's surrounded by food doesn't mean he'll make the right choice. If I didn't bring him somethin' from home, he'd probably sit behind the counter, snackin' on donuts."

Smiling, and hoping to make her feel at home, I crooked my elbow into hers and walked her into the parlor. "Everyone, this is Savannah. We work together at the newspaper. She's the *Trib*'s one-woman bookkeeping department."

Savannah began working there part-time while still in twelfth grade. College wasn't an option, so she remained at the *Tribune* after graduating high school. She'd started at minimum wage but now made almost as much as she would have if she'd worked for one of the big dailies in Atlanta. Good thing, because she and her new husband were still paying off their wedding debt from the previous year.

"I understand your hubby has to work today," Mama said, offering a glass of sweet tea as Savannah eased into an overstuffed chair.

"Yes, ma'am. He's low man in seniority."

Mama patted Savannah's arm. "Well, I'm sorry he couldn't join us, but I'm pleased you're here."

"Me, too. This is a real treat. I'm not much of a cook, so a bag of popcorn and a pile of DVDs was gonna be my Thanksgivin'."

Savannah first told me about her plans a week ago. I couldn't imagine her spending Thanksgiving alone, binge-watching a bunch of gangster movies or sappy romances, so I included her on our guest list.

Our anxious appetites took seats around the dining room table. Mama had outdone herself. The afternoon was an absolute food fest, with ample opportunity to gorge ourselves on all kinds of traditional delicacies.

The turkey, all golden brown and dripping with mouth-watering juices, *should* have been the star, but it wasn't. Don't get me wrong, it looked and smelled wonderful, and the flavor was excellent. But Miz Olivia was the one to take the lead in our cast of characters. She had the most amount of dialogue. We didn't need to go to the theater—the theater had come to us.

She probably knew more than our mayor knew about what was going on in Willoughby. She spouted updates concerning every resident in our immediate neighborhood. Then she started on other areas of town. My back tensed ramrod straight when she mentioned Mr. Smith's street.

"Y'all might not have heard, but earlier this year, some outsiders moved into a Roseberry Lane rental." She raised her eyebrows. "They're *Yankees.*" As the word hung in the air, she scanned our faces. "Bet y'all are wonderin' how I know."

Her Cheshire cat grin couldn't have been wider. Undoubtedly, she hoped to impress us with her knowledge of insider information. And it worked. Like curious fish, she reeled us in. We leaned forward and waited to hear.

She scooted to the edge of her chair to whisper. "Y'all heard of Millie Logan? Welcome Wagon volunteer? Knows whenever anybody new comes to Willoughby. She's just full of information…and she's my closest friend." Miz Olivia settled back and wound her fingers in her imitation pearl necklace.

"Anyways, Millie said she stopped by the new folks' house several days in a row with a basket of welcome goodies. She thought she saw the curtains move, but no one answered the door. She'd 'bout given up. Then a week later, she was drivin' up Roseberry and saw a gardener mowin' the grass. She stopped to ask him if the tenants were home. He said the folks livin' there didn't like to be bothered. In fact, he made it clear she was not to come back again. Can y'all imagine?" She scowled. "How rude."

Mr. Brown appeared to be the only one buying into her story. He tsk-tsked his tongue and shook his head to echo her disgust.

Miz Olivia dabbed her mouth with a napkin. "Well now, I didn't think much more about it, until I was havin' my nails done." She set her napkin beside her plate and glanced at the pampered hand resting on the tablecloth. Reaching across the centerpiece, she displayed her shiny red nail polish. "Don't y'all just love this color?"

Everyone nodded politely…everyone except me. I tried to be polite and contain myself, but my gums hurt from clenching my jaw.

She tucked the hand into her lap but continued to look down and admire the set of polished nails. Her smile faded and she glanced up. "Now, where was I? Oh, yes. My nail girl. She was tellin' me 'bout *her* new neighbors and the strange things goin' on over there. She said those folks hardly ever go out, and they peek through their blinds all the time." Miz Olivia gave her chin a firm nod. "Yep, you guessed it, same family. And, come to find out, the man Millie talked to that day wasn't the gardener—he was the *tenant*."

Bile rose in my throat. I couldn't resist setting things straight. I laid my hand on Mama's to keep her from interrupting. "Your nail girl doesn't happen to be Francine Lothner, does she?"

"Yes, as a matter of fact. She a friend of yours?" Miz Olivia grinned and batted her eyelashes.

She was sadly mistaken if she thought she'd found

someone who would corroborate her story. My neck muscles tensed. "Not really," I answered, straight-faced, determined not to let her use me as an accomplice. "Let's just say Francine's stories are well-known, but they're not always reliable."

"Well, in this case, they just might be." Miz Olivia leaned forward, lowering her voice. "Back in June, Matthew Gordon's real estate office got a call from a Mr. Smith who was lookin' to find a furnished rental. Matt asked the man when he'd like to see the only one available. Mr. Smith said it weren't necessary, he'd take it. Can y'all imagine?" She scowled and sat back to fold arms across her chest. "Who rents somethin' without actually seein' it?" She waited to let the comment sink in while swirling ice cubes in her glass.

"Anyways, Smith said he'd be sendin' first and last months' rent immediately, but he wouldn't be comin' to the office to pick up keys. He wanted 'em put under the mat 'cause they'd be movin' in after dark."

Outrage made me grip the tablecloth. "I don't think that's strange. Some people have to work during the day."

"Well, maybe, but just you wait." She held up a finger. "Gets even weirder. When the check arrived, Matt noticed it was from a medical clinic in *Chicago*. Doesn't that seem peculiar? All I'm sayin' is, I think these little things add up to make one giant, strange total. Whadda y'all think?"

My mind whirled. At the moment, I wasn't sure what to think, but I refused to leave anyone with the impression the Smith family was abnormal. The dinner roll in my hand had already been squashed by tense fingers. My face turned hot. Some angry words were about to burst forth from my mouth. I dropped the roll onto a plate and dusted my hands. "What I think is—" I winced when Mama's foot kicked me under the table.

An instant later she sprang from her chair. "Where are my manners? We still have dessert. Callie, you can help me in the kitchen. Now, who wants whipped cream on their pie?"

What a mother won't do to save her daughter from total embarrassment. I would have made a fool of myself. An outburst would have only confirmed everyone's suspicions—that I wasn't quite right in the head. I mean, after all, I had gone to school in *California*. And everyone knows how weird those Californians are.

When Mama lifted the wax paper cover off the pumpkin pie, a mixture of cinnamon, ginger, and nutmeg wafted from her homemade dessert. She slid it from the cooling rack to the counter and began cutting slices.

My angry fists were pressed against my thighs. I still fumed from the conversation at the table and needed to vent. "Of all the nerve—"

Mama pointed the spatula at me, her words barely audible as she mouthed, "Shhh. Not now. We can discuss this later."

Balancing dessert plates on my hands and arms was quite a feat. I couldn't envision myself as a juggler in the circus, but if the writing thing didn't work out, I was positive I could find a job as a waitress. I could have used a little help, but Mama was the one who got the assistance.

Pastor Dan jumped up when he saw her carrying the coffee pot and a stack of cups. "Here, let me take that, Grace." He accidentally brushed her arm.

I'd have to be dumb as a stick not to notice how

flustered my mother became at his touch. I do believe if everyone had been a little quieter, we would have heard her heart pounding.

Almost immediately, Miz Olivia began to tell stories about Mama's competition— *Wanda*. It was *Wanda* this and *Wanda* that, and how many wonderful things *Wanda* had done for our town and how many charities had received *Wanda's* donations. I could sense everyone's unease with each new exaggerated story. But later, when Mr. and Mrs. Brown finally left for home, they took that cloud of awkwardness with them.

Savannah had been quiet as a mouse during dinner, but she was the first to start lugging dirty dishes to the sink. She nodded her chin at Mama and Pastor Dan. "Why don't y'all move into the parlor and relax. Callie and I can take care of cleanin' up." She glanced at me over her shoulder with a secret wink. "Right, Callie?"

Mama shook her head. "I wouldn't feel right lettin' you do that."

"No, no. I insist. It's the least I can do to thank you for such a grand meal."

In the kitchen, I held fingertips beneath the faucet, waiting for hot water to arrive before setting the stopper in place. I often wished we'd owned an electric dishwasher, but Mama couldn't bear to give up cabinet space. That wasn't the only reason. I knew she doubted the dishes wouldn't come out clean enough to meet her strict inspection. Washing them by hand was forever destined to be the routine at our house.

Savannah picked up a dish towel and nudged me with her shoulder. She giggled. "How cute they are together. Don't you get a thrill seein' old folks in love?"

Shrugging, I squirted dish soap into the sink. Guess

I wasn't the only one who noticed what was going on.

After all the dishes had been washed, little bits of food floated in cold dishwater. I drained the empty sink while my friend dried the last of the silverware. Only halfway paying attention to Savannah's friendly chatter, I kept my other ear tuned to the parlor. Things seemed awfully quiet in there. Under the pretext of being a good hostess, I popped my head around the door jamb. "Would either of you like another cup before I unplug the coffee maker?"

Startled by the sound of my voice, the couple facing each other on the sofa flinched. They'd been lost in quiet conversation. Had I interrupted something intimate?

"Uh…not for me. I have to be going." Pastor Dan rose and turned to my mother. "Grace, will you walk me to my car?"

She didn't have to answer, her bashful smile said "yes."

"See you Sunday, Callie," he called out as they headed for the door. "Thanks for everything."

"I need to get goin', too," Savannah drawled. She folded the dish towel over the edge of the sink before giving me a warm hug. "Thanks for invitin' me today. The meal was a whole lot better than I woulda fixed. A frozen dinner couldn't hold a candle to home cookin' like your Mama done it."

I stood outside on our front porch and waved as she drove away.

Two figures, silhouetted by an occasional passing car, leaned against Pastor Dan's humble sedan.

They were oblivious to my world as I stared into theirs. How impolite of me. I spun and trotted back into the house. The dining room needed attention to return to its everyday look, so I had something to keep me busy while waiting for Mama to come back into the house.

I transferred the centerpiece to the sideboard and removed my grandmother's damask tablecloth, spot-treated the stains, and started a delicate cycle. After packaging the leftovers, I snagged a few yummy remnants of turkey still clinging to the carcass, and even tossed a few to Rascal. A dustpan in my hand, I had just bent over a pile of crumbs in the center of the room when I heard the sound of a car leaving.

The front door opened and then closed behind Mama's footsteps as she headed upstairs.

Was she humming?

She had stayed out way too long in the driveway, acting like a schoolgirl with a crush on some teenage boy. Even though I was tempted to scold her in jest, I decided against it—she might not appreciate my humor.

My smile faded as a sobering thought flitted through my brain. How much more time did we have together until Mama no longer needed me? I had expected her to eventually find solace in the company of others, and that was my prayer in the beginning. My plan was to wait for her heart to heal and then return to school. I would no longer see her as often, but I'd be her daughter forever, and our shared grief would only strengthen our bond. I shook my head to expel the melancholy. No sense in carrying sadness to bed—the act of leaving was still some time away.

Rascal followed me around the house as I turned off all the lights, then we climbed the stairs to my room. He jumped up onto my bed, wove himself into a tight circle, and settled in his usual place near the footboard.

I changed into pajamas and stood by the window in

the dark, gazing out across my moonlit garden. I'd allowed myself to be lured back into a world that felt safe in my childhood. Leaving for college hadn't been difficult, my whole future lay ahead. But leaving a second time wouldn't be as easy. An image floated through my mind, one of Mama helping me pack my luggage and then dropping me at the airport.

Would I be ready to go, or would I want to stay?

Chapter Sixteen

Most of the time, my duties at the *Trib* were simple: Show up for staff meetings and turn in my article each week. End of list. That was it. With so much free time, I would never need a vacation.

Then Mr. Barton declared, "I'm pleased to announce our office will be closed during Christmas week. I'm sure y'all can use a little time off."

What? You've got to be kidding.

The *Willoughby Tribune* always stayed on schedule, kind of like the post office. Neither snow, rain, heat, nor gloom of night would keep us from publishing. Our subscribers had signed up for a weekly read, and that's exactly what they would get. So, despite our upcoming vacation, we still had to make sure the paper showed up on their door step. Of course, the edition would be printed in advance. Each of us was asked to submit our Christmas week column two weeks early, plus we also had to turn in the regularly scheduled one.

On top of my *Trib* assignments, I'd picked up a couple of freelance jobs…with December 20 as the deadline. Realizing a good part of that month would see my fingers attached to a keyboard, I came to appreciate the idea of a vacation. And at the end of it, I might even look forward to my laptop gathering dust for a few days.

I only earned a tiny salary at the *Trib*. On the flip side, I had fewer responsibilities and plenty of hours to pen freelance articles. Although I wasn't exactly pulling in buckets of money, I earned enough to help with household expenses and even put a little into a savings account. Thank God, my parents had paid off the mortgage years before. Mama received Daddy's retirement pension, and when we added in my income, we didn't have to worry about a bill collector knocking at the door.

In the past, I received a fairly steady stream of work from various periodicals. That meant the money coming in was almost equal to a regular paycheck, albeit modest. I had to work with whatever subject the editors requested, so not every assignment was interesting. My new approach involved writing about subjects that appealed to me personally, and then crossing my fingers and hoping someone would buy. I was apprehensive at first, venturing into unknown territory. If no one liked my stories, my writing career might turn into a hobby…without pay.

My first human-interest article would be published in April. Soon I'd have to admit what I'd done. Even though I dreaded Mr. Smith's initial reaction, I didn't totally regret submitting the article. Surprising fringe benefits came my way because of it. The editor liked my style and referred me to several other periodicals. One of them, headquartered in New York City, asked for a sample piece. If it passed committee approval, I would receive a contract to do a series of short stories over the coming year.

Being in water-up-to-my-neck mode, I worked all hours to keep from drowning in a sea of digital writings. Even so, prior experience told me I functioned best when pressure was involved. With that in mind, I challenged myself with *Bring it on.*

I shouldn't have been so bold.

The flu hit our little town in a big way. Someone told me approximately twenty-five percent of our population was down with the virus. We had only two people in our household, and fifty percent of us got it. Yep, me. That twenty-four-hour bug wiped me out completely for one day and zapped my energy for almost a week afterward.

As soon as I felt well enough, I returned to my laptop. Luckily, the inspiration was there. Playing catch up, I wrote through the night until five a.m. the next morning. I finally dragged my recovering body out of bed at noon, and when passing by the mirror, I did a double take. My bed-head hair caught my attention, as did the dark under-eye circles accentuating my sickly pallor. The effect was totally gruesome. If I had to look like this, too bad it wasn't October. At least I might have won a prize at the Halloween carnival.

My zombie disguise seemed a small price to pay for making some headway. I continued writing that day and every day thereafter and conquered all deadlines. I was definitely ready for that vacation now.

Mama tackled the holiday baking by herself, not wanting to infringe on my work schedule. But when she realized my assignments were done, she handed me an apron.

I can't ever remember a Christmas season when our kitchen wasn't cozy from the warmth of the oven. The smell of butter, vanilla, and cinnamon permeated the entire house. Our baking ran nonstop from just after Thanksgiving until the twenty-fourth of December. A gazillion cookies, breads, and, yes, even fruitcakes, passed through my mother's hands on their way to ribboned baskets and cookie tins. Those homemade presents would cover every surface on the dining room table and sideboard where they awaited delivery to our friends and neighbors.

That year, we decided our holiday traditions would continue as usual. This was my first Christmas without Daddy and my mother's first without the man she'd agreed to follow through life. In the beginning, her tears flowed freely. I never knew when some little thing would set her off. It could be as simple as finding a pair of Daddy's old slippers under the bed, or hearing a song they both loved. The grief I experienced wasn't as deep as hers, but we both needed each other to lean on.

Six months had passed, and the healing was slow, but for the most part, meltdowns were under control. I sensed Mama needed me less and less. Maybe her involvement in church activities was part of the reason. One morning, she headed out the door and told me not to worry if she didn't come home for lunch. She'd be at the church, then off to run errands. Less than a minute later, she walked back into the kitchen.

"Wow, that was fast," I teased. "Got your errands done?"

"Very funny, Callie. I was about to get into my car when I noticed oil runnin' out from under your truck. Thought you'd wanna know right away."

I squeezed my eyes shut and groaned. My trips to buy motor oil had increased with each passing week, so an oil puddle didn't surprise me. However, I wasn't ready for a repair bill. "I should take it to Fred's garage right now. Will you give me a ride home?"

"This morning?"

With a nonstop nod, I pleaded while sandwiching

palms under my chin.

She looked at her wristwatch and tapped the crystal. "Okay, but we need to hurry. There's not much time before my docent meetin'."

****

New, bright red lettering on freshly painted stucco announced Fred's Auto Repair. I assumed my repair costs would help pay for the garage's latest improvements. Yet, that was a fair trade-off, because Fred had kept my aged truck alive for longer than it deserved.

I slammed the truck door and pulled the key from the ignition.

Fred came out of the repair bay, wiping his hands on a greasy rag. "Nice to see you, Callie, but I assume you didn't just stop by to visit."

"As a matter of fact, I know how much you love my truck. Thought you two might like to spend the day together."

He heaved a sigh. "So, what's the problem this time?"

"Leaking oil. A lot." I crossed my fingers. "How long before you can fix it?"

He released the hood, pulled the dipstick, and wiped it clean. Then he got down on his knees and peered underneath. He pushed himself up from the pavement and shook his head. "Wish I could take care of it right now, but we're all backed up. If we don't have the parts, Monday is probably the earliest we can have it done." He scratched his stubbled chin. "Ya know, I'd have to check my invoices, but I think this vehicle's been coming in for repairs a lot more now than when your daddy drove it. Have you thought about gettin' somethin' newer?"

"I've been considering it, Fred, but I'm not ready yet." I donned my jokester smile. "A few more repairs and I can claim it as a dependent on my tax return."

He lifted an eyebrow, but he didn't laugh.

My mother pulled into Fred's driveway and jerked to a stop next to us.

I stood back as he politely opened the passenger side door. After I settled into the seat, and he closed the door, I stuck my hand out the window and dangled the keys until he opened his palm.

He ducked to look across at Mama. "Mornin', Miz James. I was just suggestin' to Callie she might want to think about gettin' a newer vehicle. Seems silly repairin' somethin' this old."

Mama gave him a quick nod. "Thanks, Fred." Her gaze wandered to me and then back to him. "I've been tellin' her the same thing. I'm sure we'll have a longer conversation this time."

Mama waved a hasty good-bye and zipped toward the main highway. With her lips pinched tight, and her gaze fixed on the road ahead, she drove faster than usual, probably anxious to get me home in a timely manner, and herself to her upcoming meeting at church.

The silence inside the car was fine with me. I preferred not to hear another you-need-a-dependable-vehicle lecture. I thought about my previous bank statement and how nice it was to see a healthy savings account balance. If I had to purchase better transportation, my balance would be zero. And I'd be stuck with a loan payment, too.

I stared out the side window, watching the scenery whoosh by, noticing the ominous, gray heavens. Not even ten a.m., but the dark sky looked like early evening.

Clouds had been building since the day before, and the weather service had predicted a storm would arrive by nightfall. My personal storm had already arrived...I might have to buy a new car.

Chapter Seventeen

Mama swerved into the driveway, almost hitting a tree at the corner of our property.

I reached across and laid my hand on her arm. "I know you're in a hurry, but please, Mama…drive safely."

A quick grin. "I will. Now jump out. I gotta go. By the way, while I'm gone, I'd appreciate you finishin' those sugar cookies. Okay?" Her hurried speech had barely reached my ears before she threw the car into reverse and raced back onto the road faster than a driver at the Indy 500.

"Will do," I called out after her, saluting military style. *Yes, I'd be delighted to finish those cookies—every last one—preferably with a tall glass of cold milk.* But I knew I couldn't get away with it, so I promised myself I'd only eat a few misshapen ones, the ones that weren't nice enough for gifts.

The final baking sheet had almost cooled when I plucked a long green plastic box from the pantry. Mama had purchased it as a celery keeper at a Tupperware party years before. However, since we rarely ate celery, it found a new life as a storage caddy for delicate baking garnishes like chocolate sprinkles, sugared crystals, jimmies, and every food color imaginable. Before me was a veritable artist's pallet for decorating cookies, and at that moment, I was the artist.

In a corner of the kitchen, an attic carton had found a temporary home. Inside were dozens of various-sized holiday tins, all of which had been returned to us after the previous Christmas baking season, empty, except for an occasional thank you note. Mama savored each note, reading it several times before tucking it back into the tin and stowing it away until the following year.

I selected the largest red container, complete with a painted snow scene, and started filling it with a variety of baked goods—lemon bars, brownies, snickerdoodles, and more. Everything got sandwiched between sheets of wax paper. For the top layer, I chose sugar cookie cut-outs of Christmas trees, which I decorated with bright green icing and silver dragées.

I tried to imagine Johnny's expression at seeing them. Too bad my transportation was waiting for repair—that meant I wasn't going anywhere.

So why not walk? The distance was only a mile or so. Rascal needed exercise and, because of my cookie taste-testing, so did I.

Bundled in a warm jacket with an attached hood, I fastened my dog to his leash and stood on the front porch, looking up at fat clouds gorged with rain. Eventually they'd burst, but not until evening, according to the weatherman. At that moment, I had an anxious dog straining against my right hand and a cookie tin in my left. Did I really need to add an umbrella to my load?

Rascal almost choked himself pulling me down the steps. He towed me for the first block, occasionally stopping to sniff the ground and mark his territory. Then his canine intuition must have kicked in, because, mostly, he walked in a straight line toward our destination.

The first few drops of rain weren't too bad, and the telltale spots on the ground produced an earthy scent. Even when the wind blew rain into my face, I only had to reach up every once in a while to clear my eyeglasses.

Then the heavens opened.

The wind whipped inside my hood, blowing it backward. Tucking the tin under my arm, I grabbed at the hood several times and held it in place. My head got drenched anyway.

"C'mon, Rascal, faster." He didn't seem to mind the downpour—I practically had to drag him the final one hundred feet.

Mr. Smith must have seen us coming, because he stood on the front porch. He yelled over the hammering rain, "What in heaven's name are you doing out in this weather?"

I bounded up the steps to enjoy the benefit of shelter.

Rascal followed. As soon as I let go of his leash, he shook his waterlogged body. Wet fur sent used rainwater everywhere.

I raised the cookie tin as a shield. "Rascal! Stop!"

He gave himself another good shake, padded over to a quiet corner, walked in a tight circle, and dropped down to rest, releasing a generous sigh.

The edges of Mr. Smith's mouth twitched as he calmly flicked water drops off his flannel shirt. I wrinkled my nose and adopted an embarrassed grin. "Sorry about that." Sweeping moisture from the red box, I held out my homemade present. "My truck is in the shop, but I couldn't wait to deliver this to y'all, so we walked."

He scowled and shook his head.

"It wasn't raining when we started out...honest." I

gestured to the container and placed it in his hands. "Are you okay with Johnny having sweets right now? I frosted the Christmas trees just for him." Leaning to one side, I peered through the crack between the frame and the barely-open door. The parlor held no sign of a squirrely toddler.

Mr. Smith lifted the lid for a quick peek but stood firmly in the doorway. "He's asleep. I'll let him know you stopped by."

My shoulders slumped. "Shoot. I forgot about his nap. Do you think he'll be up soon?"

He glanced at his watch. "He's usually awake by now, but a fever has kept him down all day. Probably the flu."

My throat constricted, remembering the bout I'd just been through—an experience I wouldn't wish on anyone, especially a helpless child. I frowned. "It's not fair. Seems like the flu doesn't care who it attacks. Tell him I said to get well. In fact, let him know I'll be back in a day or two. I'm working on a Christmas gift for him."

In his usual stoic manner, Mr. Smith offered a quiet nod.

I rocked back on waterlogged sneakers and glanced to the growing puddle created by my dripping clothes. "I apologize for the mess." Bending over, I retrieved Rascal's leash, and wrapped it around my wrist. "Well, bye for now. Hope y'all enjoy the goodies."

"Thanks. We will."

Snugging my jacket's zipper against my chin, I moved to the edge of the porch. An occasional boom of thunder now punctuated the heavy rain. As I gripped my hood, I looked toward the menacing sky, dreading the walk home. Tugging on Rascal's leash, I urged him to follow.

He refused to move and looked up with sad eyes while delivering a mournful groan.

I kneeled to stroke his head. "I know. But we gotta go, big fella."

My reluctant dog and I were partway down the steps before Mr. Smith spoke. "Wait. Callie, you can't go back out in this storm. I'd drive you home if Johnny weren't asleep. Can't you call your mother to come get you?"

I shook my head. "No, sir. She's out. Her church meeting may be over, but she planned to run errands afterward…and she refuses to use a cell phone."

"She can't be gone forever. Why not call home and leave a message? You do have an answering machine, don't you?"

I sat on the porch swing, drew out my phone, and hit the speed dial. The Smiths' front porch wasn't exactly a cozy place this time of year with blustery wind swirling above the half-walls, but the roof overhang kept us from getting any wetter. I was grateful to be there, even though my soggy clothing made me shiver visibly.

Mr. Smith huffed a sigh. "You'd better come inside and wait."

Glancing back at Rascal, who had already settled himself for a nap, I stepped into the living room and the pleasant warmth radiating from a glowing fireplace.

"Go sit on the hearth." Mr. Smith pointed to a row of hooks embedded in the thick mantel. "Hang your jacket there."

I smiled, noticing a readymade place where Johnny could hang the almost-finished Christmas stocking I was crafting for him. I removed my wet parka and hung it at one end, then rubbed palms together before holding them up to the blaze, hoping my circulation would soon return.

Mr. Smith walked toward the kitchen to deposit the red tin. Over his shoulder he asked, "Would you like some hot cocoa and a cookie?"

I'd probably already eaten enough cookies to last me for a year. "No thank you to the cookie, but yes, sir…the cocoa would be nice."

From the kitchen came the clatter of a spoon and the whir of a microwave. A memory tugged at my heart. How many times had Daddy done that for Mama and me?

"Thanks," I mumbled when Mr. Smith handed me the cocoa. The smell of warm chocolate wafted to my nostrils. I wrapped my numb fingers around the stoneware mug and immediately felt my hands start to defrost. I took a sip, which threatened to burn my throat, but I chanced it anyway and swallowed. Raising the mug as if toasting his effort, I smiled. "My compliments to the chef."

He raised his mug in salute. "Thank you, madam." He bowed. "The chef will be glad to fix you another if you like."

This was probably the first time I'd noticed him be less than serious. Maybe he was finally feeling comfortable around me. "Have you always been the chef?"

He settled into a chair. "No. I only cook because I have to. Mary's not here for a lot of our meals, so the job falls to me. Cooking isn't really my thing."

"Not my thing either. When I lived in campus housing, my roommate had a microwave. She told me to use it anytime I wanted. I think I used it once…to burn a bag of popcorn."

His easy smile assured me my joke had improved his usually tense demeanor. Was this an opportunity to find out more about him and his family? "I assume you went to college. Did you cook then?"

Looking right at me, he didn't answer for a few seconds. "No, I didn't like cooking then either."

"You've never mentioned Johnny's grandmother. Did you meet her in college?"

His eyes narrowed. "You're sure full of questions today, aren't you?"

My face heated. "I'm sorry…didn't mean to pry."

He swirled the liquid in his cup and tipped it to his mouth to drink the final gulp. Rising from his chair, he asked, "Would you care for more?"

I drew my finger midway on the mug. "Maybe half a cup."

With our two cups, he started for the kitchen but turned in the doorway. "I'm sure you weren't prying. Sorry if I indicated that. The answer is, yes, I met her in college. But that was a long time ago and a lot has happened since then. Does that answer your question?"

My embarrassment prompted a silent nod. I'd barely turned to warm my hands and watch the fire when a high-pitched ringing made me jump.

Mr. Smith bolted from the kitchen, throwing a quick glance to the telephone resting on the end table and then to a closed bedroom door. Our cocoa mugs clattered against each other as he set them down and grabbed for the receiver.

Although I turned my back to warm my hands on the open fire, I couldn't avoid listening to a one-sided conversation.

"Do you think you left them in the restaurant? Hmm. Where's the owner today? I see. Do you have another set here at home? Never mind, that won't work, Johnny's still asleep. I don't want to take him out in this storm anyway." He paused. "No. Absolutely not. An hour is much too long to wait. What about a locksmith?"

By now, I'd guessed the caller was his daughter. Maybe I could help. I turned and mouthed the words, "I can babysit while you deliver keys."

"Hold on, Mary." He cupped his palm over the mouthpiece. "Absolutely not. Um…your mother might show up before I return."

"Then I'll have her wait with me. You probably won't be gone for more than fifteen or twenty minutes, right?"

He hesitated. His brow wrinkled.

Was he questioning my sincerity?

He lowered his gaze. "Yes, Mary, I'm still here. I was speaking to Callie. She dropped by to deliver Christmas cookies. No, she can't, she walked." He rolled his eyes. "I know it is. She and her dog got drenched." He looked at me, but his focus seemed elsewhere. "Callie offered to stay with Johnny so I can deliver your car keys."

His knuckles tightened on the receiver just before he turned away and mumbled something I couldn't make out.

Several times, he nodded in silence to the caller. His shoulders slumped as he audibly sighed. "You're probably right. Give me a few minutes."

He hung up but continued to stare at the phone. After a moment, he raised his chin and offered the details. Mary had gone to the dinner house prior to opening time.

She'd planned to collect her paycheck. Since no one was there, she let herself in. When she left, she re-set the burglar alarm and closed the locked door before realizing her keys weren't in her pocket. Currently, she was standing under the eaves of the building, avoiding the rain, but needing her father to come and rescue her. Here, a little boy was sick—he needed someone, too.

Mr. Smith's nervousness told me he wanted to stay in control of the situation. To me, the solution was a no-brainer. Why couldn't *he* see that? Why didn't he trust me? "Just go," I insisted. "It'll be fine. You won't be gone long, and I'm not going anywhere until you get back."

Evidently, he finally realized he had no other option. Leaving me in charge, he pulled on a jacket and rushed for the door.

I drew the window curtain aside and watched him back out of the driveway and disappear into the storm. The fire popped to draw my attention across the room. My fingers smoothed the curtain fabric back into place. Then I turned and walked over to encourage the dwindling embers with the fireplace poker, concerned that Mr. Smith might come back to nothing more than warm ashes. From the pile of logs laying on the hearth, I picked up two hefty ones and rolled them onto the coals, poked the bark, and waited until the fire grew.

I'd only been in this parlor once before. Briefly. That was in September, the day my cell phone and I met with an accident, and I'd been forced to use the Smiths' landline. Today I had the luxury of checking out the surroundings.

I knew this house had been rented furnished, so I wasn't surprised by seeing furniture that wasn't the most fashionable. However, everything was almost hospital-clean.

Oak bookshelves held a fair amount of reading material, the diversity impressive. I ran fingers across each spine, reading the titles of classics written before I was born—heck, before my mother was born.

I saw fix-it books for household repairs, a well-used paperback about gardening, and a dozen thick medical volumes I assumed were text books. A hefty collection of magazines, with *The Journal of the American Medical Association* topping the stack, occupied one corner. Alongside was another pile bearing names such as *Time, Reader's Digest,* and *Newsweek.* Did they have any issues of the magazine to which I'd submitted Mr. Smith's article? I quickly thumbed through the piles but found nothing that even resembled *American Portraits Magazine.* Thank heavens. A possibility existed that he'd never find out I'd written about him.

In the center of one shelf, just out of the reach from Johnny's inquisitive little fingers, a small bronze statue rested, functioning as a bookend. I didn't know much about sculpture, but I could appreciate how skilled the artist must have been to create this version of an eagle-in-flight. I picked it up to examine the finely chiseled feathers. *Beautiful, just beautiful.*

Afraid my clumsy hands would drop what was possibly a valuable art piece, I gently pushed it back against the books. As I adjusted it to the same position as before, I noticed an inscription on the pedestal. Someone had obviously tried to scratch off the words. I couldn't be sure, but it seemed to read, *The Society of...Presents the...Award to...for His Dedication to Saving Lives.*

S. Hansberger

Were the scratches making the words fuzzy or was it my glasses? I removed them and used my shirttail to clean the lenses. Before I could return them to my nose, a strange coughing sound emanated from the baby monitor atop the mantel. Then Johnny cried out, and I nearly tripped over my own feet while flying to the bedroom. When I opened the door, a sour smell stung my nostrils.

I could barely detect a small figure sitting in the middle of the crib. Even on this dark, cloudy day, every window shade had been drawn. The glow from a tiny nightlight offered the only relief. As my eyes adjusted to the dim surroundings, I realized Johnny had coughed up whatever he'd eaten last. In between his cries for *Gampa*, I stroked his soft cheek and whispered, "It's okay, Johnny. It's me, Callie."

"Cow-we, Cow-we," he whimpered, reaching up.

My heart melted. I gathered him into my arms, fully aware both of us would now be a mess. But that didn't matter. He needed my comfort. I stood there, swaying back and forth. "Shhh, it's okay, it's okay."

He laid his head on my shoulder and promptly stuck a thumb in his mouth, his body still shuddering with an occasional sob. When he finally quieted, he lifted his head, removed his thumb, and said distinctly, "Cow-we, I hungry."

The change was obvious. One minute he was crying like his world had come to an end, the next he'd easily moved on. His innocence amused me. I tried not to laugh but couldn't help myself. He joined in, although he probably didn't understand the humor. His contagious giggle set me off again. I finally had to sit on the edge of Mary's bed to avoid peeing my pants.

As his amusement subsided, he repeated more insistently, "Cow-we, I hungry."

I wiped away my happy tears. "Okay, you're hungry. I get it. But first, we need to get you out of these yucky jammies. Then *Cow-we* will fix you something to eat."

I rose to turn on the little Humpty-Dumpty lamp topping the dresser. The lighting was only slightly better but allowed me to see what needed to be done. Johnny cooperated by standing on the bed so I could unzip his footed sleepers. Still amused by his naive request for food, I couldn't stop smiling while I helped him step out of his clothing.

Then I froze in horror.

Scars covered his back from his waist to his neck.

The sight yanked me sober. I gasped. "Oh my God, what happened to you?"

"What the hell are you doing?" The voice roared from across the room.

The intensity of the sound caused me to whirl before stumbling backward onto the bed, throwing Johnny off-balance. I grabbed him before his head hit the wall. I don't know if he cried out from surprise, or because I clutched him so tightly. My startled brain took a moment to recognize the figure filling the doorway, illuminated by only the faint light from the nursery lamp.

Mr. Smith rushed forward and seized Johnny from my arms.

Johnny's crying slowed.

I realized I'd been holding my breath. Swallowing hard, I gathered my composure. "I...I...I had to get him out of his jammies." My gaze darted between the crib and Johnny. "He'd thrown up."

The only response offered was a cold stare.

I knew I wasn't guilty of anything and was determined to defend my actions. With hands on hips, I barked, "I couldn't just leave him in what he was wearing."

Johnny finally broke the silence. "Gampa, I hungry."

Mr. Smith's gaze softened before he turned away. He quietly opened a drawer, plucked out a clean long-sleeved tee shirt, and, with one hand, pulled it over Johnny's head.

I followed them to the kitchen. Leaning my shoulder against the door frame, and arms folded across my chest, I braced myself for additional angry words. I was, however, ready for his response and even hoped for an explanation of what I'd seen.

Johnny rode his grandfather's hip, and when *Gampa* opened the cupboard, the boy pointed excitedly to a box of fish-shaped saltines. With a sippy cup of water and a handful of crackers, he was eased into a shiny, chrome-framed highchair.

Mr. Smith gave a sideways glance at my soiled shirt. Turning to the sink, he reached for the paper towel roll, pulled off several sheets, dampened them with water and dish soap, and then, without meeting my gaze, held them out at arm's length.

He didn't make eye contact, but I assumed this simple gesture was meant as an apology, so I accepted his offering. After I cleaned my shirt, I dropped the dirty wad of toweling into the trash can and leaned against the wall, determined to remain silent until he spoke.

He added another handful of crackers to the highchair's tray before sealing the box and returning it to the shelf. With his back to me, he gripped the edge of the counter and leaned his head against the cupboard door. "Callie, once again I find myself apologizing." He turned to face me. "You're entitled to an explanation. I'm not at liberty to say much without speaking to my daughter first, but I beg you not to repeat anything you hear. Mary and Johnny's safety depends upon it."

My eyes widened. "I would never risk their safety…I hope you know that. If something happened to them because of me, I would never forgive myself."

His eyes softened, yet he suddenly seemed older, like worry had been beating him down for a long, long time, possibly because of a secret burden he carried. I prayed he would accept me as a true friend with honorable intentions, and that he would trust me not to betray that friendship if he confessed his problem at that very moment.

The muscles around his mouth relaxed. With his lips barely moving, he whispered, "I don't want Johnny to hear this—it might bring back traumatic memories." He gestured toward the parlor. "Let's talk in there."

We could still see the distracted toddler in his highchair, but we stepped maybe ten feet away. I seated myself on one end of the raised hearth.

Mr. Smith rested an arm on the mantle. "Not long ago, Mary lived in Chicago with Johnny. He was almost a year old. Mary and her husband had—"

Rascal barked from the front porch as a horn sounded in the driveway.

Mr. Smith's hands tensed into fists. He strode to the window and peeked between the curtains. He exhaled. "It's your mother."

Darn. I'd forgotten I'd left a message about picking

107

me up. *Darn. Darn. Darn.* I looked at Mr. Smith in a panic. Would the story-telling stop because of this interruption?

Mama honked again.

I huffed a frustrated sigh. No choice but to open the door and compete with the pounding rain by yelling. "I'll be right there, Mama."

From the fireplace hook, Mr. Smith lifted my parka and held it out. "You shouldn't keep her waiting."

I took the parka and opened my mouth to object.

He ignored my gaze by shoving his hands into his pockets. He stared at the floor.

I knew what he must be thinking—he had a secret bottled up inside and was willing to share, but now was not the time to condense this confession into a quick sentence or two. "I'd still like to hear what you have to say. We have church tomorrow. But on Monday, I can come back. Is that okay?"

Without smiling, he nodded and held open the door.

Rascal's barks evolved into quick excited yelps.

I stepped outside onto the porch and picked up his leash in one hand. With the other, I pulled my hood into place and hugged it to my neck, pausing one final moment to savor being dry. Then I bounded down the steps and out into the rain.

Once we were safely inside Mama's car, I fastened my seatbelt and glanced up through frantic windshield wipers to see Mr. Smith standing in the doorway, holding Johnny.

Mama backed out of the driveway and across a swollen torrent that consumed both sides of the banked road. "Young lady, why in the world would you go out on a day like this?"

I pushed wet bangs from my forehead. "Cookies, Mama."

"Cookies, huh?" She skewed her face into a frown. "You'd better explain."

But how could I explain without causing Mama concern?

Chapter Eighteen

Monday, December 23rd

Over the weekend, I conjured up all kinds of scenarios to finish the story Mr. Smith had started. Ten movie scripts could have been written from the various plots I created. However, none were even close to what I heard that Monday.

Mama dropped me off at Fred's so I could pick up my repaired vehicle. The scent of used motor oil permeated his shop's tiny office. I avoided laying my arm on the greasy, stained counter while Fred explained how this minor fix-it was merely a Band-Aid. I stifled a yawn—I'd heard this sad tale before. What my truck really needed was major surgery. Or a funeral.

After coming to a stop in front of the Smiths' house, I rolled down the window halfway. Although freshly washed air breathed winter's chill, it suited me just fine. Zipping my parka, I stepped outside and allowed bright sunshine to warm my face.

Johnny's happy squeals traveled over the fence. Apparently, the flu had flown and an abundance of energy now danced within that little body. A reprimanding voice followed him. Things had obviously returned to normal.

I tiptoed around the puddles lurking between the curb and the Smiths' backyard. After failing to hop over the last one, I looked down to scowl at mud now clinging to my sneakers. This was absolutely the wrong day to break in new shoes. "Hey there," I announced, closing the wooden gate behind me.

"Hey there," Mr. Smith answered in return as he walked my way. He held a fistful of wilted leaves, pruned from storm-pelted plants.

At the sound of garden tools clattering to the ground, we twisted our necks to see Johnny stomping across the muddy rows, dragging a shovel.

"He's supposed to be playing in the sandbox...but I guess that was my idea, not his."

Johnny needed a distraction if Mr. Smith and I were to talk. I held up a package smartly wrapped in brightly colored Santa Claus paper.

"What's that?"

"A Christmas stocking. Is it okay if he opens it now?"

Mr. Smith beckoned to Johnny, who was happily pulling up baby carrots one by one. The voice sent him giggling, running in the opposite direction. His determined grandfather gave chase, scooping up the toddler at the precise moment when perfect little teeth clamped onto a muddy vegetable.

"Don't do that." Mr. Smith scolded. With his free hand, he detached tiny fingers from the dirty carrot and tossed it aside. Using his shirt sleeve, he attempted to clean the boy's mischievous face.

But Johnny wasn't having any of it. He wriggled free and ran to hide behind me, throwing his arms around my knees.

I bent over until my face was upside down and stared into his precious blue eyes. "I brought you something. What do you think it is?" I waved it just out of his reach. "Wanna see?"

His eyes widened.

I took Johnny's hand and guided him to a bench by the back door.

When he finally got through the wrapping paper, he looked at the Christmas stocking, dropped it on the ground, and opted to go searching for the dirty carrot.

My ego plummeted at the rejection.

Mr. Smith picked up the gift and laid it on the bench. "I'm sure he'll want to play with it later."

"That's okay," I shrugged. "Doesn't look like a toy anyway."

"Well, on his behalf, I thank you. We both appreciate your sewing skills."

"Gluing skills."

"Excuse me?"

"I glued it. My sewing skills aren't the greatest." I pantomimed removing an imaginary pistol from a holster and blew across the tip of my finger. "But I'm a wiz with a glue-gun."

He smiled, all tension gone from his face.

Was this a good time to remind him of his promise to explain Johnny's injuries? I shuffled my feet. I wouldn't broach the subject, but if he wanted me out of his hair today, he needed to fess up.

He glanced at his grandson and then at me. "It's time for Johnny's nap. Will you wait while I put him in bed?"

I nodded, hoping my expression didn't appear too eager. In an effort to kill time, I walked the garden's rows, admiring mature vegetables. Now and then I stooped to pull ratty leaves from various greens damaged by the heavy rain, each one reminding me of Saturday's storm, not only outside the house, but inside the house, right after I discovered Johnny's injuries.

Mr. Smith called out from a slightly ajar kitchen door "Would you like a soda?"

I stood upright and shoved hair off my face. "Yes, sir. That would be great."

"A cola?"

"Yes, sir."

I discarded the final batch of plant debris into the compost bin and rubbed my hands together, but the dirt under my nails wasn't going anywhere. I stared at grungy cuticles and sighed. Too bad Francine Lothner was the only decent manicurist in town. I could have used some pampering, but I refused to listen to her gossip. Besides, I was about to hear my gardener friend's secret. And after that, no way could I risk a slipup that would give Francine some juicy tidbits to share.

Chapter Nineteen

The sandbox lip couldn't have been more than seven or eight inches high. I brushed off wet sand and took a seat on the top plank. Sitting with knees almost up to my chin, I dug at dirty fingernails that looked as if they belonged to a country farmer. Hmm…I guess they did.

My elbow bumped Johnny's sun-faded blue plastic bucket. It stood on the edge and had conveniently collected fresh rainwater, creating a makeshift basin in which to dip fingertips and rinse off soil.

When Mr. Smith came outside, I wiped wet hands against my jeans and reached up to accept one of the colas. "Thanks." I had already made a mental note to keep my usual chatty remarks to a minimum so he'd feel free to talk.

He sat on the opposite corner and kept his voice low. "Callie, the other day I was about to tell you something very private when our conversation got interrupted. Truthfully, after I'd had a chance to think about it, I wasn't sure about continuing." He focused on the ground and pushed at a smidgen of leaves with his shoe. "Then I discussed it with Mary…she wants me to tell you. She says she trusts you to keep the secret."

He stared at me, as if his comment required a response, so I didn't hesitate. "I'm pleased she does, but I hope you know *you* can trust me, too."

"I do. But that's not why I'm cautious." He looked

me straight in the eyes. "I'm about to drop a horrific story into your lap, and I don't want it to overwhelm you. I'm concerned you'll be dragged into this. Possibly, along with us, you'll be in danger, too."

My throat tightened. Did I want to be in danger? No. But I'd given my word to keep his secret, and I wasn't changing my mind. I sat straighter and grinned. "I'm tougher than I look...all five feet five of me."

He didn't smile. "Callie, this isn't something to joke about."

Casting an embarrassed gaze to the ground, I plunged tense hands into my pockets.

He glanced over his shoulder.

Was he checking to see if someone else might be listening in? Why was he so nervous? I glanced in the same direction and saw absolutely no one.

He turned to me, letting a sigh escape before speaking. "Once I've told you this, I can't take it back. You can walk away right now, and I won't think any less of you."

My sneakers wondered if they should trot my anxious body out of there. But I knew I had to stay. After all, how bad could it be? "I have no idea what you'll say, but it sounds like your family needs a friend. I'd be honored to be that friend...if you'll let me."

"Mary especially needs a friend. Since she's closer to your age than mine, I'd be relieved to know she has someone she can confide in...just in case something happens to me."

I swallowed at the thought of such an awesome responsibility, but I wouldn't allow myself to back out. I twisted both knees in his direction and laced my fingers. "Understood."

He took a long drink from his soda and nestled the can in the wet sandbox. "I need to preface this with an apology. The story is long, but you need to know what led up to Johnny's injuries."

"That's okay." I shrugged. "I have nothing more important than this."

He gave a weak smile, took a deep breath, and exhaled slowly. "A few years ago, Mary was getting her life in order after being dumped by a boyfriend. My wife and I always assumed they'd get married. Mary did, too. Her friends practically had to drag her out into public after that, but sensing her depression, they refused to let her stay home. Then she met Karl. Mary was like a new person, happy again. Almost *too* happy. We wondered if drugs were involved." He clasped his hands and rounded his shoulders while exhaling.

"She'd only known Karl for three weeks when they eloped. To say the least, her mother and I were upset. During those three weeks, we'd seen him only twice. We didn't know anything about him. We worried that Mary didn't either."

With lips pressed tight, Mr. Smith shook his head. Reaching behind him, he lifted the soda and brushed away grains of sand before gulping a mouthful. He continued to hold onto the can with both hands, resting elbows on his thighs. "Mary had a job, but Karl was out of work, so they moved into our basement. From time to time, we heard angry voices filtering up from downstairs." He shrugged. "But we vowed to stay out of it. Of course, Anita and I were there for moral support, but we didn't want to meddle. Then Mary's first black eye appeared."

I gasped. My fingers flew to cover my mouth. "A

black eye?"

He nodded, his knuckles turning white as he squeezed the soda can tighter. "Mary laughed it off—said a wall walked into her. A few nights later, my wife hugged her goodnight. Mary winced—claimed she'd shut her arm in the car door. They went to the emergency room. Later, with her arm in a cast, Mary kept to her story. But she wasn't fooling us."

I held my breath, afraid to make any sound that might throw him off track. Did he notice?

He shot me a look. "Should I go on?"

By controlling my breathing, and looking attentive without being terrified, I hoped to ease Mr. Smith's concern. Should he continue with the story? Finally, I nodded, even though I was beginning to have doubts.

I shoved the beverage can into a corner of the sandbox after deciding I couldn't finish it. The smell had tempted my taste buds, but the fizz burned my tongue when I couldn't swallow because anxiety constricted my throat.

Mr. Smith also set down his drink. He rolled his head in circles and massaged a neck muscle. "We kept a closer eye on Karl and listened for arguments. We even invented excuses to go into the basement—delivering a late-night snack, putting towels into the washer—any pretense to interrupt whatever was going on. Karl kept his cool when he was around us, but his erratic moods were showing up more often.

"Then, after a weekend away, Anita and I returned home to find the basement empty. A note in Karl's handwriting said he and Mary had moved into a rental across town. He said they'd need more space soon—Mary was pregnant."

I silently mouthed, "Oh no." Luckily, Mr. Smith wasn't watching, so he didn't see my expression. But I could see his—it wasn't the joyful look people have when they speak of grandchildren. "A grandchild. Were you happy?"

He studied me. "Happy?" He skewed his mouth to one corner. "Yes and no." He picked up his soda can and took another swallow before wiping a wayward drop from his lip with the back of his hand.

A limb from a redbud tree cast a dark shadow across his shoulder. The weekend storm had selectively pruned the tree, discarding a few orphans into the sandbox. My storyteller paused while he picked up a twig and randomly stripped lengths of bark, watching as pieces fell to the ground.

He occasionally glanced my way. "We should have looked forward to becoming grandparents, but we were already concerned for Mary's safety. Now we knew we'd worry about a baby, too." Still gazing to where the bark pieces had landed, he leaned forward and rested elbows on his knees. "We didn't see Karl for a long time after that, but Mary would stop by to shop in our pantry. Obviously, things hadn't gotten any better, judging from her fresh bruises. We encouraged her to get him into counseling. We even offered to cover the cost."

"She must have been relieved."

"She was. But Karl refused. We insisted Mary file charges against him. If she didn't, we would. We gave her a week to decide." Mr. Smith looked to the ground, his profile revealing tense jaw muscles.

I flinched when he snapped the twig in half and forcefully flung it halfway across the yard.

"Mary called a few days later to say they were

moving again. Karl had gotten a job in another city. She said his temper hadn't flared for ages, and he'd apologized for past behavior. She was sure unemployment had had a lot to do with his anger."

Mr. Smith lifted his soda. Tipping it to his mouth, he emptied the last of it. While still seated, he set the container on the ground and crushed it flat with one quick stomp.

The angry sound of crumpling metal echoed in my ears. I flinched and sat upright.

Not looking at me, he picked up the smashed disk and rotated bent edges between his fingertips. "Months went by. We heard nothing. We were worried sick. Surely the baby had been born. Was the baby okay? Was our daughter okay? Then one afternoon, I got a call. It was Mary."

Mr. Smith let the spent can fall to the ground. He stared after it and let his shoulders slump. "She said she recognized the date and wanted to wish me happy birthday." He raised his chin and looked directly at me with clouded eyes. "You can't imagine how good it was to hear her voice."

Even though hugging Mr. Smith wouldn't have been proper, that was my first instinct. I held back, but compassion gripped my heart, making me wish I had some other meaningful gesture to offer. When I felt tears forming, I tried not to cry. Yet, I knew if I failed, at least the emotion of it would telegraph my sympathy.

He looked away to wipe his eyes, then sniffed and cleared his throat. "I questioned Mary. Where was she? Could we come for a visit? How was the baby? Boy or girl? Did they need anything? If I sent money, would she and the baby come home?"

He again faced me. "Her answers were jumbled, slurred. She seemed to be having trouble concentrating. Told me she was tired, needed sleep. When I asked for a phone number, she said she didn't have one. A stranger had loaned her his cell." Mr. Smith exhaled. "Well, that scared the hell out of me."

With each new fact, my stomach churned. Afraid it would rumble, I wrapped an arm around my mid-section and hunched over, pretending to flick dirt off my shoes.

"After Mary hung up, I hit Redial. Sure enough, a stranger answered. Said he'd seen Mary stumbling through an intersection, dazed. He helped her to the curb. She told him she desperately needed to call her father. He lent her his phone. Afterward, she gave it back and disappeared."

My white knuckles gripped the edge of the sandbox. "What about the police, couldn't they help?"

"I *went* to the police. They said since I'd heard from her, that proved she could leave if she wanted. They said even if they knew her whereabouts, they couldn't do anything—Mary would have to file a complaint."

"No way! I can't believe—" My conscience immediately reminded me I was here to listen and not here to rail against unfair circumstances. Tempering obvious indignation, I softened my tone. "So, what did you do next?"

"Hired an investigator. He found her three days later."

"Where?"

"New York—in a crumbling apartment in the worst possible section of town."

I could feel tension balling my hands into fists. I shoved them into my armpits. "Were you horrified?"

"Yes. But relieved. At least we knew the location and could make a rescue plan."

We were startled by a rustling in the tree overhead, causing us both to look up. There, among the leafless branches, a menacing raven crept toward a nest holding a small bird who refused to leave. Out of nowhere, a bird similar to the nesting one, dived into the tree, squawking and flitting from one perch to another until the darker, predatory bird gave up and flew away.

Inhaling, I glanced to Mr. Smith. "And what did the plan involve?"

"I booked a round-trip ticket from Chicago to New York for myself and a one-way ticket home for Mary. The baby didn't need a ticket, but we weren't leaving without him. I guess by now you realize the baby was Johnny?"

I nodded anxiously, encouraging him to continue.

"In New York, the investigator drove me to an area worse than I had imagined. He'd studied Karl's patterns of coming and going. The window of opportunity was a narrow one. He said we'd grab Mary and Johnny and leave immediately. We wouldn't be packing any of their clothes, or anything else for that matter. Whatever she and the baby were wearing, that was it. From there, we would go directly to the airport and fly home."

I folded my sweaty palms, hoping to disguise nervousness for fear Mr. Smith would end the story right there. "I can't even imagine how scared you must have been. Or were you?"

"Petrified describes it better. My legs shook so badly I could barely stand."

He must have been envisioning that tense event, because he rubbed his thighs as though trying to bring circulation to them.

"The investigator had spoken to the locals—Karl was selling drugs and keeping Mary sedated whenever he went out. Callie, I've never been much of a religious person, but I prayed to God almost continually that day."

I could read the honesty in Mr. Smith's voice as he looked directly at me. I bit my lip and swallowed to clear a lump from my throat. "And your prayers were answered? Right?"

He nodded. "We never ran into Karl, but Mary was drugged. We had to carry her out."

"And Johnny?"

"Asleep…until all the commotion started when we woke his mother. He cried most of the way to the airport, but once we boarded, he slept all the way home." Mr. Smith's shoulders relaxed. With slowed breathing, he picked up a twig and drew a series of circles in the dirt, each overlapping until all were joined—almost like an abstract bouquet.

I smiled, inhaled deeply, and blew out a stream of air. "Thank heaven…a happy ending." I cocked my head and threw him a puzzled glance. "You still haven't explained about Johnny's injury. When did that happen?"

He stiffened. "Not until months later."

"Really? I thought maybe Karl caused it."

"He did."

Chapter Twenty

Perched on Johnny's sandbox, I gripped the splintered edge. Mr. Smith's previous statement had caused my heart to pound and my eyebrows to rocket upward. "Karl showed up again?"

He nodded. "Mary lived with us for a while, knowing she couldn't stay because—"

"Because she was afraid Karl would find her? I'm sure he wondered where she'd gone after disappearing from New York."

Mr. Smith brushed wavy hair from his forehead. "Right. But it didn't take long before he guessed. Karl made a nuisance of himself, calling at all hours, threatening to go to court if he wasn't allowed to see his son."

I scowled. "A judge wouldn't give in to a drug-dealing father...would he?"

"Probably not. But Karl didn't have a criminal record, and he's one of the most persuasive people I've ever met. As for drug dealing, it would be Mary's word against his."

"But wasn't he still in New York? Did Mary have to go to New York to face a judge? Did she—?"

Mr. Smith stilled my hand. "Slow down, Callie. Let me explain. Karl didn't care about his son. He just wanted to get back at Mary. She knew it and sometimes ignored his calls."

I held my breath. "And Karl's reaction?"

"When he couldn't reach Mary on her cell, he would call our house. If we weren't home, he'd go ballistic on our answering machine. Mary reached the end of her rope and decided to phone him back. She told him he was wasting his time calling her parents. Swore we'd all quarreled, and she'd moved out."

I raised my brow. "She hadn't. Right?"

"Right. But she hoped to mislead him."

"Did it work?"

He snorted and shook his head. "No. He continued to call and accused us of hiding her." The muscles in Mr. Smith's jaw tightened. "My wife nearly had a nervous breakdown."

I curled fingernails into my palms as my own frustration grew. "Maybe you should have changed your phone number."

Mr. Smith scowled. "We did." He lowered his head and mumbled. "Finally, Mary chose to move out. Even drove to another city and placed a call from a public phone, hoping he'd see the number on a digital readout that would convince him she lived elsewhere. His calls to us stopped, but our house got ransacked. We were sure it was Karl, looking for clues to Mary's whereabouts."

"But you knew where she was?"

He nodded. "Less than ten miles away. She'd gotten a job managing an apartment complex in exchange for a small salary and free rent. Since she worked from home, she could easily care for Johnny. And when she considered taking college courses, a neighbor lady volunteered to babysit."

"Thank God." I inhaled, pressing a hand to my chest, relieved Mary's life had regained some balance.

"But what about y'all? Did the harassment stop?"

The veins in his neck pulsed. "It got worse. Karl stalked us. That was the final straw for Anita. She packed up and moved to a relative's house in Idaho until things could get back to normal."

"And did they?"

"Normal? Ha! Hardly. Karl was on a mission. Mary knew he would be. She was careful not to leave a trail—no forwarding address, no land line. But he found her anyway."

"On the Internet?"

Mr. Smith snorted. "Mary bought a computer once, Karl pawned it. I doubt the Internet occurred to him. Besides, Mary was smart enough to adopt a fake name. The only thing she kept under her legal name was her old cell phone...just so Karl wouldn't realize what she'd done."

I squeezed shut my eyes and groaned. "The GPS."

"No. She used an old flip phone without GPS. Sometimes she'd answer, thinking she could soothe his temper. But one day, she slipped up. Told him she'd enrolled in an accounting class." Air exploded from Mr. Smith's mouth. "At least half a dozen junior colleges exist in our area. You'd think that would have deterred him, but no. We later found out he visited at least four schools before finding her."

I stiffened. "They're not allowed to give out information!" My hands squeezed into fists. "That's privacy invasion!"

He patted my arm. "Relax, Callie. I said he *visited* them. Determined, he waited outside classrooms—watched for her."

"Oh." The sun shining on my back was still warm,

but I shivered. "And?"

"He found her. He followed and blocked her car in the babysitter's driveway. He started a yelling match, but the police arrived and asked him to leave. By then, everyone in the complex knew Mary's situation. Several volunteered their guest bedroom to her and Johnny."

"God bless them for caring! But…what if Karl came back?"

"The police warned they'd be patrolling. Even so, Mary didn't want to put the neighbors in danger, so she thought it best to return to her own apartment. If Karl knew which condo was hers, she was ready. She sat on the sofa, holding a fireplace tool until the sun came up."

"Then he must have come back at some other time."

Mr. Smith gritted his teeth. "Two weeks later—when Johnny turned one. Most grandparents would want to be there to celebrate a first birthday. But Anita…" He leaned forward, rested elbows on knees, and laid his forehead in his hands.

For what seemed like an eternity, he sat motionless. Then, after a noticeable sniff, he sat upright, running fingers through his gray hair. "Sorry. Where did I leave off?"

"Johnny's birthday."

"Right." He inhaled a gulp of air while stretching a leg forward and bracing a hand on the edge of the sandbox. "I brought tulips for Mary and a cake for Johnny. She hadn't heard from her crazy husband in a while. We relaxed, ate pizza, and lit the birthday candle—several times—because it tickled Johnny every time he blew it out. Then the doorbell rang."

My body went rigid, even though I knew evil Karl was bound to reappear.

"Holding a little stuffed animal, there stood her ex. Mary had the security chain fastened, but when Karl shoved the door, the chain broke. He walked straight to the highchair and yanked Johnny into his arms. I moved to intervene, but Mary shot me a look that said, 'Don't.' Regardless, I was ready to pounce if I had to."

Shaking his head, Mr. Smith closed his eyes. "For God's sake, I don't know what Karl expected from Johnny." He turned his gaze on me. "Unbridled affection? Karl hadn't shown any interest prior to that, so his son barely knew him. Johnny tried squirming back into the highchair and reaching for the birthday cake. Karl shook him hard. That's when Mary snatched the boy and escaped to another room. Karl clenched his fists and started after her, but I grabbed his shoulder. He swung at me. I ducked and took a few steps back. He grabbed the fireplace poker and hit me in the shins. My knees buckled. Collapsing against the brick hearth was the last thing I remembered before waking to smoke searing my lungs."

I sucked in a startled breath and glanced at Mr. Smith, but he hadn't heard me.

His voice quivered. "I only know about the rest of this incident because Mary described it days later in the hospital. Evidently, Karl kicked open the locked bedroom door. Mary cowered in a corner and tried reasoning, hoping to stall until I could regain consciousness. When she told Karl about the birthday candle game, he wrenched her arm, forced her to the cake, grabbed the baby, and wedged him into the highchair. Then he yelled at Mary to relight the candle. Johnny cried. Mary never made a sound, even though her wrist was broken."

My mouth dropped open.

"That original candle wouldn't relight, so Karl jerked one from a nearby sconce, thrust it into the cake, and ordered Mary to strike a match."

Mr. Smith stared off into space. "But Johnny wouldn't stop crying. Mary shielded him with her body, afraid of Karl's mounting frustration. He picked up the cake and hurled it toward the window. The draperies caught fire. Mary rushed for the kitchen extinguisher. Karl stopped her by grabbing her ponytail. He dragged her outside and down the stairs while screaming that their problems were all her fault."

My heart went into overdrive. I pressed a hand to my throat and felt a racing pulse. Eyes wide, I froze and waited for his next words.

Mr. Smith's breathing quickened. "Karl threw Mary onto the sidewalk. She said she noticed smoke pouring through the open doorway and tried to crawl back upstairs. Like a wild dog, Karl wouldn't stop attacking her with his fists and feet. She said that just before she passed out, she felt strangely peaceful. She knew we would all be together in heaven that day." Mr. Smith's voice halted, and an enormous sob burst from his throat.

I'd never seen a grown man experience such raw emotion. Not even my father. Yet, Mr. Smith was a father to Mary and a grandfather to Johnny, and the three of them had become a second family to me. I couldn't speak to say I shared his anguish, so I squeezed his arm and then silently laid my head on my bent knees and allowed the tears to flow.

A gentle hand touched my shoulder. I glanced up to see the handkerchief he quietly offered. I nodded and then sniffed one last time, determined to get a handle on my weeping. I was a serious reporter and didn't want him to view me as a crybaby. "I assume there's more."

He nodded.

"It's okay if you can't finish."

He stared at the ground. "I don't know if we made it outside on our own, or if the firemen helped, but I remember collapsing on the lawn with Johnny and later waking in a hospital bed. We spent weeks in recovery. The doctors were amazed at Johnny's resilience. But they didn't expect Mary to survive." Sighing, he closed his eyes. "The pain from second- and third-degree burns are nothing compared to the thought of losing your only child."

My eyes were barely dry from the previous crying jag, but after hearing Mr. Smith's new heartfelt words, I couldn't stop an errant tear from sliding down my cheek. I brushed it away before reaching across to pat his hand.

"The day of the fire, a group of tenants tackled Karl and held him until police arrived. Unable to post bail, he was jailed until the trial. His sentence was based on temporary insanity; he was transferred to a psychiatric facility. From there, he escaped and hasn't been heard from since."

Pity and fear mingled in my thoughts, along with hopelessness. I offered up a silent prayer.

My storyteller's shoulders drooped. "Mary quietly divorced Karl, but I knew no judge's decree or restraining order could keep Karl from harming her. She and Johnny had to hide. The Witness Protection counselors suggested several towns. Instead, I closed my eyes and put a finger to a map. Luckily, it landed on Willoughby, Georgia."

Luckily?

Did luck have anything to do with their arrival here? Or was it God who sent them to Willoughby, knowing they needed a friend? That friend was me, of course. Always. But by agreeing to listen to the gardener's secret, I'd just taken on a whole heap of baggage. Only time would tell if I had enough strength to carry it all.

Chapter Twenty-One

Music from a toddler's wind-up toy floated through a barely open window, alerting us to the end of Johnny's nap.

Mr. Smith's chest expanded as he inhaled. He glanced toward the house and then back at me while rising from the sandbox. "I'd better get him. Want to share a snack with us?"

I stood and brushed off the seat of my jeans. Although my pulse had calmed, a tangle of thoughts still twisted inside my brain. "Thanks, maybe another time. Mama asked me to pick up some things from the store."

With sad eyes, Mr. Smith stared at me. "Callie, are you okay?" He squeezed my shoulder. "I hope this wasn't too much for you."

I nodded. "It was a lot to take in, but I'm okay." I swallowed hard. "Is there more?"

He cast his gaze to the ground and shoved hands into his pockets. "We hope not."

****

At last, in my truck, I plugged the key into the ignition. I had lied about needing to go to the store—what I needed right then was to drive aimlessly on peaceful country roads. I rolled down the window and pulled away from the curb, hoping the rush of a healing breeze would clear my head and return my pulse to normal. I gulped fresh air, but my brain still felt like it had been tattooed with a branding iron. What remained was an indelible mark that would stay with me forever. I sorted pieces of the story and labeled each one as disgusting, horrendous, or terrifying. Simply put, Karl was a villain and his every conceivable action was evil.

Poor Mr. Smith and his family, they had to be living in a constant state of anxiety, afraid Karl would show up at any minute. Their story almost resembled a Dean Koontz suspense novel. I'd read one…only one. My first was my last. Afterward, I had to sleep with the lights on for a month. On the day the gardener's secret took my mind prisoner, I wondered if the Smiths slept at all.

I didn't really want to be dragged into their nightmare, but I was afraid for them and would have done anything to help. Was there anything?

Then the realization hit. I slammed on my brakes, causing the driver behind to almost collide with my truck. I pulled to the side of the road and waved him by. Obviously, he wasn't pleased with my driving ability, even though my shrug offered an embarrassed apology.

He deftly swerved and let his raised finger speak volumes.

While the engine idled, I smacked the steering wheel with my palm. Of course, there was something I could do, something I had to do—kill the upcoming magazine article about my favorite gardener. I shuddered, knowing there was a possibility that my article, although meant to be a tribute to Mr. Smith, might actually be a roadmap for Karl.

Even though I'd already signed a contract, and had since received an advance, I needed to squelch the piece before the April issue hit the newsstands. That was four months away. Surely there was still time to stop the release. But if word got out that I had refused the opportunity to be published, would all my upcoming submissions be rejected? And, ultimately, would this action affect my job at the *Trib*? The answer was simple—my future as a journalist might be at risk, but the Smiths' future couldn't be.

After cruising every road in Willoughby, giving myself time to think, I motored into my driveway. I continued to sit in the truck, mulling over ideas on how best to renege on my commitment to the magazine without inciting a lawsuit.

The curtains in the laundry room parted; Mama opened the back door. "What you doin', hon?" She didn't wait for me to answer but walked around the truck to rest her hand on my rolled-down window. "Comin' in soon? I sure could use your help with the refreshments."

I pulled myself back into the moment and gazed at Mama, thankful for her naïve smile. Her prayer group would gather at our home in a few minutes for their weekly meeting. If I could share the gardener's secret, the ladies would willingly pray for the Smith family. But since I'd promised not to divulge anything to anyone, I knew I would be the only one down on my knees.

Chapter Twenty-Two

With the telephone receiver mashed against my ear, I thought I detected the sound of an office chair creaking as if the editor in New York had bolted upright.

"You want me to *what*? Callie, you know I can't pull the story."

Despite her initial reaction, I remained hopeful. By the end of our conversation, I needed her to see things my way. Miss Graham had been the editor of *American Portraits Magazine* for more than a decade and had probably dealt with dozens of demands from *prima donna* writers. I hated being one of them, but I saw no alternative. "I normally wouldn't ask this, but it's just occurred to me the article might stress out my gardener friend. I will definitely return the award money, and I promise to put it in today's mail." I crossed my fingers. Surely, she'd yield…wouldn't she?

"Callie, I think you already know your article is part of a series we're running. You and the other authors have each been assigned a specific issue."

"But—"

"You're wasting your breath. This is a done deal."

My shoulders slumped. What kind of ammunition would fit this situation? I bit my lip. "Suppose I told you I didn't have permission to photograph my subject?"

Dead silence.

"Miss Graham—?"

"Hold on a minute."

Canned music played on the line while I waited. My white knuckles gripped the phone as I prayed for leniency. A minute passed…then four, then five. As I pulled away the receiver to massage my numb ear, Miss Graham's voice returned.

"Yes, yes," I sputtered, "I'm still here."

"Okay, Callie. First off, do not *ever, ever, ever* send us an article without including a signed release from the subject. I'm surprised we didn't catch that." She cleared her throat. "But I've spoken with the art department. We're willing to make a small concession. As much as we love the subject's photo, we obviously can't use it as is without his permission—unless we manipulate it. Maybe backlight him so his face is obscured."

"But—"

"Just hear me out. We can also give your subject and his grandson fictitious names. I think that covers the liability issues…don't you?"

Her suggestion wasn't what I wanted to hear. I was fully prepared to argue, but arguing wouldn't achieve my goal unless I brought out the big guns. Time to reload. "No. We still need to kill the story. When I first submitted it, I didn't realize my subject was in danger. Now that I know, I don't want to contribute to his problems. I promised not to say anything, so I probably shouldn't but…the subject is hiding under the Witness Protection Program."

She exploded in laughter. "Callie, you must think I'm a gullible idiot."

I shook my head furiously as though she could see me through the phone. "Please, Miss Graham, I'm telling the truth. You've got to believe me!" Her exhausted sigh told me she was on the verge of giving in.

"Let's just say I do. Because if I don't believe you...you might as well kiss goodbye your career as a freelancer."

Our phone call ended on a better note than when we'd first begun. She finally agreed to hold off for six months, possibly repositioning my article as the final one in the series. We'd revisit my concerns later. But if Karl was apprehended by then, she wanted an exclusive on the story.

Chapter Twenty-Three

January

Another Christmas under my belt...literally. Two weeks into the New Year, and my resolutions were already being tested. Number one on the list—lose five pounds. I should have aimed for more, but I reasoned that success might be achieved with a conservative approach.

Unfortunately, three employees at the newspaper had birthdays in January. Custom dictated that the birthday gal—or guy—be celebrated with a sheet cake after the weekly staff meeting. The skinny people knew how to fend off temptation. Me? "Leftover cake? Sure, I'll take some home."

Mama had always been on my side. She regularly told me my "curves" were beautiful. But isn't that what loving mothers are supposed to say? She shook her head in disbelief when I announced my decision to drop the weight.

Early morning, just after first light, seemed the best time to jog—fewer folks would be awake to gawk as I lumbered down the road. And what a perfect time to let Rascal investigate the neighborhood.

A biting breeze accompanied us on our first outing. I layered two sweatshirts beneath a windbreaker, some stretchy thermals under my sweatpants, thick wool socks inside my sneakers, and fluffy mittens on my numb fingers. I doubted that expert runners would approve of my attire, but what the heck, I refused to freeze in my tracks.

Rascal's fur must have kept him adequately protected, because he wasn't fazed in the least. In fact, the cold seemed to infuse him with even more energy than usual. Remembering that fateful day when his leather leash had become my literal downfall, I thought it best to purchase one of those retractable nylon cord leashes so he could run far beyond where my feet were about to land.

Perhaps he could have run all day, but half a mile was more than enough for me. We rounded the corner and my gaze focused on the finish line—the faded blue siding on our house.

A vehicle approached from behind, the engine downshifting as it slowed. I kept jogging and moved closer to the curb, expecting the car to pass. It didn't. Instead, it pulled even with me.

I snapped my head to the side and saw the words *Willoughby Sheriff* emblazoned on the door of a patrol car. The driver's window rolled down. "As I live and breathe, if it isn't Callie Lou James."

His familiar lopsided smile made my pulse race. I set the thumb lock on my dog's leash and stopped short.

Unfortunately, Rascal kept going.

His momentum jerked me sideways, making me feel like a clumsy cow, which was probably how I looked to that pair of baby blues locked on mine. I smiled. "Jackson Beauregard Taylor, how are you?"

His eyes narrowed, but a grin twitched at his lips. "It's J.B., if you please."

I giggled. "As you wish, sire." I bent in a quick

curtsy. "How long have you been with the sheriff's department?"

Glancing down, he smoothed his uniform. "Ever since I graduated from the police academy last June." He looked up. "Heard you moved back to town about the same time." Almost immediately, he traded his grin for a sober expression. "Sorry about your dad."

My gaze skimmed the ground while I swallowed the knot in my throat. "Thanks." Tucking a frayed piece of yarn under my knitted stocking cap, I looked up. "Your folks okay? I mean…I haven't run into them since I've been back."

"They're great. Both retired now, so they have time to watch the grandbabies."

"Grandbabies?" I forced a wobbly grin. "When did you get married?"

"Me?" He chuckled. "I didn't. My sister did. Two years ago. She just had twins."

I sucked in a hopeful breath. "Well, congrats…uncle."

He glanced at his dashboard clock. "Guess I'd better head to the station. My shift is almost up. We'll have to get together and talk over old times." He waved goodbye as he revved the motor and sped away.

My heart hiccupped. I watched him drive out of sight and savored his words, hoping he hadn't spoken idly. I'd had a crush on him since sixth grade. I was surprised he even remembered me—we rarely spoke, and we'd shared only one slow number at a middle school dance.

I scurried into the house and shoved the door tight against winter's chill. As soon as I unclipped Rascal's leash, he wandered into the parlor and plopped onto the braided rug in front of the sofa, exhaling a heavy sigh. Every sound he made reminded me how much I loved him. With a smile on my lips, I turned to lay his leash on the entry console. After slipping off my mittens, I rubbed bare hands on my jacketed arms, hoping to transfer heat and get the blood circulating again.

And then I glanced up at the hall mirror.

There I was, in a giant ball of an oversized puffer coat staring back. J.B. had seen me this way! It shouldn't have mattered, because I wasn't looking for a boyfriend. Long ago I'd promised myself my only tie to Willoughby would be my mother. A love interest might distract me from my goal—a college degree. But, in spite of my iron will, I realized seeing J.B. had stirred something within. I sighed, resisting the temptation to dwell on that subject, and promptly marched upstairs.

After a hot shower and a lean breakfast, I headed to the *Tribune*. At this early hour, I'd have the whole place to myself, and the solitude would result in a plethora of ideas bursting forth from an undistracted brain. At least I hoped they would, because a rough draft of my next column was due by the end of the day.

Sitting at my desk, I was disappointed to find the invigoration I'd felt earlier didn't transfer to my writing. I stared at a blank screen for ten minutes, waiting for creativity to kick in. Finally, I gave up and signed onto the Internet to see if some nifty idea would grab me. An ad caught my attention—*Now enrolling students for the spring semester. Submit your application online.* Was God telling me it was time to return to school?

My finger twitched, announcing readiness to click on the link. At the same moment, a key turned in the lobby door. I looked up and saw Mazie.

She walked straight to the coat rack. "Mornin', Callie. Yer sure in early." She slipped arms from her blue fake fur jacket and sniffed the air. "I don't smell coffee. Want me to make a pot?"

"Gee, thanks. I should have thought of that." I yawned. "Maybe it'd wake me up."

She winked. "Hot date last night?"

I laughed. "Me?" Swiveling my chair, I faced her. "Nope. Just tired. Didn't sleep well and then went running at daylight."

Mazie raised an eyebrow. "Runnin', huh? Nothin' I'd ever try." She touched a lengthy polished fingernail to an excessively rouged cheek and smacked her hot-pink lips together. "My makeup might melt."

Her three-inch heels clicked across the worn oak flooring as she marched to the counter where day-old, stale donuts languished in a grease-stained box. After emptying yesterday's coffee grounds, she bumped the trash cabinet door closed with a hip, and then swished a stiff brush inside the permanently discolored carafe. "I got friends with eligible bachelor sons if you wanna be fixed up."

Thankfully, she was busy measuring spoonfuls from a giant tub of coffee and didn't see my flushed face. "Thanks, but I'll pass. Not looking for entanglement just yet. But when God drops a special man into my life, I'll be ready." An image of J.B.'s face floated through my mind. "Hmm. Come to think of it, I saw someone this morning I used to have a crush on…maybe I still do."

She didn't say, "Really?" but might as well have because of the way she dipped her chin and eyed me over the top of her glasses.

"Yep." I tucked a lock of hair behind an ear. "He

141

was super friendly today." As soon as the words left my mouth, an opposing thought hit. Pursing my lips, I folded arms across my chest. "Is there a rule that says policemen have to be nice to everyone? Even fat girls?"

She gave me a limp-wristed wave. "Ah, c'mon, Callie. You ain't fat. Yer just curvy. Be thankful you ain't got a scrawny bod like mine."

She may have been waiting for me to compliment her with a comeback that denied her skinniness. But how do you contradict the truth? At least my sappy smile thanked her for making me feel better.

Enough with the idle chit-chat. I told myself to get back to work. Since inspiration hadn't magically sprung from thin air, I knew I had to get serious. I leaned down, dragged my trusty backpack out from underneath the desk, pulled out a yellow legal pad, and flipped through pages of notes from gardening sites I'd browsed. My gaze landed on a possible topic—*Winter pruning.* Yes! Maybe now I could lay down a few semi-intelligent words for my next article. I hunched over the keyboard, hoping to make it obvious I was no longer open to casual conversation.

Mazie's potent perfume followed her as she strolled to the reception desk. She hummed while riffling through the stack of yesterday's messages. "Callie?"

"Yes, ma'am," I answered, not looking up, thoughts still attached to my fingertips as I finished typing the end of a sentence. Glancing up, I only halfway listened—my screaming creative juices were drowning out her voice.

She fanned the air with a scrap of paper. "Callie Lou James, I asked if you got this message from *Newsworthy*?"

My eyebrows scrunched. "*Newsworthy*?"

"You know...one of them syndicators offerin' news stories to subscribers." She grinned ear to ear. "Looks like they picked up your article about plantin' tulips."

My mouth dropped open. Now she had my full attention. In a panic, I spun around while gripping the chair's arms. "What? Have they published it yet?"

She studied the slip. "It don't say." She shrugged and walked over to drop the message into my lap. "But since they's an Internet service, I 'spect your article is already online."

Praying Mazie was wrong, I grasped the paper with both hands and leaned toward the glow of my computer monitor to illuminate the scrawled writing. Squeezing eyes shut, I sagged against the back of my chair.

Mazie tucked her chin. "Hey, you look a little green. You okay?"

Like a firework, a crystal-clear image exploded in my brain—the full-color photo of tulips in bloom that accompanied my article. Those hybrid tulips existed nowhere else on earth except in the inventor's garden—Mr. Smith's. I remembered being surprised by his anger the day my tulip column appeared in the *Tribune*. But now, ever since the day he'd shared his secret with me, I fully understood his initial reaction. Undoubtedly, his family was aware of his hobby, and that probably included his ex-son-in-law. Was there a chance Karl might spot the photo and recognize Mr. Smith's tulips?

"I'm fine," I said to Mazie, offering a tightly controlled grin to dismiss her concern.

She twisted her neck in the direction of the front door as it opened. Three employees entered the lobby. "Mornin', y'all," she greeted, striding to the reception desk, a cup of coffee in her hand.

I immediately reached for the phone and called the number on the message slip, hoping to do damage control. Cradling the receiver close, I hovered over the desk and kept my voice low. "This is Callie James. May I speak to Mr. White, please?" I chewed a fingernail and waited.

"Ms. James!" his voice boomed when he came on the line. "Congratulations on a fine article. Went live yesterday. What can I do for you?"

In less than ten seconds, my hopes had crumbled. I was too late to keep the article from reaching millions more eyes than originally intended. Now I had to decide how to explain this to the Smith family.

Chapter Twenty-Four

Just like ripping off a bandage, I knew it would hurt, but the pain would be short-lived if I took immediate action. However, the real pain came from watching their expressions sink. The three of us sat on the Smith's porch steps, a wide canyon between us. With Johnny down for a nap, we had a chance for uninterrupted adult conversation. I had just dropped the bomb on them about my article hitting the Internet. I waited for Mary or Mr. Smith to say something...anything. The silence made my head throb.

Mary tucked herself close to her father and leaned her chin on his shoulder.

He stared at the ground. Finally, he drew a deep breath and exhaled slowly. "I suppose you've figured out why I was so upset when I first saw the tulip article in your newspaper."

I nodded. "Now that I know about Karl, I assume you were worried he'd recognize the photo of your hybrids."

"Overly paranoid, huh?" He shook his head. "After all, Karl running across a small-town paper like the *Willoughby Tribune* would be highly unlikely." He leaned bent elbows on his knees and combed a shaky hand through his hair. "But now..."

Mary patted his arm.

I swallowed hard. Who'd have thought they'd have

to worry about my article popping up nationally? "Remember when the article first appeared in the *Trib*? You asked me to tell people I took the photo myself. But since no one ever questioned where it came from, no explanation was needed. The Internet changes that. Not only does it have a wider audience, any site using the article will have to assign credit to the *Tribune,* and to me as the author. That opens the door to a new batch of readers who might ask questions."

Mr. Smith glanced at his daughter. "Are we getting ahead of ourselves? Karl never had any interest in yard work…did he? There's probably a one-in-a-million chance he'd check the Internet for gardening tips."

A faint smile played on Mary's lips. "Probably less than that. You've forgotten, Dad…the only time Karl used a computer was to play video games."

A light bulb lit inside my head. I sat taller. "What if I go into the *Trib* tomorrow, act all excited about making it onto the Internet, and maybe confess an out-of-state fan sent me the tulip photo in the first place?" My gaze flicked between the two staring faces. "Don't you see? I want to remove any connection I have to you. I can forge a letter from a fan giving me permission to use the photo in one of my columns. Then, if someone ever calls in, everyone in the newsroom will innocently recite my bogus story." I raised anxious eyebrows and shrugged with open palms in a whadda-ya-think gesture.

Stone-faced, Mr. Smith responded. "And what will you do if someone doesn't just call? Suppose one day they walk into your office and ask for you. And it's Karl."

Chapter Twenty-Five

Over the next week, the *Tribune* received three phone calls regarding the tulip article. None were from Karl…unless he'd become an expert at disguising his voice as female. The first two callers asked where they could purchase the ready-to-plant bulbs, and the third needed to speak to the grower because her company, an online seed catalogue, wanted an exclusive contract to carry the product. All three people received the same story—the photographer had given us permission to use the photo but didn't want to be contacted because work was still underway on a patent.

A smug grin occupied my brain until the second week when the fourth person called—a man with an accent, similar to the one Mary had described as Karl's. With sweaty palms, I clutched the receiver. A few of his words were unclear. What *was* clear was his anger.

"Someone has stolen my hybrids! Lady, I demand you give me the developer's name and number right now. If you don't, my lawyer will subpoena you and your boss for a lawsuit."

"I'm sorry, sir, but we no longer have contact with the person who lent us that photo."

"Impossible," he roared. "You'd need permission to use it."

"We have permission. I have a confirmation letter that arrived just before the article was first published in our newspaper. Now it appears the grantor has moved."

"Ha! Sounds like you're covering for him and—"

"Her," I boldly interrupted. "It was a she. And I'm not covering for anyone."

Silence.

"Her?" His blustery tone softened. "A woman? You're sure? I...uh...I assumed the thief was a man."

Since he'd hesitated when I mentioned the photographer was a woman, his fumbling words only reaffirmed my fears—I might be speaking to Karl.

"I'm positive it was a woman. We spoke on the phone." My pulse raced as I exaggerated. "She's almost seventy—a real gardening enthusiast who's been cultivating tulips for years with her gardening club." I held my breath. Had I diverted suspicion from Mr. Smith?

"A woman, huh?"

"Yes, sir," I said firmly. "Definitely a woman." I held my breath as he took his time to respond, like he'd been chewing on my answer and needed time to think.

"Hmm." His breathing slowed. "I don't know of any woman who has had access to my tulips."

"Well then, just in case, why don't you leave your contact info with me? I'd be happy to report back if we hear from her again." When he recited his name and phone number, sure enough, he matched the caller I.D. on my readout. Thank heavens for digital technology. He wasn't hiding anything.

We hung up on friendly terms. I leaned back in my chair, still wondering what he was after. I could hardly wait to discuss my concerns with the Smith family.

****

I hadn't exercised my dog for two days, so I clipped

the leash to Rascal's collar, left my truck at home, and off we went. He seemed hesitant. Most days he bounded with the carefree abandonment of a pup, but today he reminded me of his age—forty-nine in dog years.

Mary answered the door. She still wore her starched uniform from the lunch shift at the Kopper Kettle. She put a finger to her lips, stepped outside, and eased the door shut behind her. Mr. Smith wasn't home, and Johnny was napping. Mary motioned to the bottom step.

Rascal and I followed. He exhaled an oomph as he dropped to the ground and settled at my feet.

The afternoon had turned a menacing gray and the increasing breeze hinted at a storm in our future. I glanced to the dark clouds and hid chilled hands inside the sleeves of my parka as I described my confrontation with today's caller. "He gets the trophy for making me more nervous than any of the others." A shiver sent chills to my brain. "He threatened me with his gruff attitude." I lowered my voice to imitate the caller's tone. " 'My lawyer is going to hear about this, young lady.' " Shaking my head, I exhaled. "Maybe he was just someone looking for his share of the pie. I mean...wouldn't there be a residual for anyone owning the marketing rights?" Tugging at my jacket hem, I stuffed the excess fabric under my legs, attempting to stop cold air from creeping inside. "Your thoughts?"

She drew her lips together and shook her head. "Doesn't sound like Karl. He *is* intimidating, but threatening to get a lawyer wouldn't occur to him. Maybe the caller is just a blowhard who's used to bluffing, hoping to get what he wants. Did he ask for money?"

I shook my head. "No. But if you think he's just

bluffing, I'm okay with that explanation if you are."

Mary grabbed the edges of her open cardigan and lapped each section across her chest. "Geeze, it's cold." She tucked hands into her armpits. "Sorry I made you sit out here. Johnny should be awake soon. Wanna go inside and have some hot cocoa?"

The first raindrop hit my nose. I extended an open palm, looked skyward, and felt the second drop immediately follow. "Thanks, but I better get home before the sky opens up." I stood and directed a command toward my slumbering dog. "C'mon, Rascal, let's go."

His eyelids fluttered as his tail brushed the ground. He didn't rise, but he stretched out and rested a golden head atop his front paws.

Crouching, I tousled his fur. "Hey, fella. We need to head home while you're still dry." I cupped his chin and stared into his eyes, almost pressing my nose to his. "Mama will be upset if you track mud on her clean floor." I shot Mary a grin. "Mama won't appreciate the wet-dog odor either."

Mary mimicked my grin. When two or three gentle raindrops tapped the steps, she moved up and under the protected area of the porch.

Rascal sighed, and again the tail swooshed.

I smoothed my hand along his back. "Are you okay, big guy?"

He grunted as he rose to stand on all four paws.

Turning to Mary, I raised my arms in a shrug. Sometimes I wondered if Rascal even understood my commands. Or was he just inclined to be stubborn so he could receive more attention? I waved goodbye over my shoulder and called out. "Say hi to Johnny for me."

Once Rascal got going, he seemed fine, but I did have to remind him to keep up with my hurried pace. Thank heavens, we only caught a few sprinkles on the way home.

Safe inside our toasty warm house, I removed Rascal's leash and watched him amble into the parlor to his favorite spot, plop onto the floor, and almost instantly begin to snore.

He wasn't usually this exhausted from a walk. How long since his last checkup? A year? I made a mental note to call the vet.

****

Dr. Atherby thrust a bottle into my hand.

"What's this?" Stroking Rascal's back, I stood beside the stainless-steel exam table.

"Vitamins. I want you to crush one of these into his food every day. Let's give him a week or so and see how he responds."

I stared at the container, my thumb tracing the label. "And if he doesn't get better?"

"We'll run some tests." He offered a dog treat and cocked his chin close to Rascal's. "You promise to be a good patient?"

Rascal answered by dragging a slurpy tongue across the doctor's face.

Chuckling, Dr. Atherby wiped his wet mouth and ruffled my dog's fur. He dropped his smile when his eyes met mine. "You do realize, Callie...he *is* getting older."

My throat tightened.

"Callie, I don't want to worry you." He bundled Rascal into his arms and set him on the floor. "His coat is shiny, his eyes are bright, and he readily swishes that happy tail...those are the type of clues we use to judge how he feels, in spite of his age. Just keep up with the vitamins and, hopefully, some of his pep will return."

A week later, relieved at Rascal's improvement, I called the vet and cancelled the follow-up appointment. We were done for another year. Weren't we?

Chapter Twenty-Six

February 19

"Happy Birthday, Callie." Mazie greeted me when I walked into the *Trib* the morning of my twenty-first birthday. She withdrew a box of tiny candles from her purse before stuffing her belongings into a cubby beneath the counter.

Surprised she'd remembered, but delighted someone other than my mother had, I blinked. "How'd you—?"

She folded fists to her hips and chastised with me with her steel-blue eyes while peering over the top of tortoise shell eyeglasses.

I could feel my cheeks redden. Silly me, how could I have forgotten? Even though Mazie was the editor's cousin, that wasn't the reason she'd been hired. "Efficient" was the word that best described her. Mr. Barton appeared to be the boss, and Mazie let everyone *believe* he was, but she was the oil that greased the cogs to keep the *Tribune*'s wheels turning. "Sorry. Should have known. Guess you have a mind for remembering dates, huh?"

"And then some." Her cherry-red lips relaxed into an infectious grin. "Hon, I may be a lot of things, but the one thing I ain't never been is absentminded." She turned and crossed to the kitchenette where a sheet cake rested, opened the box of candles, and arranged twenty-one of them among the hot pink roses piped onto white frosting. A minute later, she sauntered to my desk and tapped me on the shoulder. Leaning into my ear, she whispered, "We'll light the candles at break time, but don't eat too much cake. Savannah and I wanna take you to lunch."

I did as she suggested, fighting against wavering willpower, and turned down a second slice. However, as the morning dragged on, I occasionally glanced between the leftovers and the clock, hoping lunchtime would arrive before I made a fool of myself by shoving my face into a mountain of frosting.

"Ya ready?" Mazie and Savannah stood nearby, winter coats draped over their arms.

Startled, I looked up. I'd been so engrossed in my latest article, I'd not only forgotten about the cake, I'd forgotten to watch the time. "Yes, ma'am. Give me a sec." I printed out a copy for Mr. Barton, trotted it into his empty office, and laid it atop the stack in his wire in-basket. With my draft finished and waiting for approval, I was ready to relax and inhale relief.

****

"A booth okay?" The hostess at the coffee shop gathered an assortment of menus. She led us down the aisle, passing a table occupied by three local policemen.

J.B. glanced up and gave me a nod.

I nodded back, pulse racing.

As we settled into the red vinyl booth in a corner of the restaurant, Savannah poked me in the ribs. "What a hottie. You know him?"

"I did in high school." Not wanting to expand on my answer, I gratefully accepted one of the menus dealt to us by the hostess and turned my attention to the food pictures. My mouth watered as I stared at juicy hamburgers and golden fries. I sighed, wanting to give in, but knowing I shouldn't.

"What would y'all like to drink?" our waitress asked, pencil poised above her order pad.

"Water," Mazie said.

"Likewise…with lemon," Savannah seconded.

I flipped over the menu and stared at a tempting photo of a frosty cola, laden with a pound or two of sugar. "Um…I'll have water, too."

Savannah nudged me again as our server walked away. "Sooo…tell us about Mr. Hot Stuff."

Unwrapping the banded silverware bundle, I arranged my utensils to one side before sliding the paper napkin onto my lap. "Nothing to tell. Barely know him. We ran in separate crowds." To signal I was done with my explanation, I opened the menu and buried my nose among the soup and salad selections.

"Excuse me, ladies." He cleared his throat. "Callie?"

Looking like an overgrown little boy, gripping his hat in both hands, J.B. stood squarely at the edge of our table. I glanced up but didn't dare look right or left—I could feel the questioning stares of Mazie and Savannah. I should have introduced them, but I was concerned my nervous brain would switch their names before the words arrived in my mouth. "Hey, J.B., nice to see you again. Have a good lunch?"

"Uh…yeah, we did." He rotated his hat between his fingers, stopping at a new place on the brim. "Callie, I ran across my yearbook the other day. It got me thinking. Our class always promised to have a reunion picnic before the five-year mark. Maybe we should get the ball rolling. You have any time to discuss it this weekend?"

I swallowed. "Just you and me?" My heart fluttered at the thought.

"Well…yes. At least to begin with. Whaddaya say?"

"I'd love to." Had my elevated voice gushed in reply? Had I appeared too anxious? Sensing the eyes of my newspaper friends darting between J.B. and me, I dialed back my tone to seem more blasé. "Hmm. I'd better check my calendar first. Can I get back to you?"

He grinned. "Sure thing. Just call me at the station." He nodded to us before leaving. "Ladies."

I glanced through the window to the parking lot.

As the officers walked toward their patrol car, one of the men smirked and teasingly rattled J.B.'s shoulders.

"Callie, mind yer manners," admonished Mazie in a stern voice. But the corners of her mouth twitched as if to hide her amusement. "Didn't yer mama ever tell you starin' was rude?"

Savannah giggled. "Gonna have to check your calendar, huh?"

My friends finally gave up taunting me when the waitress arrived to take our orders. I think the rest of our lunchtime conversation centered on work at the *Trib*, but I don't exactly remember. My distracted mind floated elsewhere, questioning why I couldn't have a *temporary* boyfriend until I headed back to college.

When we returned from lunch, I overheard someone say Mr. Barton had taken off for the rest of the day. That meant my draft wouldn't be edited until the next day. *Darn.* I printed out another copy. At least I had time to drop it off to Mr. Smith so he, the authentic gardener, could check for any technical errors.

Then I thought, what the heck, it's my birthday…why not escape like the boss had? I told Mazie my plan, and she gave me her blessing.

"Since yer goin' out, do you mind droppin' these off at the post office?" She held out a rubber-banded stack of letters that had missed the mail pick-up.

I tucked them into the front flap of my backpack, but before I could slide my arms through the straps, a muffled ring sounded in my pocket. I paused mid-step and pulled out my cell phone to answer.

Mama's voice arrived from the other end. "Sorry to bother you, Callie, but my car won't start. I'm at the beauty shop. Can you pick me up?"

"Sure, Mama. But what about your car? We can't just leave it there."

"Well, we can for now. I called Fred at the garage. He thinks it's the battery, so he's bringin' over a new one. But he can't get here until later, and I still need to fix a casserole for tonight's potluck."

"Okay. But I have to run by the post office first, so plan on fifteen or twenty minutes."

****

The bell over the beauty shop door jingled as I stepped inside. The acrid smell of permanent wave solution instantly accosted my nose. My mother, her white hair perfectly coiffed and sprayed, sat in front of Francine Lothner's manicure table with her hands lying flat under a bright gooseneck lamp.

Mama twisted her head toward me. "You're sure quick. You said twenty minutes, so I decided to get my nails done. You mind waitin' a bit? I'm almost finished." She gestured with her chin toward the manicurist. "You remember Francine, don't you, Callie?"

Stiffening, I nodded, recalling the rumors that supposedly had come from Francine's own gossipy mouth.

She grinned and retuned my nod. "How ya been, Callie?"

"Fine. And you?" I forced a reluctant smile for the sake of not embarrassing my mother, who'd always taught me to be gracious in every situation.

"Fine. Just fine." She returned her gaze to Mama's hands while applying perfect strokes of peach-colored polish onto each nail. "Your mama told me you were writin' the gardenin' column for the newspaper." Holding the polish brush held midair, she glanced up with a wink. "Everythin' goin' okay?"

"Great. Really great." I smiled the widest smile I could manage, even though my throat tightened in anticipation of what she might say next. Francine knew I had no prior experience with gardens before beginning my job at the *Tribune*. Would she expose me as a novice? I was well beyond the fledgling I'd been five months before, but I still couldn't imagine having to publicly admit most of my gardening education had come from Mr. Smith.

The shop was dead quiet, except for our two voices and the occasional snip of scissors. Had the beauticians locked onto our conversation? Were the clients listening, too? I decided to wait elsewhere. "Mama, I saw something in the store window next door. Come get me when you're finished." I practically sprinted to get outside.

Striding up the sidewalk, I paused in front of the only jewelry store in town. The sun glaring on the glass blinded me. Rather than press my nose to the window, I shaded my eyes with a cupped hand and squinted at the various displays.

"Wouldn't it be easier to see if you just went inside?" The stranger had mumbled with a foreign accent.

I flinched. I hadn't heard him approach, but now he stood unnervingly close—so close I could smell cigarette smoke on his clothing. This couldn't be Karl, could it? "Uh…I'm not a serious buyer." My weak smile quivered while my feet froze in place.

He didn't smile back; he just stared.

Goose bumps rose on my arms. "On second thought, you might be right. I should go in." With trembling fingers, I reached for the door and opened it just wide enough to slip through, praying he wouldn't follow. My hand was still on the knob when I stole a nervous peek at the man on the sidewalk.

His gaze lingered on mine for a moment before he turned and walked away.

The sound of someone clearing her throat made me spin and flatten my body against the door.

"Welcome to Marco's Jewelry," the saleslady chirped. "May I help you find something?"

"Uh…thanks. But I'm just going to look around while waiting for my mother." I moved about the store, occasionally glancing to the window, hoping the stranger had vanished for good. I stopped at a locked rack of gold-plated chains. *So many smart styles.* Although I wasn't into collecting jewelry, I caressed the length of several, and actually thought about buying one. My grandmother had left me a petite cameo brooch when she died. I'd always planned to put it on a chain and wear it as a necklace. *Well then…happy birthday to me!*

The clerk unlocked the rack and draped my favorite chain over a black velvet pad. "Lovely, isn't it?"

Fingering the delicate golden links, I nodded.

"Would you like to try it on?"

"No need. It's perfect. I'll take it." I fumbled through my backpack, found my wallet, and handed her a credit card.

She swiped the card through a reader then laid the receipt on the counter and tipped a pen toward me. "Will this be a gift?"

Without looking up, I scribbled my name while skewing my mouth to one side. "Sort of."

She turned on her heel and called out over her shoulder, "This will only take a minute. Our gift wrap is complimentary."

I opened my mouth to stop her, but she had disappeared into the back room. Was it permissible to buy your own present and then have it gift wrapped? Doing something so foreign to my practical nature left me giddy. I pressed fingertips to my mouth and giggled.

"What's so funny?"

My hand flew to my chest as I whirled. "Oh, Francine. You startled me. What are you doing here?"

She scowled. "Pickin' up my repaired watch. Is that okay with you?"

Embarrassment climbed my neck and heated my cheeks. "Of course. I just meant…well, I thought you and my mother were busy with her manicure."

Her face relaxed. "We finished. Fred came early to install her battery. I think they're still in the parkin' lot out back if you wanna catch her."

The saleslady reappeared with a tiny, royal blue velvet bag, cinched with a white satin bow. She placed it in a paper sack, imprinted with the store's name. "Thanks for shopping at Marco's. Come back anytime," she drawled, handing the package across the glass display case. "Have a good day."

I mimicked her smile then turned to Francine, offering her one, also. "Good to see you, Francine. Take care."

Standing outside, I couldn't resist opening the paper sack and stroking the velvet bag with a fingertip, excited about the only precious gift I'd ever given myself.

Approaching footsteps made me look up. The stranger from earlier strode toward me, again not smiling, but with his dark eyes riveted on mine. A whoosh of warm air escaped the jewelry store as Francine exited and bumped into me. I spun toward her, crooked my arm around her elbow, and held on for dear life. "I've been meaning to make an appointment with you. Maybe I should do that right now."

She drew back her chin and blinked. "Uh...okay."

My gaze flitted from Francine to the advancing stranger and back to Francine. "What do you think?" I gestured with my chin to an outstretched hand. "Have a miracle for these gardening fingernails?"

She came to an abrupt halt and grabbed my hand to study it. "Geeze, Callie, those are gross. Why didn't you come see me before they got this bad?"

"Well, I'm here now." I tightened my grip on her arm and urged her toward the beauty shop. "Let's go see how soon you can get me in." I kept my eyes lowered as the stranger passed. A second later, I shuddered.

Francine rested a hand on my shoulder. "You okay, Callie?"

I pulled her inside the beauty shop and craned my neck to peer out the window, wondering if the stranger would stop in front of the jewelry store. "That guy gives me the creeps. You don't suppose he's going to rob the store…do you?"

She snorted a laugh. "Only if he's goin' for the insurance money."

"Huh?"

"That's Marco. It's his store."

My mouth dropped open.

"Yeah, weird, huh?" Francine's eyebrows gathered. "You're not the first to think he's creepy. At least he's smart enough to let his daughter wait on the customers."

I mentally punched myself for my jump-to-conclusion attitude. Maybe a sedative existed in my future. How else could I relax and not expect to see Karl around every corner?

Chapter Twenty-Seven

Was seven thirty too early to stop by? Standing on the front porch at the Smiths' household, I leaned an ear toward the door. No toddler sounds, just a lot of quiet. I took a chance and knocked softly. My knuckles had barely grazed the surface when the door opened.

With a phone pressed to her ear, Mary held back the screen and whispered at me, "Come in. I'm in the middle of returning a call." She cautioned with a hold-on-a-minute finger as she spoke into the receiver. "Hi, Stacy, this is Mary. I just got your message about coming in early. I have to wait until my dad gets home to babysit Johnny. Call me if you'd rather ask another of the wait staff."

Huffing a sigh, she flipped shut the outdated cell phone. "Sorry, Callie. Work stuff." She pushed hair off her forehead. "You're early. I know Dad promised to look over your next column, but he went to get gasoline for the mower. Do you want to wait? I've got coffee brewing."

"No to the coffee. But yes, I'll wait." I followed her into the kitchen and spied her son sitting in his highchair. "Hey, Johnny." I bent over to ruffle his hair. "Mmm, pancakes. Yummy." I nearly kissed him, but the sweet scent of maple syrup told me my lips would stick to his.

He smiled, syrup and soggy crumbs clinging to his face. Agile fingers, alternating with a toddler-sized fork, helped him pack food inside his cheeks, making him look like a satisfied squirrel. When he squeezed his hand into a fist, remnants of breakfast oozed between his knuckles. He held up a limp pancake, offering to share.

"No, thanks." I giggled and tapped his sticky nose "If you want to grow up big and strong, you need to finish those all by yourself."

Mary pulled the final dish from the drainer and wiped it dry. "I can make you some. Griddle's still hot."

"Thanks, but I'm eating lighter these days. Besides, Johnny's table manners just killed my appetite."

She grinned.

"So, your boss wants you to come in early?"

Rolling her eyes, she nodded. "A waitress didn't show."

I leaned back against the counter. "Would you like me to babysit?" I moved out of the way so Mary could open a drawer and put away a handful of utensils. "Rascal's waiting in my truck. We're headed to the park. Johnny could go with us. By the time we get back, your dad will be home." With raised eyebrows, I waited for Mary's consent. I could almost hear decision wheels turning in her head. "Well?"

She glanced to the clock above the kitchen sink as she slid a stack of clean plates into the cupboard. While hanging the damp dishtowel over a drawer pull, she inhaled a ragged breath. "Okay, but only for thirty minutes. Dad would have a fit if it's any longer. He prefers I keep Johnny home as much as possible."

I sighed. "Mary, I know it's difficult, but your dad needs to lighten up. Can't keep his grandson in a bubble forever. What will he do when Johnny gets older?"

****

"Faster, Cow-ee! Faster!" Johnny squealed as he hugged my hip with his chubby legs.

We had jogged along the park's running path for several minutes, Rascal straining on his leash well ahead of us. But that wasn't working. Adding an extra twenty-five pounds of toddler weight to my frame probably burned enough calories to make me smile for a week, but catching a breath was my immediate concern.

I jerked on Rascal's leash to bring us all to a stop. "Let's walk for a while, Johnny. Callie doesn't have as much energy as you." I set him on his feet, and he broke free, scampering across grass still wet with morning dew. His destination was the brightly painted playground equipment in primary colors, totally devoid of small children at that early hour.

I followed, lowered myself to the ground, and leaned against a tree. When a notification dinged my cell phone, I reached into my pocket to swipe the readout and spotted an annoying advertisement. Since nothing had been deleted for several days, I scrolled through one email after another, discarding ads and messages. Occasionally, I glanced up to check on Johnny who entertained himself by draping his body over the seat of a swing, knotting and unknotting the chains as he twisted first one way and then another.

Rascal stood abruptly, drawing taut the leash still wrapped around my wrist.

I drew him close and slipped my fingers inside his collar. "What is it, fella?"

He stared off into distant bushes while a low growl rose from his throat.

"You see something?" My gaze searched for the slightest movement but found nothing. When he growled again, pulling against my effort to restrain him, I tightened my hold on his collar. "Rascal, stop that. You're making me nervous."

He again strained at the leash, this time barking wildly.

I shivered, realizing my dog wanted to be released. By this time, I'd had enough. Hurrying the few steps to the swing set, I glanced back over my shoulder before swooping Johnny into my arms. We made a run for the parking lot, his earlier words pounding in my brain— *Faster, Cow-ee! Faster!*

With not another vehicle in sight, except for the driverless car sitting next to mine, my nerves went on increased alert. My gaze darted right and left while I reached for the truck door and yelled to Rascal, "Up! Now!" As he bounded across to the passenger side floor, I grabbed the steering wheel, and in one continuous motion, vaulted myself and Johnny into the cab, locking the door behind us. Johnny must have sensed my urgency, because he scampered into his car seat. Hands shaking, I fumbled with his safety belt and probably winched it too tight, judging from the look on his face, but I'd deal with that after we escaped. Steadying the key with both hands, I aimed for the ignition slot.

The truck refused to start.

"No, no, not now!" I tromped the gas pedal until the engine burped an encouraging backfire, allowing me to slam the gearshift into drive. Racing from the parking lot, I saw two speed bumps ahead but didn't slow— bruises were of minor concern at that moment. I sped out onto the highway, still feeling unsafe. Every few seconds, my gaze flitted from the road to the rearview mirror. Were we being followed?

Yes. We were. By a black and white car. I'd never been so glad to hear the woop-woop of a siren, knowing it was meant for me. Feeling my pulse settle, I pulled to the curb and rolled down my window.

The officer emerged from his patrol car and approached, shaking his head. "You've probably broken just about every traffic law in Willoughby—speeding, failing to yield, failing to signal, erratic driving." He gestured to the metal clip dangling near my window. "And seat belt not fastened." He slapped a citation pad against his open palm before sliding a pen from his breast pocket. "What do you have to say for yourself, Callie James?" J.B. pushed up the brim of his hat with the pen tip and glared at me.

I laid my wrists on the open window. "Cuff me. I'm guilty." My attempt at a joke brought only a tiny smile to his lips.

He scowled. "Callie, you can't be driving this way. It's dangerous."

"I know it is," I admitted, biting my lower lip. "This isn't how I usually drive. I thought we were being followed."

His eyebrows rose. "Followed?"

"Well…yes. Rascal sensed someone…or something…lurking in the bushes at the park." Now that I'd had a chance to regroup, my excuse seemed pretty foolish. I ducked my chin. "Turns out, we weren't followed after all."

Silence. Except for the tapping of J.B.'s pen against his citation pad.

Slipping my hands from the window and into my lap, I laced fingers together and mentally prayed I wouldn't have to go to court, or worse yet, explain my bizarre behavior to Mama. "Please, J.B., my insurance will go up if you issue a ticket."

He breathed a heavy sigh. "Consider this a warning." He wagged his pen in my direction. "But if this happens again—"

"It won't." I raised my palm in a pledge. "I promise."

Before we parted, J.B. said he'd cruise by the park and check out my concerns.

I didn't mention the incident to the Smith family. Why add to their paranoia? I couldn't imagine anyone discovering how irrational I'd been. Besides, nothing bad had happened—except for me looking like a fool in front of J.B..

Chapter Twenty-Eight

My birthday just happened to coincide with our monthly church potluck. Dinner was served on paper plates in the church basement—simple food, lots of starches, quite filling. But no recognition of me experiencing my special day was noted…no presents, and no happy birthday song. Actually, I was okay with that. At twenty-one, I now considered myself to be an adult. Birthdays no longer needed to be the festive affair they'd been during childhood. However, later that week, when my mother suggested we keep the celebration going, I purred. "Out to dinner? I'd love to, Mama."

The tempting aroma of grilled steaks and freshly baked bread welcomed us as we exited Mama's car in the parking lot at the Lakeview Dinner House. The smell made me instantly nix my plan of ordering a Cobb salad. Heaven knows, I didn't need anything else to increase my hunger pangs, but what might be considered a free-of-charge hint about the waiting food now gently wafted on the evening breeze and floated straight across the parking lot to my susceptible nose…compliments of the restaurant's kitchen vents.

I stopped and sniffed the air. "You know, they do that on purpose."

Mama continued walking but glanced back. "Who does what on purpose?"

I scurried to catch up. "The restaurant owners.

S. Hansberger

They're pretty shrewd. They lure you in with those irresistible smells, hoping you'll rack up a huge tab."

Mama rolled her eyes and held open the door to the restaurant.

She would have found it impossible to pick a nicer place. The Lakeview Dinner House was the only eatery fancier than the various coffee shops doing business in Willoughby. It was Wednesday, which meant the dining room wouldn't be as packed as on the weekend, but the wait staff would still offer their customary professional service to top off water glasses or deliver hot entrees, beautifully plated with just the right amount of garnish.

I caught a glimpse of Mary pouring a glass of red wine for a guest. When she turned, she flashed a smile our way, and her eyes lit. Normally, her warm countenance wouldn't have surprised me. But tonight, I knew she must be tired—she'd already worked an earlier shift at the Kopper Kettle. She probably hadn't had much time to rest in between finishing there and then changing her uniform to show up here. I hoped we'd be seated in her area, knowing we wouldn't be as demanding as the average guest and wear her out even more. But the hostess showed us to a table on the opposite side of the room.

I refrained from gorging on the mega-calorie selections, but later, I pushed back from the table and groaned with contentment anyway. "I wish I'd stopped sooner."

My mother wasn't very good at being subtle. She excused herself from the table, saying she needed to go "powder her nose." But I knew what she had in mind. One whisper to our waitress would send a candle-lit bowl of ice cream to our table.

Mama returned with a goofy smile.

Within minutes, bearing a complimentary dessert, several of the wait staff gathered to offer a rousing version of the birthday tune.

Of course, my part was to look embarrassed and chuckle, "Oh, you shouldn't have." I squeezed Mama's hand and acted surprised so she could enjoy the moment as much as I did.

I wasn't the only celebrant there that evening. At a nearby table, Mary and three other servers crowded around a family of partiers. Instead of accepting a single serving of ice cream, the group had furnished their own cake, lit with three sturdy candles—one, zero, zero.

"Happy birthday, Pop." Grinning, the man's daughter, undoubtedly in her seventies, cautioned, "Don't blow them out yet. Let me take your picture." She peered through the viewfinder of a disposable cardboard camera. "Smile."

The camera clicked.

"Wait. Don't move. It didn't flash."

While the candles flickered their glow under his chin, the man exhaled the puff of air his cheeks had been holding.

His daughter tipped the camera in every direction, squinting at each panel before turning to the young woman beside her. "Megan, I don't know how they expect people to use these stupid things. They print the instructions too small."

Megan stood. She leaned in to rest her hand on the older woman's shoulder. "It's okay, Grandma, I got this." Cell phone in hand, she aimed at the birthday boy and then moved around the table, scanning faces of each guest as they belted out their song in tribute to one hundred years of living.

Mama and I left the restaurant with satisfied stomachs and full hearts.

A day later, even though I didn't need to go into the *Trib*, I stopped by midmorning to drop off some of Mama's freshly baked goodies. Leaning an elbow on Savannah's desk, while the two of us picked away at a shared blueberry muffin, I described the restaurant event. "Can you imagine living to be one hundred? Everyone had tears in their eyes...him, too. He was so sweet...such a good sport, wearing that silly party hat."

Savannah blinked. "What a coincidence. That sounds like—" Her hands flew to her keyboard to log onto the Internet. She glanced at me. "Do you ever watch YouTube?" She clicked on a video and waited for it to load. "This has gone viral. All of us here wondered if it took place in Willoughby. Looks exactly like our local dinner house."

I scooted my chair closer. "Yes. That's him. Too cute, huh?" I craned my neck and pointed. "Ah ha! There it is...absolute proof this was taken in Willoughby."

Savannah's gaze studied the computer screen where my finger rested.

"I'm surprised none of you noticed," I proclaimed smugly. "Look at the middle of the table. See the restaurant name on the wine list?" My chest swelled with pride at my detective-like skills just before my grin grew even wider. "Oh my gosh, that's us in the background." Not waiting for the video to finish, I bounded out of my chair. "Gotta go. Can't wait to share this with my mother."

****

"Mama, come in here," I shouted. "I have something

to show you." Plunking my belongings onto the kitchen table, I drew a leg under me as I sat and booted up my laptop.

She shuffled into the room with a Bible in her hands and slid a ribboned bookmark between the pages. "What is it, hon?"

"You'll see." Smiling, I patted the chair beside me. "Come. Sit. You'll love this." I waited for her to cross the room and lower herself into a chair. "Ready?"

She shrugged. "I guess."

I angled the laptop so Mama could see. "Drum roll, please," I announced, rapidly drumming my index fingers on the table edge. "Ta-duh." After a quick tap on the pause symbol, the action began.

Mama adjusted her glasses and leaned in. "What...?" Her lashes fluttered. "Well, for heaven's sake. That's in the restaurant, isn't it?"

Both of us chuckled as we viewed the celebration, watching it to the very end.

"Look at that, Callie." Mama directed a finger toward the screen. "There's...what's her name?"

I hadn't noticed individual faces in the background earlier. My smile withered when I recognized a friend. There, standing directly behind the one-hundred-year-old man was Mary.

Earlier, I'd boasted I was a mystery solver. Now, my shoulders sagged while a reprimand slapped my pride. But this wasn't about me. Once again, the Internet had sent out a clue as to the Smith family's whereabouts. Would this one find its way to Karl?

Chapter Twenty-Nine

That fateful day when Mr. Smith shared his secret, he questioned whether I could handle the danger I might face, along with the responsibility of not telling anyone. At the time, I considered myself invincible, so I let my curiosity give him the go-ahead. Now, I had so many frightening concerns bottled up inside, I sometimes worried I'd explode and confess everything to the nearest person.

Whenever the stress seemed overwhelming, I'd run to my garden for relief. Working there was a mindless task—the best way to escape whatever troubled me. I had rescued an old, shabby throw pillow from a donation carton before it got loaded into Mama's car. It was my go-to cushion whenever I sat on the ground to pull weeds. Because I wasn't crazy about sitting in the mud from the previous day's rain, I wrapped the pillow inside a plastic grocery bag. If I'd been wearing shorts, the surface would have stuck to my bare legs, but since it was only late February, I still needed the warmth of long pants.

Each time I shifted the pillow to the next row, the plastic would crackle in reply. If Rascal had been there, the sound would have caused him to lift his head to check on me. He'd been my shadow recently, and I felt protected in his presence. But at that particular moment, he was at the vet's office, recuperating from whatever ailed him.

I'd grown fond of Rascal sleeping on the end of my bed each night, especially in winter whenever my cold feet located the warm spot beneath him. Thank goodness, he'd be home later that day, and I wouldn't have to wear socks to bed.

The night before, at two in the morning, Rascal awakened me when he sprang from my bed and rushed to the window. Paws on the sill, he growled. And he did it again twenty minutes later, and again ten minutes after that. Each time, I'd stumble to the window only to discover nothing but a light drizzle of rain along with reluctant moonlight finding its way through patchy clouds. Feeling like an insomniac, I finally gave up just before three thirty, staggered downstairs, let out Rascal, went back to bed, and instantly welcomed uninterrupted sleep.

The next morning, my mother gently tapped on the door before poking her head into my bedroom. "Not like you to sleep this late. Aren't you joggin' today?"

Barely lifting my eyelids, I rolled over to squint at the alarm clock. "No, ma'am."

"Where's Rascal?" she asked.

"Outside," I mumbled, eyes still closed, patchwork quilts up over my ears, wishing Mama would leave so I could drift back to sleep.

"That's odd. I crossed the field when I saw Olivia Brown. We talked for about twenty minutes, but Rascal never came to greet us. Olivia gave me a dozen eggs. Can I fix you some?"

I sat straight up, my eyes fully open. "What did you say?"

"I asked if you wanted eggs. They're fresh from her

coop."

"No, no. Did you say Rascal never came to see you?"

Not waiting for her answer, I heaved the quilts to one side, threw my legs over the edge of the bed, and crammed my feet into navy blue sneakers, yesterday's laces still tied. With heels extending over the backs, I shoe-horned a finger inside each shoe before hobbling down the stairs as fast as possible.

I burst through the laundry room door, shouting, "Rascal! Rascal!" While I stood in the middle of the driveway, crisp air traveled up the sleeves of my pajamas. I turned every direction, whistling and calling, over and over again.

Nothing stirred...nothing except for a red-tailed hawk, riding the air currents and swooping low to collect an unsuspecting field mouse. Normally, the sight of a hawk's victory would nauseate me, but the immediacy of locating Rascal had taken possession of my senses.

Just beyond the driveway, in the drying mud, I spied paw prints—Rascal's. They chased one way and then another. Relief washed over me when I discovered no sign of human prints. However, several sets of small animal paws had left their marks just slightly ahead of Rascal's. Again, I called. Again, nothing. I knew my garden might be the target of night creatures, so I rounded the corner, looking for telltale signs. A scattering of half-eaten veggies littered the rows, but the clues didn't stop there.

Daddy's overturned aluminum fishing boat lay near the shed. Surrounding it were dozens of doggy paw prints, and a fresh mound of earth, resulting from what appeared to be the spot where Rascal had dug underneath, trying to reach whatever was hiding. Then various indentations wandered through the garden and around the house, so I followed them.

A subtle moan came from the front porch.

I scaled the steps and dropped to my knees beside Rascal, who only partially raised his head. "What happened, fella?" While stroking his fur, I noticed dried blood on one of his legs. "Raccoons?" Thank God, Rascal's rabies shots were up to date.

He moaned again and closed his eyes, but at least his tail thumped.

"Let's go see Dr. Atherby." My voice cracked with emotion. "He'll make you good as new."

I knew my attention should be on the road as I drove but couldn't help stealing an occasional peek at my quiet dog, lying on the truck seat beside me. When I carried him into the vet's office, we were immediately led to an exam room.

After treating some minor bites on Rascal's leg, the vet turned to me. "We can't put all the blame on raccoons, Callie." He frowned. "Something else isn't right. I'd like to keep him today. Is that okay with you?"

Not really. But I didn't say it aloud. Even though I hated being separated from Rascal, I wanted him healthy again. My expression drooped as I nodded.

Dr. Atherby patted my hand. "We close at five thirty. He can go home then."

****

Holding a fresh batch of photos, I turned off the printer in my bedroom and stared at the clock. Four twenty-five. Oh, no. I'd been distracted by my garden, whipping the rows into decent shape so I could take up-to-date shots before losing the afternoon sunlight. I looked down at my soiled jeans and realized I still had to clean up before leaving.

Even though I sped through a hot shower, steam lingered in the bathroom, making it almost impossible to pull on my clothes. I opened the door to fan the fog with a wet towel. When I wiped condensation off the mirror, my reflection stared back, complete with freshly shampooed hair. Frustrated, I groaned my discontent while twisting a ponytail band around my overly-thick mop—my tight schedule wouldn't allow for time with a blow dryer.

Mama walked down the hall and paused. "You're not goin' out like that, are you?" She scowled. "It's near to freezin' out there. You'll—"

"I know, Mama. I'll catch my death from a cold." How impolite of me, interrupting my own mother. My manners were presently on hold, positioned somewhere behind my concern for Rascal. All I could think about was getting out the door. "Sorry. Gotta go. The vet closes in thirty minutes, and I have to run by the *Trib* first." My lips brushed her cheek with a hasty kiss before I took the stairs two at a time.

She called over the railing. "You're on your own for dinner. I'll be at church tonight."

Without turning, I waved a hand to signal I'd heard. I didn't have to see her face to know she was wearing one of those lighthearted looks that had become part of her everyday appearance. She couldn't help herself. Her expression probably had less to do with being at church, and more to do with seeing Pastor Dan. I was getting used to the idea of his presence in her life, knowing she'd have someone to salve her loneliness when my quest for education lured me back to a college campus.

Outside the back door, a chilly, newborn breeze assaulted my wet head, allowing the scent of coconut shampoo to follow me as I scurried the short distance between the house and my truck. Sitting inside the cab, I wrenched a key into the ignition. The engine growled several times but refused to start. *Stubborn truck.* I pounded the steering wheel with the flat of my hand. "Please, please," I begged, furiously tromping the gas pedal one more time. *Finally.* I shifted into reverse and raced onto the road, watching the winter sun slowly vanish below the horizon.

I'd been so worried about picking up Rascal on time that all my other thoughts had seemed trivial…until now. Had I remembered to grab the packet of garden photos? Keeping my left hand on the steering wheel, I dipped my right hand into the backpack lying on the seat beside me. The tension eased somewhat when my anxious fingers found the manila envelope, but a nagging voice inside my head suggested I might have left something behind.

****

After leaving a precious layer of tire rubber on the curb, I squealed to a stop in front of the Tribune. Clutching my backpack, I emerged into a cold wind. My wet bangs blew sideways, but I gripped the stem of my eyeglasses and lowered my chin against the gust. Halfway up the stairs, I collided with a UPS deliveryman and nearly knocked him off his feet.

He politely nodded as he grabbed for his brown cap.

But I was the guilty party, and if I hadn't been in such a hurry, I would have offered a more effusive apology than just, "Sorry."

Once inside, I refused to slow my pace and gave an overzealous push to the stubby gate separating the lobby from the newsroom. It banged against the paneled railing with a resounding thud. Someone must have oiled the hinges. At least no spectators were there to view my clumsiness. Except for Mazie.

Gripping a roll of black plastic trash bags, she twisted her neck to scowl at me. "Whoa, missy. Ya break it, ya fix it." She tore one of the bags across its perforated line and shook it open with a loud snap.

Startled, I blinked and mumbled a timid reply. "I'll be more careful next time." Feet already in gear, I scurried to Mr. Barton's office, faster than an escaping mouse. With one hand braced on the door frame, I flung the photo packet onto his desk, spun, and then dashed to my corner of the newsroom.

Mazie's gaze followed. "Didn't mean to bark at ya." She rubbed her stomach. "Guess I need to eat. Insides are growlin' louder than a bear comin' outta hibernation."

I grinned as I bent down to rifle through a desk drawer. My fingers bumped something way in the back. *Yes!* The subject of my search had been misplaced ear buds. I freed the trapped cable and slipped the set into my backpack. Then, concentrating on the in-basket, I thumbed through a stack of papers. "Mazie, did Mr. Barton leave something for me?" Hearing no response, I looked up.

Her silent, incredulous expression might as well have asked, "Are you blind?" She pointed to the reception counter I'd passed seconds before. There in plain sight was a page of editorial comments clipped to my draft...exactly as Mr. Barton promised.

Mazie continued her circuit from desk to desk, collecting waste basket litter and humming a country tune until the phone rang. "Dang," she huffed. "Don't they know it's after five?" She crossed to the reception desk and gawked at the flashing light before turning to me with knit eyebrows. "Who'd be callin' on our private line?" She pressed the phone to her ear. "Good evenin'. *Willoughby Tribune*," she drawled, in a tone more sugary than sweetened tea. "Mazie Lewis speakin'."

I turned my attention to Mr. Barton's scribbled suggestions and kept both eyes focused on the page, edging my way toward the exit. With one hand on the draft and the other on the doorknob, I gestured a goodbye nod over my shoulder.

"Hang on a minute." Mazie aimed her voice at me and offered the receiver. "It's yer mama."

As I marched over to answer the call, I glanced up at the wall clock and exhaled a desperate breath. "What is it, Mama? I'm running late." I pinched the phone between chin and shoulder, chucked my backpack onto the counter, flipped open the front pocket, and shoved my draft inside.

"Dr. Atherby wanted to save you a trip. He's keepin' your dog overnight."

Mama's message hit as sharply as if she'd pushed a pin into a bubble and let out all the air. "Overnight?" I repeated the disappointing word before thrusting my lip into a pout.

"Yes, overnight. He said you can pick up Rascal tomorrow."

"Did he say why he's keeping him?"

"Somethin' about waitin' for test results."

Irritation caused me to dig a fingernail into one of the stacked boxes on the counter. "You mean I didn't have to rush around after all? I wish he'd called earlier."

"He tried your cell phone, but you didn't answer."

Her statement made me pat my pocket, which yielded no results. "Darn. I guess I left it at home."

She didn't reprimand me...she didn't have to. I had the words memorized from hearing them so many times through the years. *You'd forget your head if it wasn't attached.* No longer having a reason to hurry, both my pulse and my voice slowed to an easy rhythm. "Okay, Mama. See you when you get home from church." I dropped the receiver into its cradle and trudged across the newsroom to slump into my chair.

Mazie's eyebrows wove with concern. "Everythin' all right?"

I shrugged. "Maybe. Maybe not. My dog's at the vet's. I really looked forward to seeing Rascal, but Doc Atherby wants to keep him until tomorrow."

She scooted onto the edge of my desk. "Callie, I ain't ever had kids. I got three dogs and two cats. But if one of them animals is sick, it's like they was my kid." She leaned toward me and squeezed my shoulder. "I think I know how ya feel. But fer now...ya gotta trust the vet."

Mazie would never be a doctor, but she had given me a needed dose of advice. "You're right, of course, I just hope he'll give me good news tomorrow."

The windowed front door rattled hard.

Eyes wide, we both jumped to our feet and turned our heads toward the lobby. Through the glass, we could see an open newspaper skittering across the concrete porch and off into the pale twilight. In unison we declared, "It's only the wind."

After we shared a laugh, she went back to emptying trash baskets.

I smoothed an open palm over my still-damp hair. If

my wet head caused me to get sick, Mama would remind me that she'd warned me. "Mazie, it's nice and toasty in here. Think I'll stick around and make the corrections Mr. Barton suggested. Is that all right with you?"

"Sure, if ya don't mind stayin' alone. I'm 'bout finished, so I'll be leavin' soon."

"I'll be fine. Don't worry." I went back to the counter where I'd set my backpack and withdrew the pages Mr. Barton had proofed.

A few minutes later, Mazie slid her arms into coat sleeves and strode toward the lobby. Her voice floated from somewhere near the front door. "Gonna lock ya in, okay? Got yer keys?"

"Yes, ma'am," I said, calling out in her direction. I couldn't see her, because the late UPS delivery remained stacked on the reception counter, so I rose to meet her eyes and offered a proper goodbye. "Have a nice evening."

When she opened the door, a blast of air fluttered papers from the counter. Mazie, already outside, had just inserted her key in the lock when she noticed. With lips pressed into a tight line, she scowled and started back into the building.

I stopped her with a go-on-I'll-take-care-of-it gesture as I scurried to the lobby. Bending to rescue papers from the floor, I heard the lock click tight. I straightened, sent Mazie a final wave, and watched her walk down the steps, her hands clutching wind-whipped lapels.

Her footsteps faded until the only sound was a new storm blowing into Willoughby.

Chapter Thirty

After Mazie departed, the *Tribune*'s empty newsroom seemed lonely. Her sarcastic sense of humor didn't play well with some folks, but I got a kick out of listening to her southern drawl do damage to the English language and seeing the reaction on people's faces when someone new stepped into the office.

I could have used some levity at that moment to keep from thinking about Rascal spending the night at the veterinary clinic, but I found nothing inside the *Tribune*'s old walls that would lift my spirits.

I looked out the front window and was mesmerized by the soft glow of a streetlamp, flickering as bare tree branches swayed back and forth in front of it, interrupting my view. A cold wind whistled through every crack in the century-old structure and rattled the entry doors once again. With a momentary shiver, I combed fingers through my damp ponytail. At least I was inside somewhere warm and safe.

Then a happy thought hit—I had the whole office to myself. What was I waiting for? *Crank up the music!* I did a little happy dance while shuffling to the opposite side of the reception desk and then spun the ancient radio's dial, searching for something more my style than the country songs Mazie listened to.

Static answered, on almost every single station.

I wouldn't let that deter me. After all, I'd just found

my headset. I could plug into my phone and welcome total oblivion from the eerie, creaking sounds that belonged to this aged building. Then I remembered Mama's words about how Dr. Atherby had called, and how each time he'd been forced to leave a message on my voice mail…on the cell phone that wasn't with me. Guess the only thing I'd be plugging in would be my revisions into an outdated office computer.

Over the course of fifteen minutes, the door rattled several times. With each incident, I flinched but blamed the sound on the wind. Eventually, thank heavens, the wind died to barely a breeze.

With the quiet came a myriad of tiny noises I hadn't noticed before—the ticking wall clock, my humming computer tower, the dripping faucet by the coffee pot, and overhead, an irritating buzz from an expiring fluorescent fixture. I only had the ability to address one of those issues, so I did—I got up and flipped off the light switch. Didn't need it on anyway, the lobby lights burned brightly, and a tarnished brass gooseneck lamp offered sufficient illumination at my desk. I slipped back into my chair, grateful for a little less noise, and finished the last few lines. Clicking the Save icon almost made me giddy.

Then the lobby doors jiggled more intensely than before.

I tried convincing myself it was only more wind. But could the sound have been a knock? A person standing outside couldn't see me, nor I him, because of the UPS delivery stacked on the reception counter. However, no way would I stand up and peer over the boxes to investigate.

The sound repeated—definitely a knock.

My gaze darted to the lobby and spied the newsroom

gate, still standing open from when I had banged it back against the railing. If someone walked to the side window, he would have a direct sightline to my chair.

My pulse quickened. I slithered to the floor, crawled under the desk, and folded knees to my chest. Normally, I would have laughed at how ridiculous I must have looked, but at that moment, fear had strangled my vocal cords.

Someone knocked again, louder this time. Then silence, except for the persistent wind that had returned. A moment later, I heard a tapping sound against a lobby window.

I tensed. Why wouldn't they give up? The whole town knew the lobby lights were always left on. Did someone notice my desk lamp glowing? I shook my head at the most obvious clue I'd forgotten—my backpack sat on the reception counter in full view.

If only I could grab the office phone without being seen. Just before determination took control, I heard the front doors rattle again…and a male voice.

"Callie? You in there?"

I blinked. Recognition flitted through my brain.

"Callie, it's J.B., you okay?"

My thoughts whirled as I tried to come up with how I would explain my silence. With cheeks growing hot from humiliation, I slid my chair out of the way, pulled myself up from my hiding place, and dusted the seat of my pants before approaching the lobby. I called out, "Just a sec, gotta get keys."

I smiled and waved at his face as it radiated from the other side of the glass door. Reaching into my backpack, my fingers tangled in the headset cable. I stared at it for a moment before wadding it up into my hand along with my key ring. Holding onto the doorknob, I turned the key and then stood behind the door, bracing it against the blast, allowing just enough space so J.B. could squeeze inside and leave the cold behind.

His wide shoulders brushed the opening as he entered the lobby. Inhaling a deep breath, he scowled. "You had me worried, Callie. Saw your truck at the curb and assumed you were here. Why didn't you answer?"

I opened my fist, revealing the headset. "Sorry about that…had music blaring in my ears." I held my breath, afraid he'd ask why he hadn't seen me at my desk nor question what my headset had been plugged into. But he didn't. *Thank God.*

Huffing warm breath into cupped hands, he asked, "So…working late?"

"Uh, huh. Almost finished. My stomach's been begging me to quit for ages."

He brightened. "You haven't eaten yet? I just ended my shift and was about to grab dinner. Care to join me?"

Even if I'd had plans and needed to say no, I couldn't have. I was so relieved the knock on the door hadn't been Karl's, and I was grateful to leave the building with an escort. Besides, J.B.'s eager voice charmed me.

"Love to. Can you give me a minute to print out my article?" I walked to the computer, hit the Print symbol, and then went over to observe the networked printer.

J.B. followed, glancing everywhere but nowhere in particular. "Haven't been in here since I was a kid. Hasn't changed much." He propped an arm against a nearby wall and studied me.

I shrugged. "Nothing much ever changes in Willoughby." The printer spit out a damp page, and I fanned the air with it until the musty smell of wet ink faded. "But maybe that's a good thing. Being so removed from the bustle of the big city allows for a simpler life."

"Simpler. Right. Makes my job a lot easier. The town of Willoughby is so laidback, and with virtually no crime, everyone feels safe."

Safe? Here? If he only knew. Oh, how I wanted to tell him, but I'd promised not to. Numbly, I refilled the paper cartridge with a fresh supply. When I shut the cabinet door, I mashed my fingers. "Ow, dang it." I sucked a rapid breath through clenched teeth, all the while cradling my injury.

He grimaced. "Let me see."

Biting my lower lip, I shook fingers in the air a few times before holding them out for inspection.

Taking my hand into his, he ran his gaze over every inch of both sides before gently bending each finger. "I don't think anything's broken."

Afraid my heated face would reveal how much his touch affected me, I retrieved my hand, opening and closing it without too much pain. "Pfft. Except for a fingernail."

"Typical woman." He chuckled. "Worried about her nails."

My eyes fluttered at his words, and I straightened. "Thank you. That's the nicest thing anyone's ever said to me."

"Huh?"

"About being a woman, I mean. I've never thought of myself as being anything more than just a girl." *Whoops.* Had I confessed too much? Something too personal? Strangely, I noticed how comfortable I felt, sharing my innermost thoughts with him.

He looked down, shoved large hands into his pockets, and scuffed a shoe against the floor. "Ah shucks, ma'am, 'tweren't my intention ta say anythin' outta line."

His phony hillbilly accent made me smile. I playfully punched his arm. "Come on, J.B., let's go eat before your corny sense of humor makes me change my mind."

Chapter Thirty-One

The scent of corned beef and cabbage drifted through the restaurant, reminding me Saint Patrick's Day would be observed the following day. That particular evening felt like an even grander holiday because I wanted to celebrate—for the first time in my life, I had an old crush sitting opposite me at dinner.

We sat in a corner booth—J.B. with his baby blues dancing while he related high school memories—me, elbows bent, both hands propping up my chin to keep my mouth closed, hoping to prevent myself from drooling over the seductive vibration of his baritone voice. I breathed a mind-clearing sigh. *Snap out of it, Callie. Do not let yourself be swept up.*

"You remember old man Willis, don't you?" J.B. asked. "He's still teaching journalism at Willoughby High. Heard he just remarried for the fifth time. The ladies keep lining up." A smile twitched. "He must have some magical power over women."

"You don't know?" I conjured a vision of one of the last chivalrous men alive—always opening doors for the ladies, always quick to compliment, and always keeping a fresh carnation in a vase on his desk, which he'd bestow on the student of the day. "He was a charmer— real considerate. I assume he still is. His one shortcoming was his hearing."

J. B. snorted. "Yeah…whenever he turned to write

on the blackboard, Francine could gossip without fear of getting caught."

"Exactly." I chuckled before guilt made me clear my throat and lower my gaze. "Shame on me for laughing. I saw her the other day. I think she's mellowed."

"Could be. We all mellow. Right? At least she was always friendly…even to me in my arrogant jock phase."

"Spoken like a true gentleman." I arched a questioning eyebrow at his defense of Francine. "Or are you hinting you had a crush on her?"

"Nope. Not my type. Besides, didn't have time for girls. I played every sport known to man and had to keep up my grades. My leftover hours were spent working at Fred's Garage."

"Really?" I'd forgotten J.B. knew about auto repairs. Maybe he could give me a few pointers about disciplining my lazy truck.

He pushed his empty dinner plate aside and folded sturdy arms on the table. "I didn't want to be a mechanic for the rest of my life, but I wasn't prepared for anything else. Mom suggested that a year or two of community college might lead me in another direction. Fred tried to get me to stay at the garage. He even offered to make me a partner. Guess I'll never know, but things might have been different if I'd stayed."

I laced hands into my lap. "You've done okay. Are you sorry you chose a career in law enforcement?"

"Not at all. I'm proud—really proud. I'm just saying maybe Fred got the last word." J.B.'s lopsided grin teased. "He may not have a fancy degree, but I'll bet he has a fatter bank account than any of us."

"You're probably right. I know I've spent more than my fair share at his garage."

J.B. spread his palms in a questioning gesture. "You're making the big bucks. Why not invest in a new car?"

"Pfft. You sound like my mother." Tracing a finger back and forth over the machine-printed, faux-wood tabletop, I kept my gaze lowered. "I hate to admit it, but I have a sentimental attachment to Daddy's truck." I looked up, eyebrows knit in false annoyance. "But one more repair bill and I'll have to have a serious discussion with my sentimentality."

He chuckled. "That's what I always liked about you, Callie."

"My dedication to a truck?"

J.B.'s laugh erupted. "No, silly. Your sense of humor." He leaned in, his gaze intense. "Why didn't you ever send it my way in high school?"

I tugged pieces of hair forward to hide throbbing temples as my pulse quickened. I shrugged. "We had nothing in common. You were a jock; I was a nerd."

"We had shyness in common."

"We did?" My lips parted as I looked into his eyes and assessed this mind-boggling piece of information. How did he expect me to react? Was he casually flirting? Or was there a chance for…I don't know…something between us? I hadn't meant to get sucked into a relationship, yet there I was, unable to help myself. "I didn't think you knew the meaning of the word." I squirmed. "That didn't come out right. I don't mean you can't use a dictionary. I just mean…well…after all, you were so popular, and…" I pushed my bangs to one side. "Well, I wasn't. I assumed popularity and shyness weren't related. You know how it is, don't you? No, maybe you don't."

Frustration slapped my addled brain. *Geeze, Callie.* Here was yet another item to add to my list entitled, *Speaking Out Before Thinking.* Anyway, this was getting way too personal. My apology was served up in the form of an awkward smile before glancing around the vacant coffee shop, looking for a clock. "Have any idea what time it is?"

He pushed up the cuff of his sleeve and twisted his wrist toward me so I could see the numbers on his watch. "Eight forty-five."

I sputtered, "Oh my gosh. We've been here almost three hours."

A waitress stood by the kitchen, arms folded across her chest. She occasionally glanced our way and mumbled something to the young teenager standing nearby with his foot balanced against the wheel of an empty bus cart. He nodded to her every so often but seemed more interested in whatever was on his phone.

I cleared my throat to get J.B.'s attention. Sheltering my right hand with my left, I pointed to the pair. Leaning shoulders across the table, I cupped a hand to my mouth and whispered, "Either she's an old girlfriend of yours, or those dirty looks are her way of asking us to leave."

He rolled his eyes. "Right."

Our unpaid tab still lay on the table. I reached into my backpack and withdrew some cash.

J.B. caught my hand and held it. "No, Callie, I invited you. Dinner is on me. Next time, you can do the inviting, and it will be your turn to pay."

I blinked as I choked out the words. "Next time?"

"I hope there will be a next time."

Outside the coffee shop, the wind had subsided, but a biting chill suggested tender plants might freeze during the night. I shivered, hugging my jacket closer.

J.B. put an arm around me and squeezed my shoulder. "Cold?" He opened the door to his shiny red Mustang.

I lowered myself into the passenger side and tucked gloveless hands beneath my legs. Sherpa-like fabric covered the bucket seat, allowing me to bury frosty fingers into welcoming fur.

He climbed behind the steering wheel and reached over to adjust the heater controls. "Sorry. This car usually takes a while to warm up."

"That's okay. It feels pretty cozy in here." I hadn't been as relaxed on the way to the restaurant, but now my gaze roamed the interior as if seeing the reconditioned Ford for the first time. "I like your car. Had it long?"

He nodded. "Since high school graduation. The previous owner had two accidents before deciding to sell. Took me two years and a whole lot of spare parts to get it looking this new." He glanced my way. "Know anything about cars?"

I shook my head. "Uh, uh. Never interested me. My father taught me how to change a tire, check the oil and water, and put gas in the tank. As long as a vehicle gets me where I need to go, I'm a happy camper."

We babbled about unimportant things for the next minute or two until we pulled up behind my truck in front of the *Willoughby Tribune*. A vision of cracked vinyl seats and a cantankerous heater reminded me I'd be a lot less comfortable on my solo ride home.

J.B. eased to a stop and let the engine idle. He angled his body to face me and draped an arm across the steering wheel. "I had a really nice time this evening. Can we do this again soon?"

The cold windows had fogged from our breath, and the car interior was barely warm, but my neck felt hot. "Yes. I'd like that." Not knowing what else to say, I unfastened the seat belt and reached for the door handle.

Before I could plant a foot on the sidewalk, J.B. bounded from the driver's seat and rushed around to hold open the door. "Madam." He offered his hand and gave me a gentle tug.

I stood upright, my face inches from his. "Thank you, kind sir." I bobbed in a quick curtsy.

J.B. pulled me close and planted his lips on mine before I had a chance to say no. Not that I wanted to say no, but he caught me off-guard, and the first thing I could think about was the garlic bread I'd eaten earlier and the complimentary mint I'd left unopened on the dinner table.

His arms stayed wrapped around me. "Was that okay?"

Calling on every bit of cool I'd seen in various chick flicks, I touched a finger to his chin. "Perfect."

Although my knees felt a little wobbly, I still managed to lift myself into the truck cab. The ignition turned over on the first try. *Dang.* I was sure a willing J.B. would have given me a ride home. And maybe another kiss.

Hovering just outside my open window, he pointed to the gas gauge. "You're on empty. Want me to follow you to the gas station?"

"No need. I filled up two days ago. That faulty gas needle hasn't risen in years."

I waved goodbye out the window, watching J.B.'s fine form in my rearview mirror. Yes, I admitted to myself, I had just dismissed all concerns about getting too close to someone. I decided I could handle this—whatever *this* was—at least for now, and when it was time to trot my body off to college, I'd simply say *hasta la vista* and be on my merry way. But I'd never dumped someone I cared about. Could I really do it?

My route home took me by the church. Mama's car was parked there, crowded alongside a dozen others belonging to choir members. Glowing sanctuary lights beamed through stained glass windows, casting rainbow hues onto the ground. I slowed, lowered my window, and cocked an ear toward the building. Accompanied by a pianist, familiar voices blended together in song—a song undoubtedly being practiced for Sunday's service. Smiling, I hummed along with them as I sped up and continued down the road.

A mile later, before I turned onto our street, my truck coughed, hesitated, coughed again, sputtered, and finally went silent as it rolled to a stop.

"Doggone it," I grumbled, suddenly angry my pleasant evening had ended on such a sour note. I turned the key—the engine refused to start. I glanced at the battery indicator. Normal. No use looking at the gas gauge, but I knew to check the mileage. "What the…?" Then I remembered one of the deacons had asked to borrow my truck for delivery of garage sale items to a church in Waycross—a round trip of at least one hundred forty miles. I had cautioned him about the truck sometimes not starting, and that the gas gauge didn't work, but he advised me not to worry—he had AAA coverage.

Why hadn't I paid more attention when Mama mentioned the deacon left an envelope for me? "It's under a refrigerator magnet," she said. Now I wished I'd taken the time to open it. Probably contained cash for the gasoline he'd used. Surely, that would have reminded me to fill up. I closed my eyes, leaned back against the seat, and slapped my forehead. *Callie, you're an idiot.*

Well, at least I was close to home. If my cell phone hadn't been left in my bedroom, I could have used the flashlight app. Mama would never let me hear the end of this. Sadly, I deserved as much.

Shaking my head at my ineptitude, I shut off the headlights, dragged my backpack across the seat, and slid to the ground. My anger suggested I kick the fender, but I skipped the instant gratification. *Maybe I won't have to return with a gas can. Maybe someone will steal the dang truck.*

Streetlights only existed on Willoughby's main thoroughfares, and ours wasn't one of them. A waning moon offered little encouragement. The scent of damp earth reminded me of the previous night's rain. I widened my eyes as much as possible, hoping my sight would spot any lingering mud puddles before my feet did.

Without stumbling, I trekked past weather-worn fencing and several open pastures before approaching the home of our closest neighbors, Roy and Olivia Brown. Of course, their house was dark—they were out of town. They'd asked me to keep an eye on their chickens and had left a bare bulb burning in the coop to discourage night critters from stealing eggs. Distant beams from the chicken house traveled across a portion of the field between the Brown's place and ours, sending a smidgeon of light toward our shared property line.

Thankfully, Mama had left on a light over the kitchen sink and one in the upstairs bathroom. Relief settled in my chest as I navigated up the driveway and approached the back door. I dropped my backpack to the ground and shoved fingers into the side pocket, searching for a house key. When I stepped up onto the stoop, the sound of broken glass crunched beneath my shoes. As though I'd been bitten, I rocked back on my heels. With the help of a faint glow spilling into the laundry room from the kitchen, I noticed a few jagged shards of glass, sparkling within the top half of the door frame where the window was supposed to be.

The door wasn't locked after all, so I pushed it open and discovered even more glass lying on the laundry room floor. As I tiptoed around the largest pieces, my mind sought to put together a scenario. Mama wouldn't have left a mess like this, even if she thought she'd be late for choir practice. Would she?

A loose board groaned in the upstairs hallway.

Someone was in the house.

I froze.

Goose bumps crawled my arms.

Quickly, quietly, my feet backed me outdoors. I meant to jump from the stoop, but one shoe tangled with my backpack, sending me to the ground with a thud. My hands groped my face, searching for the fractured eyeglasses that dangled from one stem. In an instant, I bounced upright but winced when I took the first step. The pain of a twisted ankle told me I needn't bother with an escape plan—hiding nearby would have to suffice. I hobbled toward the garden shed.

A fastened padlock?

I scowled, remembering I'd been the one to lock it earlier.

Panic swept my mind.

My gaze darted from place to place, desperately

seeking a hideaway I could reach via a bum foot. The giant walnut tree in the front yard still held the tree house Daddy had built, but no way could I scale the trunk as I had at age nine. And the bare limbs of the peach orchard across the street wouldn't provide enough camouflage.

My lungs stopped producing air.

With a shaky hand, I pushed against my chest. *Breathe, Callie, breathe.* Then I spied Daddy's overturned fishing boat. *Spiders be damned.* I flinched with every step toward the far side of my garden and then hefted the hull just high enough to slide beneath. The curve of the gunwale between rear and aft provided a partial view of a lettuce row growing just across the path. Knowing the sound of my panicked breathing would expose me if anyone came near, I flattened my body against the ground until my lips tasted dirt.

Suddenly, light as bright as noon sunshine flooded the yard. Someone had flipped the switch that controlled the spotlight mounted on a tall pole. My rapid pulse reverberated in my ears when I noticed a long shadow roaming the garden.

It disappeared from view.

The shed's rusty padlock rattled.

Nothing but silence for three or four seconds.

Heavy footsteps approached my hiding place.

I held my breath, watching as the black soles of a man's scuffed boots passed by.

The sound faded as he walked toward the side yard. Then he returned. And stopped.

Abruptly, the edge of the boat was lifted and rolled back against the bushes.

I gasped and scooted away from the opening, tensing my hands into fists, ready to defend myself against the large, menacing figure towering above me.

With his back to the light, his face was hidden in shadow.

"Sis? What are you doing?"

My eyes fluttered in disbelief. "Zack?"

He grabbed my arm and pulled me to my feet.

Overwhelming relief flooded my brain, but in the next moment, total outrage made me pound fists against his chest in uncontrollable fury. "I hate you, Zackary James! You scared me to death!"

"Hey," he yelled, gathering my wrists. "Is that any way to greet a brother you haven't seen for a year?"

Still seething, I wrenched away from his control and marched toward the house, barely limping, determined not to reveal the pain in my ankle. Then I stopped just inside the back door and folded arms over my chest.

He ambled behind. When he caught up, he shoved his hands into pants pockets and let his gaze roam the broken glass at our feet.

I huffed an impatient sigh. "Well. Don't just stand there." I swept a hand toward the kitchen. "Come in." Holding open the door, I warned with a sneer, "Watch your step. *Someone* broke a window."

He mumbled, "Don't worry. I'll clean it up." After stepping into the laundry room, he turned to face me, a sheepish grin on his lips. "No hug for a homesick brother?"

My eyes burned. I flung myself into waiting arms and gave him one final punch before resting my head on his chest. I couldn't hold back the flood of tears that dissolved my anger—he was the only sibling I had…scoundrel or not.

Chapter Thirty-Two

While Zack taped cardboard over the broken window, I prepared a grilled cheese sandwich for him. Even though I burned the edges, he devoured all of it, including the crumbs, which he picked up one by one with a spit-dampened finger. Then he slurped down two bowls of homemade chicken noodle soup.

Between mouthfuls, he regaled me with his adventures from the past fourteen months, during which he'd been living in South America. Some of his experiences involved working in the oil fields, and those were the stories that excited him most.

I had my leg propped up on a neighboring chair with an ice pack on my ankle while we sat at the kitchen table, warming our hands on hot mugs of coffee. I stared at his features.

He paused. "Are you even listening?"

I blinked and sat straighter. "Sorry. I can't get over how much you look like our father." Reaching across, I ran fingertips over his stubble. "If Daddy had worn facial hair, he probably would have had the same wiry scruff you do."

Zack massaged his chin. "Think so?" He tipped his head and tugged on a lock of hair. "Notice the gray creeping in? Premature, just like his."

"Premature? You're what...almost thirty-six? I understand Daddy was totally gray by your age. You should feel lucky Mama wasn't."

He shrugged before smoothing unkempt strands behind an ear.

"You need a haircut. How 'bout I get the scissors?" I lifted the ice pack from my ankle, set both feet on the floor, and stood. "We can have you trimmed up before Mama gets home."

Headlights skimmed the kitchen window.

Zack stretched to one side, peering around me as he looked toward the driveway. "Too late." He pushed his cup to the center of the table. His moist eyes were focused on the back door.

A wave of sentiment washed over me as I set aside our sibling rivalry. "Well? What are you waiting for? Go. Go."

His bare feet slapped the linoleum floor as he rushed through the laundry room, letting the door bang back against the wall.

I longed to see Mama's reaction, but I stayed behind. This was their time alone. Her prodigal son had finally returned.

****

On his first night home, Zack and I drank coffee until four in the morning. Our mother, on the other hand, could barely keep her eyes open and gave up shortly before one o'clock. But her excitement at hearing his big news probably made falling asleep difficult—Zack had admitted he'd gotten tired of globetrotting. He even hinted about settling down. He failed to mention that it wouldn't be in Willoughby.

After she went to bed, he confessed his plan. "Please, Callie, let me be the one to tell Mama. I need to do it in stages. Let her get used to the idea I'm in love, and eventually, I'll explain my woman just happens to live in South America...and I want to live there, too."

He'd met the love of his life, Valentina, through her father, a manager in the government's oil business along the Orinoco Oil Belt, not far from Caracas. At the time, Zack had just been hired on as a rookie roughneck—raw, with no prior experience in the oil industry. Knowing Zack was alone, the boss had invited him to join his family for a holiday celebration in their home. Valentina, who had somewhat of a boyfriend at the time, ignored Zack throughout the entire weekend. But with dogged persistence, my brother, a real charmer, worked his way around her obstinate nature. Eventually, she gave in.

I fidgeted, afraid of the answer to the question I wanted to ask. "Will you give up your U.S. citizenship?"

He shook his head. "I'll apply for a temporary visa. The physical kind of work I'm doing right now, I can't do forever, and I don't expect to live in Venezuela permanently. Since both Valentina and I see the value in having our children born in America, we'll come to the States when we're ready to get pregnant."

A grateful smile sprang to my lips. I tilted my face heavenward. "Thank you, Jesus." Zack's words made me forget about my ankle until I jumped up. I winced at the pain but couldn't keep from throwing arms around his neck, nearly toppling him and his chair over backward. "My playboy brother is going to make me an aunt."

He peeled away my arms and glanced over his shoulder. "Shhh! Keep your voice down or I'll have to deal with the grandmother-to-be." He squirmed. "It'll be at least two years before she can even think about sewing baby clothes."

Disappointed, I sat down and whined, "Two years?"

"Maybe three." He squeezed my hand. "Be patient. I promise it'll happen eventually. What about kids of your own?"

My gaze avoided his as I toyed with the handle on my coffee cup. "Someday. But not yet. I want time for other things first."

"Good for you, Callista James." A broad grin wrinkled his nose while he slapped the table with an open palm. "My plan exactly. Party hardy while you're young."

His flippant attitude made me bristle. "Evidently, you've forgotten our father died not too long ago. I put my education on hold for Mama's sake. If I don't go back, I won't graduate." My chair legs scraped the floor as I rose abruptly with the intention of storming out. "At least one of us was responsible enough to be here."

He caught my arm. "Please, Callie." His voice softened as he pleaded, "Sit down."

I glared at his grip on my arm.

Fingers loosening, he let his hand fall to his lap. "I need to tell you something."

I thumped into my chair, folding stiff, obstinate arms across my chest, refusing to meet his gaze.

Without saying a word, he pulled a plastic pill bottle from his pocket and set it on the table.

I took the bait and leaned forward to read, but the words were written in Spanish. I tossed him a snarky response. "So? What's that for?"

He rolled the bottle between his fingers. "These keep me normal."

"Normal?" I narrowed my eyes, not yet ready to simmer. "What are you saying?"

"When Daddy died, your letter took two weeks to

find me in the Amazon. I'd had a headache for days, and my muscles ached, but I knew Mama needed me. Then, in the airport, I passed out. Woke up five days later. In the hospital. 'Malaria,' they said."

In his apologetic phone call, weeks after the funeral, he'd left out the part about having malaria. He didn't sound well but blamed it on hard work for a boss who threatened to fire him if he left. I'd swallowed my angry words and passed the phone to Mama. Since she knew last-minute flights were almost impossible to schedule, she forgave him. But I didn't...until now.

I stared in disbelief. "Why didn't you tell us that when you called?"

He snorted. "You think Mama needed something else to worry about?"

At that moment, I respected my brother more than I ever had. He'd always had my love, but my respect? That was something I'd been stingy with. A lifetime of guilt made me reach across the table and lay my hand on Zack's. "If only I'd known."

He shook his head. "No way. You were taking care of Mama. You had enough going on."

My shoulders sagged. "Tell me about the malaria."

He filled me in on the details of his illness...and the possibility of a relapse. That's why he was taking the pills—*not* taking them could result in death. After our discussion, I felt like I'd been to medical school. When I finally went to bed, I had trouble sleeping. The culprit might have been those three pots of coffee we'd consumed. Or maybe my concern for Zack had led to a whole new batch of worries stomping around in my head. I prayed the day would never come when I'd have to share them with our mother.

Chapter Thirty-Three

After tossing and turning for what seemed like hours, I fell into a deep sleep. My mind eventually wandered into dreams—dreams that let me believe all would be well if I had the protection of my big brother. When I awoke, I found myself wishing Zack would stay forever. The feeling grew stronger later that day when he suggested we go fetch a can of gasoline and retrieve my truck. I didn't need to ask; he volunteered.

We went to church early on Sunday morning, hoping to secure a prime spot in the pew closest to the altar. Mama's idea. She'd already asked Pastor Dan to announce Zack's homecoming. Since Zack had expressed an interest in settling down, Mama had visions of the congregation welcoming him with open arms, reminding him what a great support system existed in Willoughby. And if he needed more encouragement to move back here, it wouldn't hurt if some of the single girls introduced themselves. After that, he'd be hard-pressed to leave, and Mama could have both of her baby chicks roosting in the nest with her. Or so she thought—because my brother had yet to confess his plan to return to South America.

After Pastor Dan called upon Zack, he rose and turned to wave at the congregation. Every eye in the sanctuary had a chance to admire my clean-shaven, newly sheared brother. Surely they all agreed what a fine young man he must be, coming back to his hometown to visit his widowed mother.

Mama donned a smile so bright, she looked like she was lit from inside.

I found it easy to swallow any sibling jealousy that might have existed years before, because now I knew about Zack's battle with malaria. Losing him would have crushed me.

After the service, the ladies' auxiliary welcomed smiling faces as everyone filed into the basement's social hall. Outside, the ground level stopped a foot or so short of coming even with the basement ceiling, which left just enough space for a series of transom windows along one wall, which allowed fresh air and sunshine to flood the room. To prevent distraction from cars coming and going in the alleyway, those narrow windows were hung with lacy white curtains sewn by Mama and another church lady.

The bounty of a freshly prepared lunch greeted me when I stepped into the church's basement. Heaping platters of finger sandwiches on white bread, with crusts neatly trimmed, sat next to divided relish trays, filled to the brim with carrot and celery sticks. Scoops of mayonnaise-laden potato salad and crisp, peppered coleslaw kept company with wiggly cherry gelatin that had been molded into clear glass bowls. All of it had all been provided by the church family—not just in honor of my brother, but as part of a monthly ritual to welcome new members into the fold.

Even so, Mama turned the event into a mini-party by donating a fancy store-bought sheet cake with frosted lettering that proclaimed, "Welcome Home, Zack." Alongside the cake was a pink cardboard box of dainty decorated cookies she'd also ordered, mindful of the need to provide an alternative dessert for toddler fingers. Normally, she would have baked it all, but she wanted to spend every precious moment with my brother, savoring his words, indulging his every whim.

After sampling a little of everything on the buffet, I moved to the dessert table, ready to reward myself with a slice of cake. The oldest member of our church appeared beside me, leaning on a hand-carved cane. A bread crumb clung to her lower lip.

I flashed a smile—not because of the crumb, but because her always-twinkling green eyes hinted at a mischievous childhood. "Afternoon, Miz Cooper."

She nodded. "Afternoon to you, too, Callie. Fine day, isn't it?"

The stiff paper tablecloth crinkled against my thigh as I reached over to grab a plastic fork. "Yes, ma'am."

Miz Cooper leaned toward my ear. "Callie dear, are you losin' weight?"

I twisted my head to look at her. As it was impossible not to concentrate on the bread crumb, I straightened and averted my eyes by glancing down, smoothing the tail of my white cotton blouse against an almost-flat stomach. "Hmm, maybe I am. Thank you for noticing."

She offered a wise grin, then moseyed off.

I remained standing at the dessert table, studying the plastic fork in my hand for an achingly long moment while listening to a voice in my head that reminded me of the promise I'd made to myself. Finally, I sighed, returned the fork to the basket of unused utensils, then walked away without a single bite of cake.

Chapter Thirty-Four

In the warmth of our parlor, Rascal slept at my feet. He'd glommed onto me like a sticky note ever since coming home from Dr. Atherby's office. The vet suspected Rascal had ingested anti-freeze. Did we have a leaky vehicle? Ha! Every liquid in my truck leaked.

Guilt made me cringe. If I needed an urgent reason to buy a new vehicle, this was it. Until I could make the financial arrangements, I vowed to keep a closer eye on the driveway and instantly mop up whatever spilled.

The hall clock had barely chimed nine o'clock, but Mama had already gone upstairs.

Even though Zack was usually asleep by now, the persistent dark circles beneath his tired brown eyes hinted he still wasn't getting enough rest. He blamed his look on jet lag.

Rascal opened an eye when my brother shifted on the sofa.

Zack stifled a yawn. "I would have been off to bed an hour ago if my stomach wasn't so queasy." He rested a hand on his abdomen. "I think you and Mama are bent on torturing me. I've eaten more in the last few days than I usually do in a month." His smile twitched. "I know. My own fault."

I grinned. "The bottle of antacids in the medicine cabinet should ease your problem."

"Thanks." He folded the current *Tribune* and

scooted to the edge of the sofa. "Does Rascal need to go out?"

My dog must have recognized his name, because he lifted his head.

I smoothed his fur and cupped his chin. "Not yet." Taking the newspaper from Zack, I laid it in my lap. "Think I'll stay up for a while and read."

My brother stood. "Then I'll see you in the morning."

I nodded. "By the way, thanks for saying you like my column."

He stretched and brought his arms down to his sides. "Like it? I love it." Bending over, he tapped my forehead. "You've got a lot of gardening knowledge in there, kiddo."

I blushed. "I can't take all the credit. I have a friend who helps."

He raised an eyebrow. "A friend, huh? That good-looking guy in the sheriff's car who waved this afternoon?"

Why did Zack always have to tease? "No. A gardener friend. A kind, generous man who offers occasional advice."

Zack thrust his nose just inches from mine. "A man, huh? Maybe I better meet him and ask what his intentions are toward my baby sister."

"Zack, get out of my face." I pushed against his chest. "He's a grandpa with a grown daughter older than me." My scowl relaxed. "In fact, if you weren't already engaged, I'd introduce you to Mary." Visions of my brother having to deal with Mary's ex-husband made me rethink my words. "Or maybe not."

His eyebrows gathered. "Why not? You think I'm

not good enough?"

"No." I lowered my gaze under the pretext of smoothing wrinkles from the sofa's brown polyester slipcover. "Thing is, she's got more problems than you can handle. She's…oh never mind. I'm not supposed to say anything."

"Now you've got me curious." Zack lowered himself to the cushions. He rested an arm along the back of the sofa and drew up a knee to face me. "Callie, do I sense you want to talk about this?"

I glanced to the stairway. Mama had retreated to her bedroom minutes before, but I could hear water running in the bathroom and the sound of a toothbrush being tapped against the sink. Leaning toward him, I whispered, "Can you keep a secret?"

Two throw pillows separated us. Zack tossed them onto the floor and inched closer, holding two fingers to his forehead in a Boy Scout-style salute. "Absolutely."

I had promised not to say anything to anyone, but surely that didn't include someone who was leaving for Venezuela in a few days, someone who had absolutely no interest in spreading gossip. Did it? I knew if I didn't confide in someone soon, I'd go bonkers. A hefty gulp of air fueled my courage. Twenty minutes later, my shoulders felt like the world had been lifted. I sagged against the sofa's welcoming cushions. "That's as much as I know." I'd left nothing out, including all the evil details about the Smiths' nemesis, Karl.

My brother's intense expression hadn't faded throughout any of it. He turned his gaze to the floor, bent his head, and combed long fingers through his fresh haircut.

Silence.

I held my breath. "Well? Say something."

His eyes searched mine. "I don't know how you've kept this a secret. But I do know this, if I were Mr. Smith...I'd get a gun and hunt down that Karl fella."

"The real world doesn't work like that, Zack. At least, not legally. Got any other suggestions?"

Pursing his lips, he shook his head. "Would Mary like to work on an oil rig in South America?"

"Pfft. Nice try...but no."

We batted around ideas until the clock startled us by chiming midnight.

Rascal lumbered to his feet like an arthritic old man. He arched his back in a leisurely stretch before propping his chin on my knee and staring with soulful eyes.

I patted his head. "You're right, Rascal. Time for bed. Solutions can wait until morning."

Chapter Thirty-Five

My mother stirred butter beans and freshly chopped carrots around a meaty ham hock before pushing the iron pot to a back burner. Wooden spoon still in hand, she bent down until her eyes were level with the stovetop and watched the flame dwindle as she turned the knob toward simmer. She glanced at the stove's clock. "Callie, it's almost noon. Shouldn't we wake Zack?"

Her words rattled me into realizing my brother had slept more than eleven hours. Afraid Mama would read the concern on my face, I kept my eyes focused on the cutting board I'd just washed. After wiping it dry, I slid the wooden plank into its usual position behind the toaster. Even then, I didn't look at Mama. "He probably needs to sleep a bit longer." I reached to the windowsill, pushed the plunger on the hand lotion bottle, and let a pool of liquid fill my palm. "We stayed up pretty late."

"If *both* of you stayed up late, then how come *you're* lookin' so bright and bushy tailed?"

I casually shrugged and kept spreading excess lotion up my arms. Before I could address her question, the sound of an engine slowed in front of our house and was immediately followed by the slam of a car door.

Rascal whined and ran straight to the entry.

Mama's gaze flitted to the clock. She pushed our gingham kitchen curtains aside and craned her neck to search the street. "He's early!" Hands fluttering to her head, she plumped up several wisps of white hair. "How's that? Do I look okay?"

I squeezed her forearm. "Yes, ma'am. You look lovely."

She put one foot into the parlor, mumbled something, turned around, removed her apron and tossed it onto the counter before giving her hair another pat. "You're sure I look all right?"

My grin teased. "Do you want me to say no?" Before she could react, the oven timer sounded, and the doorbell rang. I pointed toward the front door. "You answer that, I'll see to this." I gave her a gentle push, shooing her from the kitchen. "Breathe, Mama, breathe."

I wrapped my hands around crocheted hot pads before plucking a pan of golden-brown homemade cornbread from the oven. I could hear Mama's elevated, giddy voice as she steered Pastor Dan around Rascal and into the parlor. Their footsteps stopped at the sofa. I knew my mother expected me to join them and be part of her welcoming committee. However, I delayed for a few moments so I could drink in the aroma of hot cornbread that begged for real butter.

At last, I emerged from the kitchen, and the three of us visited in the parlor. When I noticed Mama stealing glances between the hall clock and the staircase, I stood. "If y'all will excuse me, I'll go see what's keeping my brother."

Mama's shoulders visibly relaxed.

On my journey across the room, I could hear her comments behind me. "Zack's a good boy. I'm anxious for you to get to know him, Dan."

Dan, huh. Not Pastor Dan?

Outside the guest bedroom, I pressed my ear against

the door, hoping to hear Zack moving about, getting ready. "Zack?" I tapped a knuckle. "Are you awake?" Getting no response, I eased the door ajar.

A bottle of antacids lay spilled onto the nightstand, alongside Zack's empty container of malaria medicine. He had several hand-stitched quilts swaddled to his chin and was tightly curled into a fetal position. His eyes were closed, and his wide-open mouth delivered a fitful snore. An occasional spasm rocked his body.

Was he having a nightmare? Or was yesterday's gluttony still giving him problems?

I didn't have the heart to wake him, so I tiptoed downstairs to deliver a fib. "He's still jetlagged. He said to go ahead without him. Are y'all ready for lunch?"

Fancy ruffled placemats protected the table from our steaming bowls of bean stew.

Mama passed the butter dish to Pastor Dan as he helped himself to another piece of cornbread. "You're spoiling me, Grace. My Monday lunches are usually dry peanut butter sandwiches."

She grinned.

Pastor Dan looked my way. "Callie, I've been following your column in the *Tribune*." He gestured to his bowl. "Is any of this from your garden?"

I selected a plump radish from the relish tray and held it up. "No, sir, except for these."

"Not the beans?"

"No, sir. My garden didn't get started until last September. Beans have to be planted in the spring."

"Hmm. Spring's just around the corner. Will you re-plant your garden then?"

"Maybe. I really hadn't thought about it." I lied. I *had* been thinking about it. A lot. And I struggled with

215

my choices. Should I keep doing what I'd done since Daddy's death and stay home with Mama? Was she tired of me hovering? Should I consider going back to school in the fall? *Think about it later, Callie.* I popped the radish into my mouth.

"What will happen to your garden when you return to school?" Pastor Dan asked.

Return to school? A nervous gulp sent a radish bite down my windpipe. Afraid my face would turn blue, I grabbed a glass of sweet tea, hoping the liquid would clear my breathing passage. When I glanced around the table in a panic, Mama must have thought I needed her help, because she jumped up and pounded my back. The help I *really* needed was in understanding why Pastor Dan thought I had school on the brain.

Still sputtering, I swallowed and held up a hand. "I'm okay."

In silence, we settled back into eating. I made sure nothing was in my mouth before speaking. "Pastor Dan, did I say something that hinted I was returning to school?"

"No. I just thought you might be thinking about it. You've done a wonderful job, seeing your mother through the worst. Maybe it's time you returned to your own life. You should pray about it." He looked at Mama, and then at me. "Callie, I hope you know how very fond I am of your mother. I'd like Grace and me to see each other more often. I'd be blessed to have you agree with that."

Mama blushed, glanced at me, and then smiled at Pastor Dan.

I watched his arm move toward her, and hers toward him. Even though I couldn't see below the table, I sensed from their rapt expressions they had just clasped hands.

Was he asking for my blessing? I hadn't heard him say the actual word "marriage," but was that what he meant? Before my addled brain could process the thought, the doorbell rang. With raised eyebrows, I looked at Mama. "Are we expecting someone?"

She shrugged and shook her head.

"Y'all sit tight. I'll see who it is." Dropping a crumpled paper napkin onto the table, I pushed back my chair and marched to the entry.

Whining excitedly, Rascal followed, toenails clicking across the polished oak flooring as he wagged his tail. Since he hadn't barked, I assumed the caller was someone familiar.

I pulled on the doorknob. Bright sunlight and brisk air sifted into the entry. "Mr. Smith! Johnny! What a nice surprise." I held back the screen and waved them inside. "Come in."

"Thanks, but we can't stay." With one arm cradling his grandson, Mr. Smith remained standing on the front porch, feet firmly planted. A terra cotta flowerpot, containing a healthy bunch of blooming tulips, was nestled in Johnny's hands. Mr. Smith mumbled toward the boy's ear, "Go ahead. Tell her."

"Happy burfday, Cow-ee." Johnny thrust the gift at me before slithering from his grandfather's hold. He dropped to the floor and wrapped his arms around my dog's neck.

Rascal licked him in the face and repeatedly whined with pleasure.

My shoulder leaned against the open screen door while my hand cupped one of the delicate flower heads. "How lovely. They're your special hybrids, aren't they?"

He nodded. "I forced the blooms, but nothing opened until this morning. Sorry they weren't ready on your birthday."

"Well, thank you. They're perfect." I smiled. "Hmm. Forcing blooms...that would make a great newspaper article."

My attention shifted to Rascal and Johnny, enjoying each other's company on the braided rug beneath my feet. I continued to hold open the door. "Those two haven't seen each other in a while. You might as well come in for a bit."

He smiled and stepped into the entry, tiptoeing around his grandson and my dog.

I released the screen door as laughter drifted from the dining room.

Mr. Smith glanced up and gave a polite nod toward my mother. He looked at me. "I'm sorry," he whispered. "You're probably eating." With his protruding thumb making him look like a hitchhiker, he motioned to the door behind him. "Johnny and I should go."

"Please stay. We just finished. We're about to have dessert. You can join us."

My guest lagged behind as I strode across the open space separating the entry hall from the dining room's wide archway. "Birthday present from a fellow gardener." I did my best TV hostess impersonation by gesturing to the tulips before setting the clay pot on the table. "Mama, you remember Mr. Smith, don't you?"

"Of course. How are you?"

"Fine. And you?"

"Very well, thank you." She grinned. "Mr. Smith, this is Dan Blair, my—"

"Our pastor." I cut her short because I wasn't ready

to hear her say boyfriend, or fiancé, or whatever title she might use. Maybe later, but not now. Even though I assumed the announcement was coming, I still needed time for reality to sink in.

While the men shook hands, I pulled out a chair for Mr. Smith next to Pastor Dan. "Please. Sit here." I called toward the pair on the entry rug. "How 'bout some ice cream and cookies?"

My mother started to rise, but I pressed my hand to her shoulder. "No, Mama. I'll get it."

When I returned bearing a tray of filled ice cream bowls and a selection of Sunday's leftover cookies, I found my mother stuffing sofa pillows into Johnny's chair, propping him up to table height.

The men were involved in a conversation, but Pastor Dan seemed to lead the discussion. Or maybe I should say…lead the questioning. "How do you like Willoughby Mr. Smith? Do you think you'll stay?"

Mr. Smith fidgeted. "Um…we like Willoughby just fine. We think it's a great place to live."

"Here you go." I set the tray between the two, hoping to interrupt. Spoons rattled in bowls as I handed a serving to each person while they passed the cookie platter around the table.

Before I could sit, a faint sound came from upstairs—stumbling footsteps preceded the click of the bathroom door. "Y'all please excuse me. I want to check on my brother."

The echo of my shoes stopped outside the bathroom. I listened. Sure enough, Zack's upset stomach had sought revenge. I spoke to the closed door. "Zack, it's me. Can I do anything to help?"

After the sound of him coughing up the last of

whatever was left in his stomach, the doorknob turned and my brother leaned against the jamb, gazing at me with rheumy eyes while wiping the back of a shaky hand across his lips. "I'm sick, Callie. Really sick."

My wide-eyed gaze riveted on his. "Food poisoning?"

"Hope so. Better *that* than malaria." He reached for a wet washcloth, wiped his mouth, threw the cloth into the sink, wobbled, and then fell back against me.

With his arm draped over my shoulder, I struggled to steady him as we crossed the hall. When he dropped to the bed, I tucked a mountain of quilts around his trembling body. "Just rest. I'll be right back. I think you need help."

Chapter Thirty-Six

Returning to the dining room, I glanced at Mama, afraid that hopeful look in her eyes would disappear if I delivered bad news.

"Zack comin' down soon?"

I figured a truthful answer would unsettle her, so I smiled while taking a breath. "Not just yet."

Before she had a chance to quiz me further, I switched my focus to Johnny who was sharing a bite of cookie with my dog before putting it into his own mouth. "Yuck, Johnny. Rascal isn't allowed to have sweets. Let's toss that out and get you a fresh one. Okay?"

Everyone chuckled as I grimaced while wadding the slimy, half-eaten cookie into a paper napkin. When I returned from tossing it into the trash, my gaze sought Mr. Smith's. I knew Mama would question me later, but at that moment, I put on a fake smile and did what was necessary. "Mr. Smith, may I speak to you for a moment?"

He followed me into the long hallway that led to the laundry room.

Safe from the curious eyes and ears of the ice cream eaters, I spun to face him.

His brows gathered. "What is it, Callie?"

Time to be gutsy. I had kept my mouth shut for weeks, but it was time to verbalize my suspicions. I held my breath. "Are you a doctor?"

He recoiled. "What?" His eyes narrowed. "What makes you think that?"

"Intuition." I swallowed. "Well…are you a doctor or not?" Desperation rose in my throat. "My brother is sick. Maybe it's food poisoning, maybe it's malaria." The weight of those words brought tears to my eyes. "If you'd rather not answer, I understand. I just want to know if Zack needs immediate attention."

He squeezed my arm. "Lead me to him."

****

In the guest bedroom, we found Zack quivering uncontrollably.

Mr. Smith approached the bed and bent over to rest his hand on my brother's shoulder. "Zack, I'm here to help. My name is—" His gaze flashed from Zack to me. He studied my face. Then he took a deep breath and turned once again to the patient. "I'm Dr. Monahan."

I tried not to let my face show surprise, but Mr. Smith's true identity had just been revealed. For me it meant finding another piece of the puzzle; for him it might result in bringing his enemy one step closer. Obviously, Mr. Smith had divulged his real name because he trusted me not to tell anyone. And I never would, even if my life depended upon it, because by him admitting who he was, he had unselfishly demonstrated complete loyalty to my family.

Mr. Smith…or rather, Dr. Monahan, shook his head. "That suntanned skin is far too yellow. Not a good sign." He checked under the patient's eyelids and inside the mouth. "Definitely jaundiced." Using the back of his hand, he touched my brother's forehead and neck. "Callie, do you have a thermometer?"

I bit my lower lip and shook my head.

The pill bottle caught his attention. Picking up the plastic container, he inspected the label. "I recognize the drug. How long has this been empty?"

Zack mumbled barely audible words that sounded like, "Since yesterday."

Panic roiled within my stomach. "What about a refill?" I took an anxious step toward the door with feet poised to dash out to the nearest pharmacy. "Should we get more?"

"Slow down." Still gripping the pill bottle, the doctor turned to me. "This may not be the correct medication, but the CDC in Atlanta will know." He patted Zack's arm. "Don't worry, son, we'll get you taken care of."

In those few minutes of doctoring, his whole demeanor changed. Gone was the shy Mr. Smith, the person who spoke in halting sentences as he sought to avoid questioning. Instead, I saw a driven professional who focused only on one task—providing hope for my brother. He held the phone to his ear as he spoke to the Center for Disease Control and never hesitated to announce his name as Dr. William R. Monahan.

After the call, he again checked Zack's forehead. "We need to lower his temperature. Callie, get some clean washcloths and a bowl of ice water."

I raced downstairs. When I flew by the dining room, Mama leapt from her chair. As though drawn by a magnet, she followed me into the kitchen.

"Callie, is something wrong?"

Dread gripped my mind. I spun to see her innocent expression, knowing it would instantly change to one of alarm. But I had no choice. "Zack may have malaria."

Her hands fluttered to her lips as she stifled a gasp.

Her eyes radiated fear, but I didn't have time to coddle her. Instead, I demanded, "Get a bowl…a big one." Reaching into the freezer compartment, I withdrew a stack of plastic ice cube trays, piled them onto the counter, and twisted the first one, expecting Mama's immediate assistance. Two cubes tumbled into the sink before I turned to check on her.

She stood motionless, her hands still covering her mouth.

"Mama, a bowl. Now!"

Balancing a blue stoneware mixing bowl filled with ice cubes floating in a sea of cold water, I watched the contents slosh as I shuffled across the kitchen floor while barking at the woman following close behind. "Mama, stop. Stay downstairs. Call Mary. Her number's on speed dial. Have her pick up Johnny. If this isn't malaria, it could be something contagious."

Soon after, cold compresses, saturated with ice water, covered almost every inch of my brother's yellowed skin. Each time we put the final one on his toes, we'd repeat the process, starting again with his head.

As we worked, Dr. Monahan explained what he'd learned from the staff at the CDC. They recommended a more potent malaria drug—but it needed to be administered intravenously in a hospital setting. Because Willoughby's only urgent care facility had limited resources, my brother would have to be transported to Putney Memorial in Albany, almost an hour away. After the explanation, Dr. Monahan ordered an ambulance to transport my brother. We listened for a distant siren, hoping the ambulance would arrive soon and close the gap between Zack's current state and, ultimately, his survival.

I didn't want to give anyone the opportunity to question Mr. Smith about his doctoring expertise, so I lied and told them he'd been a medic in the military, and he'd had lots of experience with malaria victims. "He belongs in the ambulance with Zack."

My mother continued fretting. Pastor Dan squeezed her hand. "Sounds like a good plan, Grace. You and Callie should ride with me in my car."

I immediately called J.B. and cancelled the plans we'd set for that evening. I couldn't possibly think about having dinner with him until I knew my brother was out of danger.

J.B. didn't hesitate. "I want to help, Callie. How 'bout I lead the way with red lights and siren through town? Maybe even all the way to Albany."

His dedication melted my heart, but I didn't want to get him in trouble with his boss. "I love you for offering, but we'll be okay."

Tormented by my own human helplessness, I slumped into a chair and closed my eyes in silent prayer. Everything within my power had been done. Time to leave the remainder to God.

Chapter Thirty-Seven

On Friday morning, glorious, awesome sunshine beamed through the window in Zack's hospital room. This was his first fully responsive day since being diagnosed on Monday. Although he was on the road to recovery, a lifeless pallor made him look much older than thirty-six.

My blanket and I had taken up residence over the four previous nights and three days in a reclining chair, pushed back into a corner not five feet from Zack's bed. I was determined to stay with him until he showed distinct signs of improvement. The time spent there allowed me to call Mama with updates on his condition.

She had worried about Zack fighting through the stupor on his own caused by the malaria, because in the beginning, she wasn't allowed to be near him. The Putney doctor had detected a nasal tone in her voice, possibly due to her incessant tears, but just to be safe, he advised her to stay away, stating there was no sense in exposing Zack to a new crop of germs.

The doctor finally pronounced Mama well enough to visit. On Friday, she sat on the edge of Zach's bed, making sure he finished whatever the hospital's kitchen had prepared. "Don't want my baby boy to go hungry."

He hadn't eaten solid food yet, but that was about to change. His rolling bedside table, holding a breakfast tray, hovered over his lap.

When she reached for an orange slice, Zach trapped her hand. His tired brown eyes chastised her. "Mama, I love you for trying, but I'm totally capable of feeding myself."

Grinning, she pinched his pale cheek. "I know; just humor me. We need to get some meat back on your skinny bones." She dangled the slice near his mouth until he caved.

He dropped the spent orange rind onto his tray and wiped his mouth. His crooked smile teased. "Why is it I feel like a chicken being fattened for one of your recipes?"

Although she laughed, tears filled her eyes. "You don't know how relieved I am to hear you makin' jokes again."

A stout figure, hands on hips, stepped into the doorway. She was one of the nurses assigned to my brother's care after the emergency room drama had subsided on Monday evening. "Good morning, Mr. James. You appear to be feeling better." She strode to Zack's bedside and pushed the tray table out of the way. "Want to take a ride?"

Zack grinned. "Out the front door?"

"Not today, I'm afraid." Her tone was brusque. "Doctor Chopra has ordered a few tests."

"Dr. Chopra?" Zack's brow creased. "What about Dr. Monahan?"

She glanced at the paper in her hand. "I'm sorry, I don't see a Dr. Monahan listed on the requisition."

"But he—"

I jumped up and went to pat his arm, afraid his comments might lead to a slew of questions. "Now, now, Zack. Just be a good patient and follow orders." Words of explanation would normally have tumbled from my mouth, but not this time. Even a torture chamber couldn't make me reveal Dr. Monahan was actually someone incognito, someone I'd known as Mr. Smith for the past six months—someone who Zack had known for only a few less than lucid hours.

The nurse rested her hand on the bed's railing. "If you can sit up, we'll take you in a wheelchair to the lab. If not, a gurney will be your transport. What's your preference?"

Mama and Pastor Dan, his arm around her waist, stood by the door and watched a hospital orderly wheel Zack toward the elevator.

I lowered myself into my chair. "Mama, why don't you two go to the cafeteria and get something to eat while Zack's out for testing?"

"Won't you join us? You must be hungry."

My stomach growled, but it would have to wait. "Not right now. Think I'll just stay here while it's quiet." I reached to the floor and withdrew a laptop from my backpack. "Gotta catch up on work stuff."

The truth? To satisfy my weekly obligation at the *Willoughby Tribune,* I had already finished the latest "Gardening with Callie." On Monday night, after the doctors had settled Zach into a room, I returned home to Willoughby and packed an overnight bag for myself. Before heading back to Albany, I dropped my article off at Mazie's house. God bless her! She volunteered to type my words into the newspaper's antiquated computer network system. This simple act of kindness allowed me to spend even more precious moments with Zack, assuaging my mother's concerns, and my own, as well.

During the rest of the week, hours of idle time were

spent in a vigil at Zack's bedside. As he rested, I continued to write and wound up completing five weeks' worth of gardening columns.

So why had I turned down the invitation to eat with Mama and Pastor Dan? My ultimate goal was to have an empty room and no witnesses present when my brother returned. I needed to fill him in on a few details, starting with…who Dr. Monahan really was.

Chapter Thirty-Eight

None of us had seen Dr. Monahan for several days. After Monday's speedy ambulance ride, he spoke to one of Putney Memorial's emergency room doctors about Zack's condition, then disappeared. He didn't come back to the hospital to check on Zack, but I didn't expect him to—he obviously feared recognition.

The day I checked Zack out of the hospital, he insisted on seeing Dr. Monahan before heading home. He refused to wait any longer to thank the man who'd possibly put himself in danger in order to save the life of a patient. And Zack was aware this needed to be done in a private setting to protect his benefactor's secret.

****

I pulled to the curb on Roseberry Lane. We climbed the steps and knocked. The house seemed deserted until we noticed delicate fingers parting the window curtains.

A moment later, a lock clicked, allowing the oak door to swing inward. Mary stepped out and held open the screen door. "Hey, Callie." She offered her hand to my brother. "You must be Zack. Dad will be glad to know you're out of the hospital." She motioned to the parlor. "Please. Come in."

Johnny looked up. His foot bumped a tower of building blocks, sending colored wooden shapes clattering across the floor as he scrambled toward me. "Cow-ee!"

"Johnny!" A rush of affection pinged my heart. I knelt to greet him with open arms. His palms sandwiched my face as we exchanged a noisy, wet kiss. I could barely resist taking a bite. "Oh, Johnny, I've missed you so much." I pulled his frosty hands from my face and pressed them between my palms and rubbed them vigorously. "Your hands are cold." I rested my nose on his and scowled. Our eyes crossed. "Have you been playing with ice cubes?"

Mary stood above us. "We've had no heat for a few hours. We smelled a gas leak, so Dad shut it off at the meter. The house seems aired out now, but I didn't want to light the fireplace…just in case."

Rising, I hefted Johnny to my hip. Only then did I realize he wore a heavy jacket. I zipped it closer to his chin and noticed his mother was also wearing a jacket. "It's way too chilly in here for you guys. Why don't you come over to our house?"

"No need. Dad went to buy a repair part for the furnace. But thanks for offering."

Still in my arms, Johnny leaned away from our group and kept a serious gaze fixed on my brother.

Smiling, I turned slightly so he could fully see the stranger. "Johnny, this is Zack, my brother. Do you remember the day you brought me the birthday tulips?"

He lowered his gaze, put a fingertip in his mouth, and nodded.

"Well, Zack was upstairs, but he was too sick to come meet you. Now he's all better, so I brought him here to say hi."

Johnny buried his head on my shoulder, hiding his face from view.

Zack held up a hand. "Hey, buddy. At least give me

a high five."

Johnny slowly twisted his head, exposing one eye to study Zack's flat palm. A few seconds later, he reached out and slapped it, and then immediately turned away to giggle.

The sound of a key in the lock jerked our attention to the front door. Johnny squirmed free and ran to his grandfather, who scooped him up. "I assumed that was your truck, Callie. Did I miss your visit?"

"Just arrived."

He walked over to shake Zack's hand. "Nice to see you upright." He moved his fingers to Zack's wrist, checking the pulse. "How do you feel?"

"Tired, but a whole lot better."

Mary tapped her father's shoulder. "Dad, maybe we should invite them to sit."

Her suggestion came as I stole a look at Zack. He appeared paler than when we left Putney Memorial. He should have been home in bed, but I didn't have the heart to refuse his request to thank Dr. Monahan.

"What can we offer you?" Mary asked. "Maybe some water? Coffee? Tea? Apple juice?"

"Appo juice," Johnny squealed, wriggling down from his grandfather's arms. He tugged on his mother's pant leg. "Appo juice. Appo juice."

Mary bent over and put a quieting finger to his lips. "Why don't you come and help me?" She took his hand in hers and straightened. "What would everyone else like?"

With our preferences noted, and her son bouncing along next to her, Mary headed for the kitchen. The clink of glassware—followed by the opening and closing of the refrigerator multiple times, and of course, Johnny's excited voice—suggested it would be a while before we saw our hostess again.

The rest of us settled into overstuffed chairs. What followed was almost like a visit to a doctor's office. Mr. Smith…or rather, Dr. Monahan, gave my brother instructions about what he could and couldn't do for the next few weeks. "The important thing is rest. Lots of it. Got that?"

Up until then, I'd withheld my curiosity. While Mary was out of the room, I dared to ask. "I hope you don't mind a question." Lowering my voice, I focused on Dr. Monahan's eyes. "You seem to enjoy doctoring. You must have had a practice at one time."

He rubbed his hands on the chair's arms. "Yes, I had a practice, a good one. I still own a clinic with three other physicians. I've had no contact with anyone except the bookkeeper since I left. She's the only one who knows my whereabouts. As far as my partners are concerned, I'm off traveling. I draw a monthly stipend, a small one, of course, since I'm not sharing in the workload. But it's enough to pay the rent and utilities."

"Hmm. So, it's true…the rumor about your security deposit being paid by a Chicago medical clinic?"

"What?" He stiffened. "Where'd you hear that?"

I waved a hand. "Don't worry. The local gossip queen announced it at our Thanksgiving table, but none of our guests reacted."

"Thanksgiving?" He ran a hand through his gray hair. "Why didn't you say something before now?"

"Because you always led me to believe you were a gardener. I mean, what reason would a clinic have for paying your bills?"

Rocking forward, he leaned bent elbows on his

knees and clasped his hands. "Do you think the gossip died at that point?"

"I can't swear to it, but I'm pretty sure it did. Miz Brown's words don't hold much sway with Willoughby's residents."

The sound of soft snoring grabbed my attention. I glanced at my brother whose head had dipped to his chest. "Zack?" I reached over to touch his arm.

He raised his chin and sat up. "Huh? Did I miss something?" A lazy yawn escaped his lips. When the apple juice arrived, it seemed to perk him up a little, but before long, his eyes drooped. He mentioned a nap would be nice.

At least he'd had a chance to thank Dr. Monahan. Now, if only Zack would follow the doctor's orders.

****

At home, my brother fell into bed and slept. For three solid hours.

Later that evening, he stood in the kitchen, clutching the phone. "But I've been ill. Can't you waive the charge for rescheduling? What if I have my doctor fax you a letter?" He huffed a sigh and hung up.

Concern drew my brows together. "You're not skipping out on us, are you?"

He traced fingertips across the lines in my forehead. "You're gonna end up with premature wrinkles if you don't stop scowling."

I shoved his hand away. "You're avoiding my question."

"Don't worry, baby sister. No plans yet. I'm merely researching what steps have to be taken in the future."

Of course, I believed him. He'd barely recovered, and he'd only been out of the hospital for half a day.

Besides, he'd promised Mama he'd stick around for a while. Had he lied?

When our mother walked into the room, Zack and I both hushed. Any mention of him leaving for Venezuela usually threw her into depression, and neither of us wanted to be responsible for causing her pain. Much smarter to talk when she was out of ear shot.

The next morning, before I left for the *Tribune,* Mama headed outside with a basket of fresh laundry and a canvas bag of clothespins. She'd be at the clothesline for at least fifteen minutes. Perfect. Zack and I could speak privately without sending Mama into tears.

His bedroom door, however, remained closed. I didn't knock, figuring he must be catching up on much-needed sleep. Yet, since he was an expert at avoiding confrontation, it occurred to me he might be playing possum. That was okay; I'd hound him later.

At noon, when I returned for lunch, I parked in the driveway next to Mama's car and entered through the back door, shutting it gently, just in case Zack was still asleep.

Rascal met me in the laundry room, wagging his tail, whining his usual greeting. "Shhh," I whispered. "Good boy." I patted his head while listening for voices and other household sounds.

Silence.

At that time of day, the aroma from lunch preparations usually filled the kitchen. Right now, the only smell that lingered was the stale coffee from breakfast. I bounded up the stairs and stopped at my brother's open door. Rumpled sheets and patchwork quilts were flung back, revealing an empty bed. "Zack?" I called down the hall toward the bathroom. No answer.

Every room was empty.

Panic turned to anger as I stood in my own room with a clenched jaw while shaking my head at Zack's cunning. Obvious clues were right in front of me: ink-smudged thumbprints on top of my home printer, plus empty packaging from a new black ink cartridge. Crumpled pieces of paper had missed a toss to the wastepaper basket. I suspected they'd provide answers. After picking up a page and smoothing out the wrinkles, I identified it as a practice printing of Zack's boarding pass and his itinerary, all scheduled for later that day.

Falling backward onto my bed, I stared at the ceiling. *You are such a fool, Zack.* I wasn't sure if I admired his stubborn determination to return to his beloved Valentina—or if I should curse his reckless behavior for leaving so soon. After a perilous bout of malaria, the likelihood of another relapse couldn't be ruled out.

I found Mama sitting on the front porch steps, wrapped in a crocheted throw from the sofa. Because her eyes were rimmed in red, I knew I didn't need to tell her about Zack's departure.

She sniffed and reached gnarled, arthritic fingers into the box of tissues in her lap. "He caught me completely off guard. I was puttin' away leftovers, and when I closed the refrigerator door, there he stood, smilin'. He was holdin' his duffle bag, and he had tears in his eyes. I barely had a chance to hug him before an airport shuttle pulled up." She put a tissue to her nose. "My boy's gone again."

Mama's pain became mine. I sat beside her and rested my head on her shoulder while rubbing her arm. "Zack has always avoided goodbyes; I hoped this time would be different." Although anger simmered just below the surface, disappointment was the overriding emotion moving within me.

Why couldn't you have stayed a bit longer, Zack? For Mama's sake. For my sake, too.

His speedy escape offered one advantage: he wouldn't be around to blow Dr. Monahan's cover. I wondered how long before someone else slipped up?

Would it be me?

Chapter Thirty-Nine

On the last Thursday in February, all three harvest-gold shampoo sinks sat idle in Francine's beauty shop. Between tilted slats of dusty aluminum blinds, the late-afternoon sun offered its final rays, sending stripes of light sliding across an avocado-green, flowered linoleum floor. Everyone had left for the day except Francine.

Atop a dorm-sized refrigerator, a vintage tabletop radio played a slightly familiar country song. Francine guided my fingertips into a soaking bowl on her manicure table before pointing to the radio. "Too loud?"

"Not at all. I love that station." Truthfully? Not exactly my type of music, but I hoped the sound would hide my nervous swallowing.

She smiled and then turned to tidy up her display rack of nail polish bottles.

I really needed this manicure, but my hands felt trapped, as if set in concrete. I fidgeted. Here I was, in the same room with the person I imagined as my nemesis—the one person who might cause me to slip and reveal the gardener's secret. Long before I made my nail appointment, I convinced myself I could be invincible. Just keep my mouth buttoned tight. However, a closed mouth had never been part of my demeanor.

She rotated her swivel chair to face me and scooted forward until our knees bumped under the table. "Callie, we're about to get your nails lookin' all gorgeous.

Promise me you won't shove them into mud anytime soon."

"I promise. At least for a couple of days."

She rolled her eyes and then withdrew my hands from the sudsy solution, first one, then the other, massaging each finger with a fresh terry towel. "Special occasion comin' up?"

"Just a basketball game."

"Oh, yeah?" Her eyebrows lifted. "Willoughby High?"

"Uh huh. They made the playoffs. I'm anxious to see how good this year's team is."

With nail clippers lingering over my cuticles, she paused. "Me, too." A wide smile crested her lips. "Maybe we could go together."

I lowered my gaze but felt telltale red crawling my neck. "Um…I sort of have a date."

She dropped her clippers into a cylinder of disinfectant from such a great height, the blue liquid splashed out and dribbled down the glass sides. She snorted. "Oh, really?"

Her sarcastic tone made me wonder if she thought I'd lied to get out of having her join me at the game. Or worse yet, maybe she thought I was undatable. *Tell her, tell her*, the little voice in my head urged. "Uh…you remember J.B. Taylor, don't you?"

She eyed me for a moment and then looked down at my nails and started filing. "How could I ever forget? A few hundred of us had a crush on him in high school."

I didn't want to encourage jealousy, but she'd led me to it. "Well, J.B. asked if I wanted to go to the game."

She glanced up and accidently nicked my skin with her emery board.

"Ow." Grimacing, I jerked away my hand.

"Sorry." She held my finger tightly as she fanned it with her free hand. "Consider me flabbergasted." Her emery board again sought my nails, more tenderly this time. "I hadn't heard about you and J.B. dating."

"Do you usually hear about who's dating who?"

"Yep." She dusted my nails with a soft brush. "Small town. You'd be surprised what kind of stories cross my table."

No, I wouldn't be surprised. Same ol', same ol' that went on in high school. I assumed more gossip was devoured here and then regurgitated by Francine than by anybody else in Willoughby.

She narrowed her eyes. "How come your mama never mentioned anything about J.B.?"

"Probably because she's fixated on her own love life."

"Love life?" Francine's nails bit into my skin. "Callie, what are you sayin'?"

I hiccupped a quick breath and then slowly exhaled as I repositioned my fingers. "Mama and Pastor Dan—"

Her hand flapped a limp-wristed wave. "I know all about *that*." She leaned in. "I thought you meant she had a whole line of suitors." She lifted my hand and gave the towel beneath a quick shake, then smoothed it back into place. "What about you and J.B.? You know...*your* love life?"

My heart fluttered at the thought. However, Francine had caught me off guard, so my chin involuntarily shrank into my neck. "I don't have one. I mean...J.B. and I have only been out a few times." I saw one of her eyebrows rise before she dropped her gaze to my fingertips and began to file furiously. Would I be left with only stubs on my wrists?

"Callie, my chatty reputation from high school must still be followin' me. Trust me, I don't gossip anymore. I'm just curious about what goes on in Willoughby. However, if you don't want to say anythin', I understand."

"No, it's not that. Really. I mean…J.B. and I are just friends." I hoped my statement was incorrect, because I wanted J.B. to be more than just a friend. But I wasn't yet prepared to deal with other people's opinions. The silence separating Francine and me grew with each moment, feeling heavier and more oppressive, making it hard to breathe.

While applying my base coat, she only spoke once—in a monotone. "What color do you want?"

I hadn't thought that far ahead, but I decided to lighten the mood. "Dirt color?"

A grin twitched at the corner of her mouth, but she didn't look up. "We don't carry that. What's your second choice?"

"How 'bout spinach green or carrot orange? Something that will match the veggies in my garden."

We transitioned to laughs. In a more relaxed atmosphere, we discussed the merits of one color of polish over another and finally decided on a subtle shade of pink. As Francine finished applying the base coat, and then the first layer of pink, I watched in silence, fascinated as each expert stroke improved the appearance of my hands.

She kept her focus on my fingernails, finishing another layer before glancing up. "Callie, you're bein' awful quiet." She reached for a bottle of clear polish and topped each nail with a final glaze. "Your column is gettin' lots of interest. You must be thrilled." Her gaze locked on mine. "Is Mr. Smith still helpin' you with it?"

She had broached the one subject I'd hoped to avoid. My pulse quickened.

"I only ask because he's my neighbor. But I guess you already knew that. The Smiths keep to themselves, and I've never met them. What are they like?"

Could Francine's curiosity be satisfied without me giving away the secret? "Um…they're nice. Just simple folk."

"Aw, come on, Callie," Francine said, wrinkling her nose. She tightened the lid on the polish bottle and searched my eyes. "By now you must know them like family." She eased my fingers under the nail dryer. "Well?"

The smell of warm nail polish wafted upward, reminding me of Miz Olivia Brown and the way she'd shown off her manicure on Thanksgiving. She had gestured with bright red fingernails while describing Willoughby's new, weird residents—the Smith family. She suggested she was only echoing words that had come straight from the horse's mouth…or rather, from her manicurist's mouth. Maybe this was a chance to set Francine straight. Yet, I had to stay clear of saying anything that would prompt more gossip. I kept my gaze riveted to hers. By not letting my eyes wander, I hoped to assure her of my sincerity. "I first met Mr. Smith when I accidently fell and he—"

Her hand flapped. "I already know that. Your mama done told me. Tell me more about what they're like." She bent her elbows, laid one arm down on her table and one arm up to support her chin.

Okay, you can do this. Just control your breathing

and, whatever you say, make sure the Smiths seem like any other all-American family. "Well…some people might call them reclusive, but I find them to be extremely shy. They're not much different than the rest of us, just trying to make ends meet. Mary is divorced. She works two waitressing jobs. You might have spotted her if you eat out much. The Kopper Kettle? Lakeview Dinner House?"

My rapt listener shook her head and switched elbows for her chin rest.

My anxiety kept me rattling on and on, speeding toward what I thought would be the finish line. "Her son, Johnny, is almost two—so cute, so full of energy. I think the world of that little guy. I'd babysit him more often if Mary wasn't so overly protective."

Francine's eyes widened at my statement.

"Um…I mean…she's probably no more protective than any other mom. After all, that's a mother's job…right?" My attempt to backpedal had me wondering if my audience had tuned in to my nervousness.

"Then there's Mary's father. He mostly stays home and takes care of Johnny. He works in their backyard garden." I glanced down and wiggled my fingertips, still under the nail dryer. "Thank God for Mr. Smith's expertise. Because of him, I've got a job I really love."

If I'd been writing this out longhand, I would have put away my pen and paper, figuring I'd come to the end of the story.

Francine barely blinked. "What else? Like, where did they come from?"

My shoulders tensed, bordering on paralysis, so I disguised it by shrugging. "They've lived lots of places…all over the United States."

"So, then why move to Willoughby?"

I inhaled an uneasy breath. Would Francine detect the lie I was about to spit out? "A friend of a friend told them about Willoughby. Mary thought Johnny would benefit from growing up in a place with a small-town atmosphere. And since her dad was widowed, she asked him to come along."

"That means they're here for good?"

I forced a grin. "Probably." Ready to be done with her questions, I glanced around the beauty shop, looking for a distraction. My gaze landed on the wall clock—hands in the shape of hair-cutting shears that told me it was after five. "Oh, gee, look how late it is. I need to—"

The phone interrupted. Francine sighed. "Francine's Beauty Shop." Her voice dripped with honey. "Yes, ma'am," she drawled, reaching for her appointment book.

I mouthed the words, "Am I finished?"

Silently, she nodded and turned her attention to the caller.

Did Francine realize I was anxious to escape? I laid some cash on her manicure table, waved goodbye, and slipped out into the cool early-evening air, breathing a thankful sigh.

Once again, I had avoided revealing the gardener's secret. I'd spoken like someone with insider knowledge, and I was pretty sure I'd been convincing. The first part of my story had been truthful. The last part? Surely, God would forgive me, because as for the Smiths living permanently in Willoughby, that could change at any moment…especially if Karl showed up.

Chapter Forty

The Pep Club's circus-striped popcorn cart sat by the entry doors, allowing the buttery smell of hot popcorn to devilishly float throughout the gymnasium. My mouth watered as we walked by, but I tried ignoring the signs of hunger, because I knew J.B. and I would eat dinner afterward.

The article in the *Tribune*'s sports section announced the upcoming basketball playoffs and recommended attendees show their support by wearing school colors. All I could come up with was a pair of denim jeans and a bright yellow hoodie. J.B., still sporting the same physique he'd had in high school, unearthed his blue-and-gold letterman's jacket. Although five years had passed since he'd quarterbacked for the Willoughby High football team, that jacket still fit. The only clothing items left over from my own high school days was an assortment of cotton socks. At least I could brag they still fit.

On both sides of the gym, three aisles of glossy stairs separated the raised oak planks that made up the bleachers. I wondered how many man hours and how many layers of shellac it took to achieve such a high shine. Years before, only stockinged feet had been allowed to tread across that sacred gym floor. Even so, uptight janitors could be seen buffing out shoe scuffs on a regular basis. That evening, the sound of tennis shoes echoed their squeaks as the general public filed into the building. Either the janitors' rules no longer applied, or they were standing in the wings, grinding their teeth, ready to plug in electric buffers when the visitors went home.

"Watch your step," J.B. cautioned as he stood on the first step, offering his hand.

He stopped a third of the way up and scanned the crowd for familiar faces, looking for former classmates attending the game. He suggested we might find someone to join our committee of two and help plan a reunion picnic.

I didn't voice my opinion out loud, but being half of a committee with J.B. suited *me* just fine, and I preferred to keep it that way. An overzealous wave on the top row just below the *Go Willoughby* banner caught our attention.

J.B. leaned close to whisper, "What about sitting with Francine? Think she's got any ideas for the reunion?"

Phooey. Where was a believable excuse when you needed one? "Sure." My lips grinned my approval, but my stomach churned its objection. Not only would I have to share J.B. with Francine, but she might dredge up yesterday's unfinished conversation about the Smith family.

"Hey there, y'all," she shouted as we approached.

J.B. paused at the end of her aisle. "Hey, Francine. Mind if we join you?"

"That'd be great. Nothin' worse than sittin' alone."

Standing aside, J.B. let me pass so I could slide in next to Francine.

"Long time no see." Her gaze fell to my fingers as

she gushed, "Your nails look great. Who does them?"

"Thanks." I stretched out a hand for examination. "You might know her. She's the best manicurist in town."

J.B. nudged my side.

I glanced toward him and noticed a scowl.

He mouthed, "Isn't Francine a—?"

"We're joking," I murmured. "Francine did my nails yesterday."

He smiled as he reached to squeeze my hand. "Well, I wouldn't want anything to damage your pretty nails, but would you like some popcorn?"

Didn't take more than a second to convince me. I vowed to balance my calorie intake later. "That would be great." I twisted my neck toward Francine. "Popcorn?"

She nodded.

Turning back to J.B., I held up two fingers. "Make that two, please." Being a liberated woman, I reached for some money to send along for my share. Almost immediately, I realized J.B. would never accept my offering, so I let the handful of coins drop back into my purse. I exhaled and watched my date's fine form descend the bleachers. *What a gentleman.*

Francine tapped my shoulder. "Thought you said you and J.B. were just friends."

I blinked. Was it the sigh, or was it the staring that had betrayed me? "Uh…we are."

"Coulda fooled me." She raised an eyebrow. "Looks like you've already got him trained."

Trained? Her statement pricked a nerve, causing me to stiffen. I bit my tongue. Dogs were trainable—unless you considered Rascal—but my mother and father's relationship told me people couldn't be trained. When my mother complained, "Rawleigh, you left your shoes in the parlor again," she knew that wouldn't be the last time. Or when Daddy would grumble, "Another cookbook?" Mama's reaction was merely a pleasant smile. No way could she pass up a garage sale where she might find a collectible title by Betty Crocker.

So, why bother trying to train someone? Either they suited you, or they did not. And, if not, you could move on, or choose to lighten up and accept them for what they were. "Trained? Maybe we're just compatible."

Her lips parted as if to comment, but she went silent when applause and whoops erupted around us. Our school mascot, the Willoughby Wildcat, ran up and down the bleachers, trailing a bouquet of helium balloons, each stenciled with triumphant words—*Go, Fight, Win.* When he reached the center of the gymnasium floor, he released the balloons and watched them float all the way up to a twenty-five-foot ceiling, giving the crowd another reason to cheer.

As the audience quieted, I took advantage of the lull that followed. "Francine, I need to clarify something from yesterday. You probably think our discussion of the Smith family got interrupted, but I want to say I have nothing more to add and—"

She sighed. "You don't have to explain. We're not in high school anymore. I know my reputation for gossipin' still dogs me. My own fault, I guess." She dipped her chin as she laced fingers into her lap. "Maybe if my mother had lived, her attention would have filled my need to feel important. That's what gossipin' did for me." Her eyes pleaded with mine. "But things are different now. A few years back, my sister complained she'd lost all her friends. Everyone avoided her—said they didn't want to be part of some story I might repeat." Again, Francine's gaze fell to her lap. "My sister is the most important person in my life, and it made me sick that I'd hurt her. I knew right then I had to change."

Had I misjudged her? Guilt nibbled at my conscience and made me rub her arm in sympathy. "Too bad we all don't realize we have traits that need changing." But had she changed? For the Smiths' sake, as well as hers, I hoped so. I looked away, deciding how to pose the question I needed to ask. "I don't want to sound skeptical, but Olivia Brown mentioned something on Thanksgiving—"

She sighed and shook her head. "Callie, I already know what you're gonna say."

"You do?" I hated repeating what Miz Olivia had said, I just needed to clear up some things. But why did I feel like now *I* was the gossiper?

"Your mama had me do her nails the day before Thanksgivin'. I told her I hadn't spoken to you in a while, but I'd seen your truck over at the Smiths' house. I was concerned because everyone on our street thought the family was a little odd, always peekin' through closed blinds. Then your mama whispered you were there because of your new job at the *Tribune*, and that Mr. Smith was givin' you gardenin' advice."

I opened my mouth to speak, but Francine plunged ahead. "Like I said…your mama whispered. No one heard about your job but me. No one. I might be curious about what goes on in Willoughby, but I stopped repeatin' those stories long ago, and I've never said a word about the Smith family. Ever."

"Okay, but—"

She held up a reproving finger. "Hold on, Callie. Let
me finish. On that particular day, Olivia Brown sat a few
feet away under a dryer bonnet. She cocked an ear
toward us. Musta been hard to hear with that noisy dryer
runnin', so she turned it off and fanned herself like she
was havin' a hot flash." Francine's mouth twisted into a
smirk. "Didn't fool me. She was hopin' to get an earful
of our conversation." Francine rolled her eyes. "Finally,
she claimed a seat at my manicure table, all fired up with
comments, so I listened—didn't speak—just listened."

Francine looked me squarely in the eyes. "I hope
you believe me, because I swear, that's the honest-to-
God truth. Olivia Brown has a way of embellishin'
things. When she isn't given enough fuel to light her
stories, she makes up things. If you've got suggestions
how I could set her straight about the Smiths, I'd be
happy to try."

Talk about lost causes…I didn't think anyone had a
lick of hope to convert Miz Olivia. "Thanks. Good to
know you're on the Smiths' side."

"I am. In fact, I wave whenever I see them, and
recently, they've waved back."

A grin settled on my lips. "Really? They're usually
so shy. At least Mr. Smith is. I'll mention your name the
next time I go over."

J.B. slid onto the bench and passed us each a bag of
popcorn. "Go over where?"

I flinched. "Oh, just to a neighbor's house." We
hadn't heard J.B. approach because our jubilant pep
squad had taken over the floor to warm up the fans. The
crowd had been stirred into a frenzy. I sampled the
popcorn. "Gee, this is great. Here, try some." I pressed a
few kernels to J.B.'s lips, hoping to keep his mouth busy

so he wouldn't pursue the questioning. "Oh, look!" I pointed to the locker room doors as they swung wide.

Our team emerged wearing blue-and-gold jerseys.

Even if I'd been chained to the bleachers, I couldn't have stayed seated. I nearly dumped my popcorn on the person sitting below me when I jumped up. I cupped my hands around my mouth to chant with the crowd, "Wildcats! Wildcats! Wildcats!"

Two hours and twenty minutes later, my enthusiasm died. Unfortunately, our high school basketball team wasn't going any farther in the playoffs. The evening hadn't been a total loss—Francine had volunteered to help plan our reunion, and I'd started thinking she wasn't my enemy after all.

We passed by subdued conversations as we made our way to J.B.'s car after walking Francine to hers. Understandably, the only rowdiness we heard came from the visitor's parking lot on the opposite side of Campus Drive.

J.B. stopped short and snapped his fingers. "Shoot, I almost forgot." He turned to glance at the last few stragglers dribbling out of the gymnasium.

"What did you forget?"

"Mr. Willis wants to talk to you. I promised we'd find him after the game." He grabbed my hand. "Come on. Maybe he hasn't left yet."

J.B. must not have seen my surprised expression, because before I could ask questions, he had me turned around and running. Our hurried pace didn't slow when we saw the interior lights dim, nor when the janitor closed the double doors and reached for a wad of keys dangling from his belt loop.

"Excuse me," J.B. called as we clamored up the rise

of concrete steps.

The janitor walked toward us. "Leave somethin' behind?"

"No, sir. Just wondered if someone was still inside."

"Place is empty, 'cept for them basketball players in the locker room. Can I take 'em a message?"

"No, sir. Thanks anyway." J.B. sighed and turned to me. "Sorry, Callie."

I took his arm, and we retraced our steps to the parking lot. "Any idea what Mr. Willis wanted to talk about?"

"He's been following your column. Said he's proud of you. He wondered if what you learned in his journalism class has helped in any way."

I didn't blush but felt a little lightheaded from the flattery. "His teaching did help. Someday I hope to tell him that."

J.B. stopped and withdrew his arm from mine. He reached into his pocket, pulled out a slip of paper. "You don't have to wait. Here, he gave me his number, just in case. You should call. He's hoping you'll be a guest speaker for his class."

Like a proud bird, I threw my shoulders back. "No kidding?"

He grinned. "No kidding."

I scanned the scrawled writing and then gripped the paper tightly, as if it were a thousand-dollar bill. All this time, I'd assumed I would have to work for a big newspaper far away from home in order to feel important. And yet, here was proof—self-satisfaction could find me anywhere. Even in a small town like Willoughby.

Chapter Forty-One

March 23

Damp pajamas woke me from a nightmare that featured Karl. I tossed back the covers and replayed the images. In my dream, he'd come to Willoughby to kidnap his son. And to take revenge on Mr. Smith and Mary. I was the only thing standing in his way. There was a weapon just out of reach, but I'd lost my glasses and blurred vision wouldn't let me see it. Sitting up in bed, I shivered and then headed for the bathroom.

A refreshing hot shower washed away my fears and allowed me to smile. I remembered Johnny was officially a two-year-old today. I felt like a family member—I was the only invited guest. But before leaving for the party, I had a to-do list weighing me down.

Outside our back door, a thermometer advertising a local hardware store hung on a rusty nail. I glanced at the temperature—perfect. The vegetable seedlings on the laundry room windowsill were ready for planting, and the weather was set to cooperate. But I wasn't prepared yet. Since I would have a larger garden this time, and because I'd developed a reputation as an expert gardener, I decided a master plan was needed. With sharpened pencils, a sketch pad, and, of course, a pink rubber eraser, I hovered over the kitchen table, drawing garden plots until the clock in the parlor told me it was time to leave for a staff meeting at the *Tribune*. The meeting ran late, as usual, but I could still pick up Johnny's gift and be on time for his celebration.

****

Toy stores didn't exist in Willoughby—the local drug store was the only alternative. I waited in line, tapping my foot. *Almost there.* Directly in front of me stood an elderly couple—him squinting, reading aloud the information on the pharmacy bag, and her leaning on his arm as she patted his shirt pocket. "Sam, put on your glasses." They finally moved to another register when a second clerk motioned them over.

Although I wasn't at the front of the line yet, I was closer. If my meeting at the *Trib* hadn't run late, I wouldn't have been in such a hurry. And, if I hadn't put off picking up a gift until today, I would already be at the Smiths' house. At the moment, my arms held a glossy gift bag decorated with cartoon animals, a package of red tissue paper, a silly greeting card, and Johnny's present.

On my first trip down the toy aisle, I stopped at the miniature cars display. Mama kept Zack's collection stored in the attic, waiting for a future grandchild. Since my brother was a lot older than me, I didn't have any idea what he'd been like as a child, but I imagined him drooling at the sight of the fifty-car boxed set I'd just seen. The price was more than I'd budgeted, so instead I reached for four individual cars, vacuum-wrapped against cardboard backing. I stood in line the first time, smiling at my choice, until I realized the cars had tiny wheels that might end up in Johnny's mouth. Back to the toy section.

Coloring books and crayons? I still loved them, even

254

at my age, but Johnny would probably decorate his bedroom walls with rainbows of purple and orange. My gaze finally landed on sandbox toys being set out for our new warmer weather. I reached around the stock clerk and selected a plastic dump truck, almost the same shade of red as the vehicle I drove every day, but a whole lot shinier. I'd found a gift that would be perfect for hauling sand on a sunny day or carrying lettered building blocks inside the house when rain kept Johnny indoors.

The final customer ahead of me was a young mother with a baby perched on her hip; an older child clung to her pant leg. The clerk tickled the baby under his chin while the mom fumbled through her purse one-handed. She apologized as she emptied the contents onto the counter. Eventually, she slid a few coins toward the register. Then she grabbed her older child by the back of his shirt just before he reached into a display of candy bars.

I admired the woman's multi-tasking. The baby, now peeking over her shoulder, was cute as a button and earned my wink. However, my impatience wouldn't let me forget I had somewhere else to be.

With money in hand, I stepped up to the register at the same moment the clerk turned to answer the store's phone. Calming my anxiety while waiting, I perused the wire racks displaying various magazines. My hands stopped. There it was. The April issue of *American Portraits Magazine*, already on the stands.

I thumbed to the table of contents and exhaled a boatload of air when I didn't see my article listed. Later I would email Miss Graham, the editor, and thank her for being so forgiving of my blunder, and for pulling my story about Mr. Smith. I'd done my part to keep his family safe…at least for now.

****

With the sun offering a wonderfully warm afternoon, we gathered around a picnic table in the Smiths' backyard. Johnny crouched on bent knees in front of a small round cake decorated with mounds of frosting that posed as red, yellow, and blue balloons.

Mary pushed two tiny candles into the cake and looked into her father's eyes. "Ready?"

He drew a deep breath. "Are you sure you want to do this?"

"I think so." She bit her lip. "Let's do it before I change my mind."

Mr. Smith struck a match. His hand trembled as it hovered above two candle wicks.

Were they really going to light the candles? Wouldn't that bring back memories of the fire where two of them almost died? I gasped. "What about—?"

Mary gripped my arm. "It's okay, Callie. We have to get back to being normal…for Johnny's sake." She reached down to wrap her son's inquisitive little fingers within hers, making sure he didn't touch the flames.

After we finished singing the birthday song, Johnny clapped his hands, smiling as he scanned our faces, possibly wondering what was next.

Mary leaned toward the cake, shoving a lock of her hair behind an ear. "Like this, Johnny." Then she pinched her lips together and blew a gentle puff. "Can you do that?"

He looked at the cake, then at his mother.

She repeated the demonstration.

Then, after hesitating a bit, Johnny mimicked her.

When the two candles flickered and went out, I

exhaled in relief and enthusiastically held up a palm. "Good job. Gimme me five."

I didn't have to be a mind reader to know what was humming in Mr. Smith's and Mary's heads—their clenched jaws and moist eyes betrayed them. Thankfully, Johnny not knowing how to blow out the candles had shown he had no memory of that fateful day the year before. Although the child had been quick to forget, the adults would probably remember forever.

Watching the birthday boy unwrap his gifts was magical, his excitement contagious. The thought of Karl's ribbon-adorned gift for Johnny continued to haunt me, and for that reason, I had purposely shied away from buying a stuffed animal. Luckily, Karl's toy had been lost in the fire. New toys now littered the tabletop. Johnny opened my gift last and promptly crawled from the picnic table to try it out.

Mary followed. Sitting on the edge of the sandbox, she smoothed a path of sand and helped her son fill the truck with a cargo of twigs and rocks.

Standing for a while, quietly watching them, I breathed contentment. I hoped the Smiths were happy, too, and that maybe they'd found a smidgen of peace that afternoon. I went back to the picnic table to tidy up what was left of our dessert. As I stacked dirty paper plates and napkins, I glanced at Mr. Smith. "You seem especially quiet."

"Do I?" He set his half-eaten cake slice on top of the pile and then leaned on a bent arm to support an unsmiling face. "Sorry."

After brushing crumbs off the bench, I sat next to him. "Don't apologize. You must be experiencing some heavy memories right now."

Nodding, he mumbled, "Yes. Mary and I have been dreading this day." He turned to me. "But with you here, it's been a whole lot easier."

I inhaled and thanked God for letting me help. "Couldn't imagine being anywhere else right now." In the middle of rising, I stopped and lowered myself to the bench again. Mr. Smith's brief smile faded. "Is something else troubling you?"

He shrugged. "Probably nothing to be concerned about, but I can't get it out of my mind." He looked me square in the eyes. "Why would someone break into the clinic and not steal anything?"

"What clinic?"

"The one in Chicago...my clinic...the one where I'm a partner. Police found a broken bathroom window and a trail of blood leading into the bookkeeper's office. They couldn't find anything missing—no drugs, no money, nothing. Even the petty cash box was untouched, and it was right there in plain sight." His eyebrows gathered. "Strange, huh? Police think it was probably a homeless person looking for a warm place to spend the night. The bookkeeper thought I ought to be informed anyway."

An ominous theory nudged my brain. "Does the office have paperwork that would point to where you're hiding?"

He cocked his chin. "No. I didn't fill out a change of address, and my house in Chicago is still listed as my primary residence. All correspondence goes to a post office box, which the bookkeeper monitors."

"Ask the bookkeeper to take a second look. If Karl found even a slip of paper with your address—" I didn't need to say anything further; I could already see the fear in Mr. Smith's eyes.

He stiffened. "Callie, you shouldn't be here."

I glanced over my shoulder at Mary and Johnny. "Can't this discussion wait?"

"No. I don't want you drawn into this anymore than you already are. It might have been a stranger who broke into the clinic, but if it was Karl—"

Even though I could see his point, I couldn't imagine deserting my new friends. "Why not just notify our local police? I'm sure they'd help. I know J.B. would."

"Willoughby doesn't exactly have endless resources for assigning unlimited protection, and that's what we'd need."

"But it's their job and—"

"It's their job to protect Willoughby's citizens. Let's face it, I'm an outsider. Besides, Karl is crazy. And smart. He vowed to use every means to find us, and I know he won't let anything or anyone get in his way." Shaking his head, Mr. Smith closed his eyes and exhaled. "Every morning I wake and wonder when he'll show up. Would he choose today?" He looked toward the sandbox. "And if he does, will I be able to protect my family?"

How could I console such hopelessness? "Have faith. Maybe the authorities will catch him soon and lock him up."

He stared at me. "They tried that. Didn't work. We were naïve to think it would." He wadded his napkin and tossed it toward the other discards. "The clinic break-in reminds me we will never be safe." His shoulders sagged. "Callie, I don't want you to come over here anymore."

My lips parted to disagree, but before I could respond, Mary lifted Johnny from the sandbox and walked toward us. Through clenched teeth, I whispered to Mr. Smith, "Let's talk later."

Picking up the stack of paper plates and napkins, I dumped them into the empty, pink cake box and folded the whole thing over on itself, ready to drop it all into the trash. "Thanks for inviting me. Guess I'd better head home and check on Rascal. I would have brought him along if I'd known we'd be outside."

"Sorry," Mary interrupted. "Sitting outdoors was a last-minute decision. We smelled gas again."

I turned toward her voice and cocked my head. "But I thought—"

"You thought we repaired it? So did we. But this is a new leak. It's coming from the kitchen stove." Huffing frustration, she grumbled, "Living in this rental, we've learned to adapt to all kinds of inconveniences. Luckily, we had nice weather today."

The first bit of shade had crept into the backyard. The day might have been warm, but the evenings wouldn't be comfortable for another month or so. I scrunched my eyebrows and shivered. "You aren't planning to spend the night here, are you?"

She rubbed her arms. "Don't worry. The landlord scheduled a plumber for five o'clock."

Headed for the trashcan at the side yard, I walked by an open window and heard the doorbell chime. I pointed my thumb toward the sound. "Maybe that's him now."

Mr. Smith looked at his watch and then shot Mary a panicked expression. "It's too early."

Wide-eyed, Mary hurried to the gate and peeked through the slats. Shoulders relaxing, she turned around and exhaled. "It's okay. There's a plumber's van out front."

By the time Mr. Smith and I had gathered all the remnants from the birthday party and stepped indoors, the stovetop rested on open hinges, and a plumber's toolbox had been positioned in the middle of the kitchen floor.

Mary, with her son straddling her hip, walked me out to the curb.

I gave Johnny a noisy kiss and then hugged Mary. "Now if the plumber can't get this fixed right away, bring your jammies and come over to my house. Mama would be thrilled to fuss over all y'all."

"And if we did come over, I'll bet Rascal would be thrilled, too."

I grinned, endorsing the truth of Mary's statement. The Smiths had become family to me. And to my dog, as well.

Climbing into my truck, I blew kisses out the window and drove away. A sinking feeling in the pit of my stomach stayed with me. There was nothing I could do except hope and pray Mr. Smith would follow through by questioning the bookkeeper. Shoving anxious feelings aside, I looked in my rearview mirror and wistfully smiled, watching as Mary and Johnny disappeared into their house. At that moment, I was blissfully unaware I would never see them again.

Chapter Forty-Two

Rascal clawed at the laundry room door, barking excitedly, desperate to get out. With a dinner fork paused in midair, I twisted my head to observe him in the adjoining room, just a few feet away. "What is it, boy?"

I'd learned something from his raccoon run-in—not to let him outside until I had some idea of what his barking suggested. My kitchen chair scraped the floor as I stood and walked to the laundry room. A new glass panel had been glazed into the top half of the door by my brother, and Mama had fashioned some checked curtains to cover it. I turned on the porch light, parted the curtain, and peered out into the night.

"See anythin'?" my mother asked from her place at the table.

A shadowy car of undetermined color sped away from our mailbox.

I shook my head at Mama, not wanting to frighten her. "Nope. Nothing." I rubbed my arms, just like I normally did on chilly evenings, but truth was, the arm-rubbing was an unconscious reflex to the concern that pricked my skin. "If it's okay with you, I think I'll leave the light on for a while, just to scare away any critters in the yard."

Rascal followed me back to the table and plopped onto the floor.

"Good dog." I patted his head, thankful for his

protective nature.

****

My mind was always less troubled in the morning light. Nighttime worries never seemed as urgent after the sun rose. The previous day's concerns hadn't totally vanished, and although I wanted to check on the Smith family, I refused to wake them with an early phone call.

My laptop was open, and I sat in my usual position on the sofa, outlining a new assignment—this one for the editor of a well-known gardening magazine who had seen my tulip article on the Internet. At least a bit of good had come from all the anxiety I'd suffered.

Mama descended the stairs and had her feet pointed toward the kitchen when the doorbell chimed. She glanced at me. "Sit still. I'll get it."

Rascal woofed a short bark and strode across the room to be her defender.

"Mornin', Miz James." Our letter carrier's young voice traveled from the front porch.

"Mornin', Paul. What brings you to our door today?"

"I have your mail."

The screen door creaked open, and then came the rustle of papers being passed between hands—probably just more advertising flyers, but Mama loved to devour them all. "I appreciate it, Paul, but you could have left these in the mailbox."

"I know. It's just that…well…we have a problem that needs discussin'."

Curiosity pinged my brain. I slid my laptop onto the sofa and scurried in sock feet to stand next to my mother. "Morning, Paul."

He greeted me with a nod. "Mornin', Callie. I was

just tellin' your mama we have a problem. This was in your mailbox." He extended a book.

I reached to accept it, recognizing the dog-eared copy of Mr. Smith's gardening manual. But why had it shown up in *our* mailbox? I smoothed the cover. "So, what's the problem, Paul?"

He looked down, shuffling his feet. "Well, your mailbox is governed by the U.S. Postal Service. It's only for official mail."

"Sorry about that. A friend must have dropped it off. We don't want to break any laws. If I pay you for the postage, will that make everything legal?"

His face reddened. "That won't be necessary. Just wanted to remind y'all of the rules." With a touch to his hat brim, he dipped his chin. "Y'all have a good day now."

"You, too, Paul." My mother closed the door, glancing to the book I clutched. "That from your gardenin' friend?"

I nodded, eyebrows knit, as I silently questioned why it had been delivered here. I couldn't remember asking to borrow it, but at least now I knew whose car I'd seen the night before.

"You oughta mention we don't want our mailman to get in trouble. Tell Mr. Smith, if we're not at home, it's safe to leave whatever he has on our front porch."

"Yes, ma'am."

Once again, I perched on the sofa. I set the book aside, choosing not to dwell on why it was here…I didn't need another distraction. However, I did make a mental note to call Mr. Smith after finishing my article.

The assignment again captured my attention until my stomach growled. I chided myself for sitting so near the kitchen—so near all the snacks. Munching on a handful of carrot sticks, I returned to the parlor and flopped onto a sofa cushion. The gardening manual lay pinned beneath me. After tugging on its binding, I tossed it to the end of the sofa and watched a taped packet of yellow lined paper slip from the pages. When I unfolded it, two keys fell into my lap. Smoothing the paper's folds, I saw Mary's handwriting.

Callie, pardon the nervous scribbles. Dad spoke to the clinic's bookkeeper. She checked his personnel file. Your suspicion was correct. One thing was missing, the check stub for our Willoughby security deposit, noting our address. We're not waiting for Karl to show up. We're leaving town. Please return these keys to Matthew Gordon, the rental agent. Whatever's left from our security deposit is yours. Consider it a down payment on the new car we know you need. We'll miss you terribly. Please pray for us.

Love, Mary

The Smiths had fled Willoughby, and I didn't get to say goodbye. I grabbed my phone, hit speed dial for Mary, hoping to at least wish them a safe journey. No answer. Just a recorded message that said the phone was no longer in service. When I realized I'd never see those friends again, sadness descended. The weight of it was as if a soggy wool coat had been thrown across my shoulders, and I didn't have the strength to cast it off.

Chapter Forty-Three

Angry clouds blanketed the skies of Willoughby that afternoon, but the weatherman didn't totally commit to rain in his forecast. So where was that stupid sunshine? I desperately needed my spirits lifted. My heart ached. I missed the friends who hadn't even been gone a day.

The Smiths had asked one last favor—I wished I could have done more. The sign on the window said Willoughby Rentals. When I stepped inside, a bell over the office door jingled.

With no one in sight, I called out, "Hello? Is anyone here?"

Silence was the only greeting for several seconds.

Then, from somewhere in the back of the building, footsteps padded toward the front. A gangly, thirtyish male emerged from the hallway with a crumpled paper towel, digging its flat edge under a fingernail. Wadding the used towel into a ball, he lobbed it toward the wastepaper basket as if trying for a three pointer from center court.

"Sorry. Had my hands in the sink. Dang printer cartridge leaked all over." He displayed ink-stained fingers. "Matthew Gordon at your service. What can I do for y'all?"

Extending an open palm, I displayed the keys. "I was asked to return these."

"Ah, yes. Callie James. The message said you'd be

droppin' by." He crossed the room, talking over his shoulder. "So, the Smiths are movin', huh?" He pulled open a file cabinet drawer and withdrew a manila folder. "Wasn't because of those gas leaks, was it?"

I hated bending the truth, but what else could I do? I shrugged. "I'm not sure. Maybe." I couldn't tell him the real reason—that their lives depended upon an escape.

Unclipping the top page from the folder, he laid it on the edge of his desk and offered an ink pen.

I moved closer to scan the title, *Notice to Landlord.*

Still holding a pen, he pointed to the blank line highlighted at the bottom. "Mr. Smith approved ya signin' for him. Said he wanted the security deposit made out in your name. Hope ya don't mind waitin' 'til after we've paid the cleanin' crew."

"That's fine," I mumbled, bending to scribble my signature, cringing when I filled in the spot, *Address for Return of Security Deposit.* It wasn't fair—me being the recipient of money that wasn't mine—money that should have gone to a family who didn't dare reveal their forwarding address. I laid the pen on top of the form. "Need me for anything else?"

"Nope. That's it." He tucked the page into the folder and glanced up. "Ya don't happen to know if they left the house unlocked?"

"I have no idea. I'd call to find out, but Mary's phone isn't working. Was the door supposed to be left unlocked?"

"Well, I hoped it would be. The plumber's goin' by to make sure the repair held. I can't leave until my secretary returns from lunch. Ya mind runnin' over there to check the door?"

Goose bumps rose on my arms. I emphatically

shook my head. "I can't."

"Please. You'd be helpin' out the Smiths." He raised an eyebrow. "Ya know, legally they could be drawn into court over breakin' their lease." He dangled the keys. "I'm sure the landlord would overlook that if ya did this tiny little favor."

Little favor? Ha! His request resembled blackmail. But even though I knew the landlord's chance of finding the Smith family would be slim, I didn't want anything illegal hanging over their heads. Someday they might be able to come out of hiding.

I huffed a sigh and reached for the keys. "Oh, all right." But it wasn't all right. At least I knew better than to go there alone.

****

I drove to the police station and found J.B. sitting at a desk. Two of Willoughby's finest also happened to be in the office. "J.B., may I speak to you?" I motioned to the door. "Outside?"

We leaned against the wall while I explained my dilemma. Other than my brother, I had concealed Mr. Smith's secret from everyone. Loyalty had been my mantra, and *his* family had become *my* family. But now that fate had intervened, and the Smiths were gone, I knew I could come clean. Seconds after confessing to J.B., overwhelming relief flooded my brain—I had unloaded several months' worth of burdensome worry. Sunshine had yet to make an appearance that afternoon, and the ominous cloud hovering inside my head hadn't totally disappeared, but I now had hope that everything would be clear by the end of the day.

With a sober face, J.B. straightened and squeezed my shoulder. "I'll get my car keys."

We settled into his patrol vehicle and J.B. turned on his headlights. His driving was swift and focused, but luckily, he wasn't speeding when we rounded the corner at Roseberry Lane.

Two cars were stopped in the middle of the street. One of the drivers had rear-ended the other. The drivers stood at the curb, arguing whose fault it was. They might not have punched each other yet, but their body language suggested they were headed in that direction.

J.B. pulled up beside the escalating tempers, and as a precaution, set his emergency lights to flash. "Sorry, Callie. I need to settle this. Can you wait a few minutes?"

I nodded, gazing at the Smiths' rental house half a block away. As soon as J.B. exited the vehicle, frustration had me drumming fingernails on the door handle. I was proud of him for being a dedicated lawman, but as I watched and waited, the knot in my stomach grew. When impatience finally got the best of me, I slid from the passenger seat and approached the fray, careful to stand back. The incident that had started with assigning blame had ramped up to a swearing contest. From a few feet away, I gestured to J.B. and mouthed, "I'll be right back."

When I turned to go, he stepped toward me and caught my arm. "Callie, wait. I should go with you."

"You're needed here." My grin wavered. "If I don't come back in a couple minutes…call the police."

He rolled his eyes before returning to the bickering drivers.

In other parts of Willoughby, shafts of sunlight had started to peek through the midday clouds, but not on Roseberry Lane. It was as if a giant tarp had been thrown over that particular area, covering it with shadow. No birds sang, and a growing breeze sent blossoms skittering across lawns as if a spring storm was on its way.

The empty house sat quiet. On the front porch, a kitchen chair had been propped against the screen door to hold it open. Turning the doorknob, I found it unlocked and breathed a sigh of relief. *Good.* I could return the keys to the rental agent with a clear mind.

On my way down the steps, I bent to pick up a toddler's lonely sock. The Smiths' frenzied rush to vacate probably hadn't allowed a second look to see what they'd left behind.

What *had* they left behind?

I glanced at J.B. down the street. He was too far away to hear my voice, so I stood there patiently and waited for him to look my way. When he finally noticed me, I raised a hand and pointed to the house, signaling I was going inside to check things out.

He waved back and watched me over his shoulder as if nervous about me venturing into the house alone. Then again, he was used to my independent nature and probably knew he couldn't control my actions.

An ominous feeling crept over me as I crossed the quiet threshold and stepped into the dimly-lit house. All the blinds had been closed against prying eyes. The pungent smell of gas stung my nose. If the Smiths had spent the night there... Shivers ran up my spine; I couldn't bear to finish that thought. When nausea from the gas odor threatened to make me sick, I held my breath, swung the front door back and forth in a fanning motion, and left it ajar. Then I rushed to the back door and did the same. Leaving the house wide open seemed far better than having to explain I'd smelled danger and did nothing to prevent an explosion.

Standing outside in the Smith's backyard, I sucked fresh air into my lungs. A few feet away, newly-turned soil and a lone shovel lay quietly next to a heap of dead plants. The previous week, Mr. Smith had dug up each row of spent vegetables from his autumn planting. "Time to seed the summer garden," he said, reminding me I needed to do the same.

While scanning the dark plot, moisture rimmed my eyes. I was on my own now. Never again would I share garden ideas with my mentor, and never again would I see the three people I'd grown to love.

Sticking my nose just inside the kitchen, I sniffed to check the air. A light smell lingered, but not enough to deter me from venturing back inside. My gaze swept the room. A few cupboard doors were flung open, but very little had been removed. I shook my head, realizing fear had won out, and the Smiths had been forced to abandon most of their possessions. I sighed, feeling a little guilty while walking through the house, searching for some small item to take as a remembrance.

An overhead bulb glowed from the hallway, lighting my way toward the bedrooms. Upended drawers, and a pile of empty hangers on the closet floor were the sad reminders of a hurried escape. As I considered each item atop the dresser in Mary's room, the front door shut. "J.B., is that you?" When he didn't answer, I ignored the sound, thinking a breeze had swung the door closed, and I continued searching both bedrooms. Not finding anything that looked like a precious keepsake, I returned to the parlor.

A collection of odds and ends rested on the mantel. I crossed the room and picked up a wallet-sized framed photo showing Mary with Johnny on her lap. Smiling, I clutched it to my chest.

The back door clicked shut.

I spun, scraping my foot against the brick hearth, and grazing my hip while falling to the carpeted floor.

Catlike, a stranger rushed across the room and jerked me to my feet.

Karl?

My heart pounded as I stared into his bloodshot eyes. He wasn't much taller than me, but he had a powerful build, and there was no way I could defend myself. A scream rose halfway to my mouth, but he grabbed me by the neck. J.B. was at the end of the block, and I doubted he could hear me from there, so I twisted away, knowing I was on my own. "Let go of me. You're hurting my—"

"Shut up!" He renewed the grip on my throat. "Where are the people who live here?"

I shook my head and my voice squeaked for lack of air. "I can't breathe."

He loosened his hold and ran a hand down my arm to yank me close. So close, I could hear his sinus congestion and detect the stench of stale cigarette smoke permeating his clothes.

"Where are they?"

I rubbed my aching neck. "I…I don't know."

"You're lying!"

"I'm not lying." The expanded pupils of his dark eyes challenged my answer. I jerked my arm away, feeling his nails etch my skin. "This house is supposed to be empty. The rental agency sent me here to inspect it."

He shoved his pockmarked face toward mine. "You

must think I'm an idiot! The agency would know the tenants' whereabouts."

"I'm not the agent, just the inspector." The lie caused my voice to waver like a young boy's at puberty. I knew exactly what Karl wanted, but he wouldn't hear it from me. I planned to play dumb to throw him off track. "But if you're looking to rent this place, you'll have to wait for our cleaning crew to clear out everything." A growing headache gnawed at my temples. "Now, if you'll excuse me, I have to go." I tried pushing by him, but he caught my arm.

"You're not leaving," he said in a hoarse voice.

His open mouth must have compensated for his plugged-up nose to help him breathe. The scent of menthol cough drops seeped between gaps in his yellowed teeth. Maybe he couldn't smell the hazardous fumes, but I could, and I wasn't sure how long before we both felt the effects.

"Why don't we go outside and discuss this?"

He sniffed, wiping a shirt sleeve under a wet nostril. "You're going nowhere until you tell me how to find those tenants."

My knees shook, promising to buckle, but I stood firm while beads of perspiration collected along my hairline. "Sorry, I can't help you."

He tightened the grip on my arm, and a wicked smile crossed his lips.

"Not even if I'm a family member?"

Could he hear my heart pounding? His fingernails dug deeper into my tender flesh, but I refused to wince, not wanting to acknowledge his power over me. Rather than allow my eyes to squeeze shut against the pain, I stared at my reddened skin, praying Karl would loosen his hand so I could run. "How many times do I have to say it? I know nothing! You should ask the agent."

He released my arm, but his gaze traveled down the length of it to my hand, still clutching the mantle photo. He seized my wrist. "For not knowing someone, you sure seem partial to their picture."

As the room's toxic fumes increased, my vision blurred, along with my ability to concentrate. How much longer would our brains function before we passed out? I had to outlast Karl. I blinked in rapid succession, fighting the urge to give in. His hold on my wrist wasn't nearly as strong as in the beginning. I pulled free of his grasp and glanced at the photo. "Oh. This?" A nervous smile twitched on my lips while another lie tumbled from my mouth. "I don't want the photo, just the frame. For my collection."

His shoes pressed against mine, pinning my heels against the solid hearth. I couldn't step backward, but I *could* suck in my chin, so I wedged the photo between us at the height of my throat. "Since the tenants left this behind, I thought they wouldn't mind me keeping it."

His eyes narrowed.

I knew not to react to his anger, or he'd turn more violent. "But if you're a relative, you should probably have it." I tipped it toward him and raised my eyebrows, hoping the sacrificial offering would cool his temper.

Pulling the frame from my hand, he flung it across the room at the bookcase, shattering the glass and sending a spray of tiny pieces skittering along the shelves. The sharp sound rang in my ears. I swayed and only stayed upright by grabbing onto the mantle, wondering if the effect of seeping gas was making him lightheaded, too.

He stumbled backward a half step and withdrew a fresh cigarette. Crumpling the empty pack, he tossed it into the fireplace with enough force to make it bounce out onto the floor.

I blinked, my vision getting worse with every breath.

He patted his breast pocket, then growled, "Do you have a match?"

The answer caught in my throat. My head twitched a frantic "no." Couldn't he smell the deadly air surrounding us?

Shoving down on my shoulder, he forced me to sit on the raised brick hearth. "Stay here. Keep quiet. I need a light." He turned toward the kitchen.

A warning formed on my tongue. Rising, I swayed and reached for his arm. "No! Don't!"

He spun. "Shut up!" He scowled as his angry backhand connected with my face. "I can't think straight with you yapping!"

His slurred words vibrated in my ears as he pushed me down onto the hearth again. Careening on wobbly footsteps, he staggered into the kitchen.

Eyes wide from the horror of his hostility, I cradled a throbbing cheek and imagined his assaults on Mary. Empathy for her pain, and a vision of Johnny's disfigured back, allowed anger to color my thoughts. I believed in the sanctity of life, but ambivalence about Karl's future had landed in my brain. Since he hadn't been willing to listen, his undoing would be his own fault. I prayed that God would forgive my callousness, but sacrificing myself made absolutely no sense. As soon as Karl rounded the corner into the kitchen, I lurched toward the front door.

My feet carried me only to the porch steps before a house-shattering explosion catapulted me outward. I'm not sure how much time passed, but I woke to find J.B.'s hand on my cheek.

"Don't move," he soothed, his eyes wet with tears as he pushed hair from my forehead. "The ambulance is on its way."

Hours later, after receiving oxygen, and undergoing x-rays and a CT scan, I was given a sedative and treated to an overnight stay at the hospital. The following day, my body ached everywhere, and scrapes and bruises covered my skin, but I was allowed to go home with nothing more serious than two broken toes, a loose tooth, and a persistent ringing in both ears.

****

Mama answered the door. "Come in, J.B., she's on the sofa."

My heart melted when I saw the man I loved looking like a lost puppy. Bending stiff elbows, I scooted up on a stack of down-filled pillows.

With a handful of drooping field flowers, J.B. strode across the room. "Can you ever forgive me?"

"For the wilted bouquet? Or are you admitting to blowing up the house?"

Although his eyelashes glinted with moisture, a grin crept to his lips. "Nice to know you still have a sense of humor."

He described the blast, how it had shaken the entire neighborhood and sent me flying, and how I'd barely missed hitting the concrete walkway by inches.

I've thanked God so many times for His mercy. Whenever someone brings up the incident, I find myself quoting an old familiar phrase: *God must have been watching over me.* The second part of that phrase is often, *He must not be finished with me yet.* And, yes, I even wrote those words in my journal…because, for sure, my renewed chance at life was just beginning.

Epilogue

One year later

My foot had barely put pressure on the brake pedal of my new *used* car. I'd only owned the vehicle for a week, but the stopping power, which was so much more responsive than Daddy's old truck, still amazed me. My taffeta bridesmaid dress rustled as I stepped onto the pavement in three-inch, pink satin high heels. I shoved the car door closed before realizing the almost noiseless engine was still running. Chuckling, while reaching through an open window, I removed the ignition key.

I stared at the house I hadn't lived in since last September. The property was barely recognizable. Fresh blue paint transformed the peeled siding from old to new, and the white trim was bright and clean. I'd always meant to give our front porch a touch-up, but someone else had tackled the job—probably parishioners from Mama's church. I hesitated to call it *my* church anymore, because I now lived in Statesboro near my school, Georgia Southern University, and I attended a local parish near campus.

In the middle of the yard, a real estate sign tilted at an odd angle. I walked over and gave it a firm push into the recently-mown lawn. Scanning the area, I saw Mama's faithful roses, now neatly trimmed and climbing along a sturdy trellis. Regret pricked my soul, knowing the roses would soon belong to someone else.

There I was, on the edge of saying goodbye to the house where doting parents had brought me after my birth. I sighed, hoping the memory of this beloved old place wouldn't fade as fate sent me along a new path.

Stepping onto the driveway, I noticed my heels no longer caught in widened cracks of broken concrete. The newly-poured, smooth surface extended into an often-wished-for carport, standing strong, its raw lumber ready for a coat of paint.

I paused outside the laundry room to study Zack's handiwork on the door's window. Rapping the glass with a firm knuckle told me the installation was just as solid as the day he repaired it a year ago. No need for improvement, much like my adored brother. His phone call, when he arrived in Venezuela twelve months ago, let us breathe easier. *Thank God.* Zack said he felt much better and was sure he was on the mend. He promised to visit at Christmas this year and said he'd bring Valentina.

My gaze landed on the doorknob. The old, rusted lockset had been replaced with a bright silver one. I caressed it with my fingers and found it unlocked. When I stepped inside, even knowing the answer, I called out, "Anybody home?" My voice echoed in reply, reminding me life had moved on.

Just inside the kitchen, almost hidden under a layer of fresh yellow paint, a series of tiny indentations notched the doorframe, indicating the heights of both me and my brother during our childhood years. Savoring the memory, I kicked off my high heels, pressed bare feet to the floor and my back against the doorframe, wishing Mama was there with a pencil to mark my growth. Funny how the mere thought of it brought a lump to my throat.

Naïve innocence had been left behind, and my evolution over the past year had been extraordinary, not in the physical sense, but in spiritual and emotional ways. Swallowing, I picked up my shoes and headed to the next room.

My lungs inhaled the scent of pine-scented cleaner rising from every surface. Newly washed and pressed curtains hung at each window, and the oak flooring glowed under a fresh coat of wax. Leaving our house in spotless condition was the undeniable sign of my mother's final commitment to the home she had cherished for so many years.

All the furniture was gone, except for the one piece that remained for me—the hall console. If J.B. hadn't been on patrol that day, he would have helped load this into my car. But it could wait. No one would complain if it had to sit in the empty house for one more day. And yet…would another twenty-four hours of procrastination make closing the door on the past any easier?

I traced fingers along the doggy scratches left by Rascal, and melancholy clouded my eyes. Opening the top drawer, I spotted his worn leather leash—the one we used for so many years before buying a modern one, complete with a reel of nylon cord. Mama chose to keep the newer version, so I tucked the old one back into the drawer and smiled, happy that a hint of Rascal would always be with me.

At that moment, he was at the groomers getting all gussied up. He would spend the weekend at the doggie board and care, then Mama and Pastor Dan would pick him up when they returned home after a brief honeymoon. Since dogs weren't allowed in my apartment complex, Rascal's new home would be with the newlyweds, but I was welcome to visit anytime. After all, Statesboro wasn't that far away, and the parsonage had a spare bedroom for me.

Eventually, when Pastor Dan retires, he and Mama will move to his modest lakefront cabin. But there is only one bedroom, so I'll have to sleep on the sofa or find another place to stay. My heart skipped a beat as a sweet thought came to mind—J.B.'s mother promised to re-do her sewing room and turn it into proper guest quarters. Just for me.

After finishing my tour of the empty house, I slid bare feet back into the shoes I carried and walked outside. Not knowing what would greet me, I steeled myself against disappointment by taking a deep breath before wandering to where my garden once grew.

A few overgrown veggies had survived neglect. I hoped they would re-seed themselves for the new owners. Maybe someone else would have a chance to enjoy working the soil as much as I had. At least pleasant memories would sustain me, and maybe I'd have a chance to share my knowledge with a child or two someday. Until then, I would be content growing radishes and strawberries in terra cotta pots on my apartment's sunny balcony.

Beckoning from the road was our rural mailbox, now painted a crisp white and looking brand new. A stack of junk mail rested inside, and a lone letter, bearing a Chicago postmark, sat atop everything. Anticipation had me giggling when I recognized the handwriting.

Flipping over the envelope, I spied a tiny heart sticker, pasted upside down, and smudges of swirly crayons decorating the entire surface. I slid a finger under the sealed flap, then leaned against my car to devour Mary's words.

Dearest Callie,

First off, forgive me for not writing sooner. Johnny helped "file" some papers and your address got lost in the process. Yes, I know, email would be easier, but I've been stuck in the Stone Age. However, my new boss requires email, and he's setting up my account next week. I'll forward my contact info soon.

I finished accounting classes and found a great job, keeping the books for a local fast-food franchise. Not yet sure if I want to go further and get my CPA certification.

My parents' reconciliation has required a lot of time and forgiveness. Mom still feels guilty about deserting us, but her fragile nerves just couldn't handle the constant state of fear. Now, with regular therapy, she's getting stronger. She's honestly putting all her energy into making a peaceful home like she and Dad used to have. Oh, and she'd be the first to say thank you for your touching magazine article and for assigning our family an alias.

Dad is back at the doctoring business and couldn't be happier. He's established a volunteer organization to assist battered women in our area. He even plans to get them involved in planting a community garden.

Johnny attends preschool three days a week. He had trouble sharing at first because he'd never had other children around to set an example. That's the cloistered way we had to live during that scary time, but without Karl stalking us, we've graduated to a more normal life.

Who knows? Maybe someday Johnny will have a brother or sister. Yes, I've met someone! The sweetest man you can imagine. He's a teacher and so good with children. We're talking marriage, possibly by the end of the year. If I mail you a wedding invitation, will you come to Chicago? If you can't, I promise to send photos.

I hope life is being good to you. Write when you have time. Please know you'll always have a special place in our hearts.

Love, Mary

Sighing, I held the letter to my chest, letting my heart absorb Mary's love.

"Hey there, Callie."

A familiar voice called out and broke my reverie. I squinted into late afternoon sun, shading my eyes with an open hand to see our neighbor dragging a garden hose through the field. "Hey, Mr. Brown. How are you?" I crossed our driveway and, not wanting to dirty my satin shoes, stopped at a swath of red Georgia soil to stand near the property line. "Missed seeing y'all at the wedding."

"Sorry 'bout that. Hated not being there, but the missus was feelin' kinda puny. Thought it best to stay clear of folks in case she's contagious."

Turning his back for a split second, he gave an over-zealous yank to his garden hose, allowing it to flip over and release a kink that had restricted the water flow. He dropped the hose into a dirt basin surrounding the first sapling in a row of recently planted fruit trees. A thought crossed my mind—were these new plantings his heroic effort to provide privacy for the new buyer?

"I understand the church is hostin' a potluck for the newlyweds next weekend."

"Yes, sir. And everyone's invited. Y'all plan on being there?"

"You bet." The gap in between his front teeth showed as he smiled. "A team of tractors couldn't keep us away." He moved the hose to the next tree, then wiped wet hands on the bib of his overalls. "The missus tells me you put Willoughby on the map with that magazine story about the Roseberry Lane family. She says everyone's talkin' 'bout it." Neck bent, he focused on the water filling the basin. "She wonders why you didn't use their real names." His chin rose, revealing a smug grin. "I told her it weren't none of her business."

Well, well, well…someone gutsy enough to stand up to Miz Brown. Good thing he had turned his back to adjust the hose, because I couldn't hide my silly grin.

He straightened; his lips formed a tight line. "Rumors say you'll probably move to New York after graduation. We'll be real sad when that happens. Gonna miss your column in the *Tribune*."

"Well, sir, things have changed. Moving to New York isn't on my list anymore. I'm actually anxious to move back to Willoughby. My boyfriend wants that, too. For now, I will email my columns to the *Trib*."

His laugh lines crinkled. "Well, I'll be darned. You reckon it's okay if I share that with the missus?"

"Absolutely." Giving my approval meant everyone in Willoughby would hear the news immediately. In fact, Miz Brown's words would spread faster than mine ever could, even if I nailed flyers to every single fence post in town.

A distant screen door banged shut, and I spotted his wife heading toward us, waving, probably hoping to acquire some new gossip. My feet wanted to flee, but I was raised to be polite, so I stood firm and waited as she crossed the field.

"Afternoon, Callie," she called out, just prior to sneezing. She dabbed her nose with a wadded tissue before tucking it inside the sleeve of her sweater. She stopped a few steps away and shook her head. "Can't decide whether to call this dang thing an allergy or a cold." Clearing her throat, she beamed at me. "My, my, can't remember ever seein' you in a dress. You're pretty as a picture."

"Thank you, ma'am." I looked down and smoothed the bodice of my bridesmaid dress. "Not sure pink is my color, but Mama charmed me into it."

She cocked her head. "How come you aren't wearin' your glasses, young lady? I thought you couldn't see without 'em."

I touched a finger to a vacant temple where eyeglass stems used to rest. "Got tired of replacing broken frames. I've switched to contacts." Her questions always made me nervous. Was she digging for gossip? I fidgeted, contemplating an escape. "Y'all have any idea of the time?"

Mr. Brown looked up at the sun and then to the shadows tracing the ground. "My guess is about four o'clock."

"Four? Oh heavens!" Both hands flew to my cheeks, probably a little too dramatically. "Didn't realize it was that late. I have to be going." I turned toward the street but called over my shoulder and waved. "See y'all at the potluck next weekend."

I scampered to my car, which, by the way, started on the first try. J.B. had worked on my previous vehicle— Daddy's old truck—repairing it as needed. But I hated asking him to keep it alive, when all it really needed was an oversized coffin for its burial. I grinned, remembering my relief when Willoughby High welcomed the vehicle into their auto shop program. Not only do the students have fun poking around under the hood, they hope to someday have it all spruced up to ferry the Homecoming queen and princesses in the annual parade.

One more thing remained on my to-do list while I was in town: satisfying pent-up curiosity about a house and garden where I used to visit. That day marked exactly one year since the explosion. Ready to see the changes, although slightly apprehensive, I swallowed my hesitation and wove my car through the streets of Willoughby.

Approaching Roseberry Lane, I slowed to a crawl, remembering the catastrophe that almost claimed my life. After the incident, I purposely skirted that area for weeks, driving far out of my way, just to avoid reliving the horror. At the time, I had no wish to return, but I did anxiously wait for rumors to educate me about the cleanup and restoration.

I'd heard the rental was still empty when I left Willoughby to begin the fall semester in Statesboro. Fast forward to the present day, and viewing from my slow-moving car, the rental looked wonderfully solid, at least the part I could see. Where the old kitchen had existed, a new one melded perfectly with the structure. Future renters would never know the evil that had visited the year before.

Long gone was Mr. Smith's garden. The blown-apart fence had yet to be replaced, but youthful laughter rose from behind the house where healthy vegetables had previously grown. A partial view of a swing set made my heart sing. The home obviously contained a family with children.

A spot of color stood among a clump of green in the front yard, making me tap the brakes and almost bump my head on the steering wheel. Mr. Smith's hybrids had survived the destruction, and one lonely tulip decided to bloom late. The last petal should have dropped long ago. Had it waited for my return? A vision of the notorious tulip photo lingered on the fringe of my memory.

I pulled to the curb and let the engine idle. The house's front door was ajar, but a new metal screen existed between the warm spring air and the tenants' voices inside.

Should I? Or shouldn't I?

I looked down and gathered taffeta into my fist. "What the heck, I'll never wear this gown again anyway." Before my sensible brain could argue, I leapt from the driver's seat, ran across the road, shoved my hands into loamy soil, and extracted as many tulip bulbs as I could carry in the folds of my bridesmaid dress. I scurried back to the car, tossed my loot onto the floorboards, and sped away with uncharacteristic bravado.

A block away, I pulled over to hold my sides and laughed until tears rolled down my cheeks. *Who is this person?* A tissue wiped my eyes but removed the makeup I so carefully applied that morning. I was glad to have it gone. J.B. would be glad, too. He always makes me feel pretty, saying he loves my natural beauty. However, even before he had uttered those words, I'd already made peace with myself about my looks. I have a lot more going for me than just superficial concerns, but I do plan to keep my weight within reasonable limits, for the sake of my health. As for looking like a skinny supermodel, that is definitely out of the question. I will simply respect the body God has given me.

In horror, I glanced at my fingernails and cringed

when I saw chipped polish and dark soil lodged beneath the cuticles. Francine would surely scold me for messing up her "artwork." Because she's my friend, she would also be sympathetic to my brazen deed. But as my manicurist? She would threaten death.

Since my suitcase and I were spending the weekend in her guest bedroom, I needed to creep back to Roseberry Lane where she lived, only three doors down from the flower bed I had just ravaged.

Suddenly ashamed of my selfish, impulsive behavior, I shook my head and prayed none of her neighbors saw me steal Mr. Smith's tulip bulbs. Then it hit me—the stolen bulbs signified an everlasting bond with the Smith family. At that moment, I was actually okay with that. Tomorrow, I might not be. But I would wait until then to go back and apologize…and repair the damaged flowerbed.

Looking down at my soiled clothing, I realized the time had come to change for my date. J. B. and I were meeting for dinner. Yes, he would understand my hasty action—he wouldn't like it, but he would understand. He has always supported my efforts and makes me want to be the best person I can be. It's easy to love a guy like that. And I do. And who knows? Maybe tonight, one of us will propose.

A word about the author...

Sheila Hansberger, an award-winning author and artist, resides in California. Her paintings can be found in permanent collections across the USA. Her 5-star rated book, *The Better Than Average Apple Cookbook,* features full-color illustrations of her apple-themed artwork. *The Gardener's Secret* is her debut novel.

Visit her website at: www.s-hansberger.com.